Visible Empire

VISIBLE EMPIRE

Hannah Pittard

HOUGHTON MIFFLIN HARCOURT
Boston   New York
2018

hmhco.com

Library of Congress Cataloging-in-Publication Data
Names: Pittard, Hannah, author.
Title: Visible empire / Hannah Pittard.
Description: Boston : Houghton Mifflin Harcourt, 2018.
Identifiers: LCCN 2017053569 (print) | LCCN 2017046216 (ebook) |
ISBN 9780544748989 (ebook) | ISBN 9780544748064 (hardcover)
ISBN 9781328551306 (PA Canada edition)
Subjects: LCSH: Atlanta (Ga.)—Social life and customs—20th century—
Fiction. | Aircraft accident victims' families—Fiction. | Life change events—
Fiction. | BISAC: FICTION / Literary. | FICTION / Historical.
Classification: LCC PS3616.I8845 (print) |
LCC PS3616.I8845 V57 2018 (ebook) | DDC 813/.6—dc23
LC record available at https://lccn.loc.gov/2017053569

Book design by Kelly Dubeau Smydra

Printed in the United States of America
DOC 10 9 8 7 6 5 4 3 2 1

For my mother, Stacy Schultz,
who first told me the story of the disaster at Orly

And for all the people who lost their lives that day
and also for the people who loved them

It was the worst disaster involving a single airplane in the history of aviation.

— "121 IN ATLANTA ART GROUP KILLED AS JET AIRLINER CRASHES AT PARIS; 9 OTHERS DEAD, 2 IN CREW SURVIVE," *New York Times*, JUNE 4, 1962

Atlanta has suffered her greatest tragedy and loss.

— MAYOR IVAN ALLEN

Many people have been asking, "Well, what are you going to do?" And since we know that the man is tracking us down day by day to try and find out what we are going to do, so he'll have some excuse to put us behind his bars, we call on our God. He gets rid of 120 of them in one whop . . . and we hope that every day another plane falls out of the sky.

— MALCOLM X AT THE RONALD STOKES PROTEST IN LOS ANGELES

"This thing is so overwhelming," said a man who had lost two of his loved ones, "that I can't feel anything. I guess it will hit me tomorrow."

— "FLAGS IN ATLANTA FLY AT HALF-STAFF," *New York Times*, JUNE 4, 1962

Visible Empire

Robert

In the first few hours, confusion.

The numbers kept changing. The French were saying 121 dead, which meant—according to the manifest—there must be 11 alive. But New York—how could they have known more than Paris? more than Atlanta?—New York was insisting on 130: the French hadn't included their own countrymen—9 dead, 2 alive—in the initial count. They hadn't thought the U.S. would care. We had our own numbers to deal with, or so their logic went.

But by late afternoon on June 3, 1962, the number finally stuck: 130. Of those: 121 Americans.

The mayor of Atlanta, Ivan Allen, he was everywhere those first few hours, those first few days. He was in Atlanta at the Cathedral of Christ the King. He was in New York, with the political bigwigs, looking at mimeographs of the evidence. He was in Paris at the crash site, kneeling, his head bowed. His photograph was on everyone's front page. He was on the television, on the radio, in your ears, in your face.

"It'll be a month," he said, "a month before the bodies will be identified."

The bodies—Atlanta's bodies—had been burned beyond recognition.

In the three days before the manifest was finally printed, the phone calls to the South were nonstop, even as they went unanswered. Artists from New York, collectors from LA, they were all calling. There was confusion in the art world about who, among their southern friends, had actually gone on the trip and who had merely alluded to the possibility.

Sidney Woolsey, for instance. Hadn't he mentioned taking his wife and daughter? Didn't he say something about showing Joan the Louvre?

What about Morgan Robinson? Investors had been calling his house forty-eight hours straight. No one was answering.

Del Paige—the president of the Atlanta Art Association—why hadn't he been in touch? He would have been able to answer all their questions, but he wasn't returning anyone's calls.

And what about the Bentleys? The lovely, lovely Bentleys? They'd talked about the trip, but surely they hadn't actually gone, not with three small children at home. Or was that precisely why they had gone? Hadn't that been exactly what Raif had told them last fall, in town for the Assemblage exhibition at MoMA? Hadn't he said that Nance needed a break? "She works herself to death," he'd told them. "We have the maid. We have the nanny, but she insists on doing it all."

There were people who knew what was going on, of course. Obviously there were people who knew.

Robert Tucker, for one, he knew something. He knew because he'd taken the call from Ralph McGill, his publisher at the *Atlanta Journal,* on the morning of the incident.

"It's bad," McGill had said. "It's everyone. I don't know what to say. I—"

Robert could hear several other extensions ringing in the background on the other end of the line.

"What do you mean, it's everyone?"

When McGill called, Robert was sitting in his leather recliner —a gift last Christmas from his in-laws—watching as water from the sprinklers hit the lowest panes of the first-floor windows of the house on Forrest Way. For several minutes, he'd been watching. Every time, the water evaporated before the sprinklers came back around. That's how hot it already was.

"I'm truly sorry," said McGill. "Tell Lily I'm so sorry."

"Are you at work?" Robert thought he could hear the relentless ricochets of the newsroom, but the noise—frenetic, intense —could have easily been from a train station or the airport. "It sounds like you're at work."

"I have to—" More phones. "It's chaos. Come in when you can. No. Strike that. Be with Lily."

Lily Tucker, Robert's wife, wasn't due for two months, but the baby hadn't been sitting right and her doctor had warned of the possibility of an early delivery. Her parents, George and Candy Randolph, had taken the flight to Paris three weeks earlier. "A last hurrah," Candy had said, "before we become grandparents." They'd sworn—sworn up and down—that they'd be back in time for the delivery. They hadn't known of the recent complications.

And now this news.

This news that was so inconceivable that Robert didn't immediately believe it. Nor did he immediately comprehend the event's necessary reverberations, its effects, its consequences on every aspect not only of his own small life but on the town, his town, on Atlanta.

Robert was still in his study when he hung up with McGill. Lily was somewhere upstairs. He could hear water being run. In the last week, since the doctor's new warnings, she'd been running baths sometimes three and four times a day. She'd be in there when he left for work in the morning, and she'd be in there when he came home. He leaned back now and listened to the water, to its gurgling through the pipes.

"It's bad," McGill had said. "It's everyone."

Robert closed his eyes and thought of Rita.

All that spring, Robert had worked to convince Rita to take

the trip. "You've never been abroad," he'd said. "You've never seen Paris; you've never seen Rome. You're so young. Look at you. You're so goddamn young. Get out there. Go see it. Go live."

"You're tired of me," she'd said. "Admit it and I'll go. I'll do whatever you ask if you just admit that you've soured of me."

"Darling, anything but sour, anything but tired. This geezer wants you to see the world." Robert Tucker was forty-two years old.

"You mean to fall in love with your wife while I'm gone," she said. "You mean to wash your hands with me." Rita was twenty-three, a little more than a year out of school and only a few months younger than his wife.

"*Of* me," he said.

"Of me." She stood arms akimbo and cocked a hip. She was playing at Bette Davis, maybe Sophia Loren. He couldn't quite place the imitation. They'd seen so many matinees by then. "You see? You agree. You've all but confessed."

"Darling," he said.

During this particular conversation, they'd been in Purgatory —what the staff referred to as Purgatory—which was the storage unit for the several thousand reams of paper housed in the underbelly of the *Journal*'s warehouse at Five Points, the intersection of Decatur, Edgewood, Marietta, and both Peachtrees.

"Yes," she said. "I see. It's all starting to make sense to me. I've got the plot."

"We're journalists," he said, "not fiction writers. Leave that nonsense to New York."

She slapped a rolled-up paper against an open palm. "Send her to Paris, you think. She's young and more than arguably attractive." She paused, pushed her hip to the other side, posed dramatically. "Ahem. I continue: Send her to Paris with one hundred–plus of the city's most fabulously wealthy art patrons and she is bound—*bound!*—to find a replacement for—how did you say it? Oh yes—this old geezer."

"Rita," he said, moving toward her, putting a hand on that extended hip. He brought her waist close to his, and let his hand travel toward the wonderful bottom curve of her ass. She wore what she referred to as string undies.

One thing Robert liked about Rita — in addition to the string undies toward which his fingers were inching nearer and nearer on that day in Purgatory — was that she'd come from almost as little as he. She'd built herself up, pulled herself from the cesspool of the DeKalb public school system, put herself through college, and gotten a job not as a secretary but as a reporter. She was a go-getter; she was feisty. Smart, tenacious, outspoken, she was opinionated about everything, including the clothes she wore, which were something of a cross between a beatnik's and a socialite's. On any given day, the bottom of Rita might pass for Katharine Hepburn (those high-waisted, wide-mouthed trousers of *Philadelphia Story*), while the top half might look ready for a night with Herbert Huncke in some basement bar in New York City.

Rita whacked Robert's hand just before it made contact with the string. "Fat man, you shoot a great game of pool," she said.

They'd seen *The Hustler* in the afternoon the summer before, and ever since she'd taken to quoting from it as though she were Fast Eddie. "But I'm not a sucker" — her words, off script now — "Your game . . . Oh sure, I see now, your game isn't for me to find a replacement in the 'it' crowd. No, you've got nicer plans for me. You think I'll meet a Parisian. Sure. You think I'll never come back."

In fact, what Robert had been thinking was that he'd complicated his life. He was about to be a father. He had a fair amount of personal debt. He was in love with his wife, but he was also in love with his mistress, a woman nearly two decades his junior, which he didn't think was fair. His age, his circumstance — Rita was right. He didn't think she deserved him. She deserved something better. He wanted her to go away and find someone else because he didn't think he'd ever be able to break it off with his wife, whom he'd once regarded as his best friend but since the pregnancy had regarded as a kind of stranger. He wasn't strong enough. It had to be Rita who did the ultimate breaking. And so he'd spent all that spring advocating that she take the swank gig and cover the trip for the *AJC*.

"You'll see France," he said. "You'll see Italy."

"I'll be bored to tears by that crowd," she said. "Snobs."

"They drink like fish," he said. "You'll fit right in."

"I haven't had a drop," she said, "not in a week. At least a week. You haven't even noticed."

"It's paid vacation," he said.

"You're the boss."

"It's not like that. It has to be your choice."

And on and on it went for many weeks until she did finally make the choice. She gave in. "You're right," she said; the trip was six days out. "I need to go. It'll give me an opportunity to think."

Of course, by that time, Robert's in-laws had also decided to make the journey, which had given him pause, which had made him slightly antsy, slightly sick to his stomach, in fact. But he'd been with Rita on and off for over a year, and she'd never threatened to tell and no one at work even suspected. So when she finally signed up—"to fly over with the lot of them," as she'd said —he was happy for her. He was heartbroken and happy.

For the past three weeks, as the socialites toured the museums of Europe, Rita had trotted behind them, writing little ditties, chronicling the day-to-day inanities of the expedition:

the Parisian chill is unrelenting . . .
the women complain constantly of their heavy coats and pine for the
breezy dresses that hang, unseen, in the closets of their
hotels . . .
half the group has drunk the tap water in Italy and caught
a bug . . .
the other half are very nearly always hung-over . . .

Her daily column had been a hit with readers. McGill had been talking about raising her up in the ranks, moving her from beat coverage to a weekly column all her own—"Girl About Town," he'd been calling his idea. "Girl About Town." He was charmed by his own generosity. It was to be a surprise when she returned. The entirety of the *AJC* staff—not just Robert, not just McGill—had been proud of their cub, of the valiant effort she'd put in rubbing elbows with the city's elite. There'd been a general upswing in the mood of the newsroom just yesterday simply because Rita was coming home. In one day, their Rita would be returned to them. They were gay as gay could be.

But something had gone wrong.

Something horrible had happened.

The jet had begun its takeoff, yes.

But in less than a minute, in fewer than ten seconds in fact, if the eyewitnesses were to be believed, the plane had returned to the runway, its metal belly slamming hotly and lethally—*and, oh god, that terrible sound!*—into the earth.

Candy and George and Rita, too, they were all gone.

The phone rang again. Robert picked it up, pushed the switch hook to terminate the call, then restored the handset to its housing. He yanked the cord from the wall and stood.

Overhead, he heard the movements of his wife sloshing about in a full tub. He heard the drain being pulled and the subsequent torrent of sudsy water through the pipes of their house. He heard his wife's voice; it was calling his name.

Lily was calling Robert's name and calling it—he was aware even then, even in that split second—in a manner she would never again be able to duplicate, in a timbre she would never quite recover, a timbre free of grief and the intimate knowledge of immediate and insurmountable loss.

Robert Tucker was about to leave his wife.

He leaned over abruptly and retched.

Ivan & Lulu

Early on the evening of June 3, the mayor's wife, being tucked into bed by her husband, said this: "Are they absolutely sure?"

"Absolutely."

"But that means it's everyone."

"That's right. Except for Bentley."

"But Nance?"

"Nance and her mother."

"What about the boys?"

"Bentley's boys are being cared for."

"How will he get home?"

"He'll fly, of course."

"I can't stand it."

"Let me say good night, Lulu. There are calls I need to make."

"Will you have to go to France?"

"New York first, then Paris. We've gone over this."

"But that means you'll fly, too? You'll get on an airplane?"

"It was a fluke," Ivan said.

"But I heard you on the phone. I heard you say it might have been sabotage."

"Nonsense."

"I can barely breathe."

"I leave in a few hours."

"Come to bed. Hold me."

"I need to make a few phone calls before my flight."

"Wait," she said. "Let me catch my breath."

"Catch your breath."

"It's Mindy, then?"

"Mindy is gone."

"Mary and Tom? Peter and Carol and, oh god, but that means it's also Sue Hill and—"

"Stop now. *Shhh.* Don't torture yourself."

"But it is torture," she said. "It is. I can't breathe, I tell you. I can't breathe."

"Think of our children. Think of me and think of our children. We need you. The city needs you. They'll be looking to us. We have to be strong, Lulu. We have to be very strong. That's right. Close your eyes. Hush. Good girl, yes. Good girl. Sleep now. Dear sweet girl, sleep now."

"But it's everyone," she murmured as he slipped out of the room. "It's everyone. It's everyone."

And it *was* everyone. It was Mindy Johnson, who went to prom four years in a row with Bobby Hanson but then married George Johnson instead, which meant it was George who was sitting beside her on the plane, but Bobby was there too, a few rows back, next to Sally Jean, the woman he finally settled on after Mindy broke his heart. And it was Nance Bentley, the wife of lovely Raif Bentley and the mother of three handsome boys who all attended Westminster and looked dashing on Sundays at First Presbyterian in their matching blue seersucker suits. And it was Nance's mother, Gillian Joyce, longtime widow and consummate drunk. It was Mary and Tom Beaker and his parents, Morris and Virginia. It was the Beakers' best friends, Peter and Carol Cummins, and their neighbor Sue Hill Cleaver. It was four trustees of the Art Association and a former president of Oglethorpe University and half the members of the Junior League and both cofounders of the Atlanta English-Speaking Union and seven volunteers of the Humane Society and twenty members of the Druid Hills High School PTA and another twelve of Westminster's PTA and three faculty members of Emory University, not to mention the very first female clerk of the Georgia Supreme Court. It was every member of the ad hoc all-female croquet team that had been founded on a whim by Sheila Stowe, and it was sixty members of Piedmont Country Club and another forty-five of the Cherokee Driving Club. It was twenty doctors, nine architects, thirteen lawyers, and too many mothers and fathers to count.

In short, it felt like everyone because to the mayor's wife, it *was* everyone; it was everyone she cared about, and they were all gone in a single, heartbreaking, unbelievable whop.

Everyone

In preparation for their flight home—having toured the art and architecture of Switzerland, Zurich, Lake Lucerne, Venice—the Atlantans returned to Paris. The trip had been a success. Money had been raised for the Art Association and the Women's Committee. There was talk that the Cultural Arts Center in Piedmont Park would finally be made a reality. Spirits were more than high, but by the end of their visit, those who weren't hung-over were laid low with a virus that had started first in Rome. *Don't drink the water,* they'd been reminded so many times. *Don't drink the water.* The virus had passed from spouse to spouse, friend to friend, lover to lover. Fifty of them had been in the lobby of the Hotel du Louvre the night before their scheduled departure. There'd been champagne, dancing, deliberately inappropriate suggestions about partner swapping always met by giggles and blushing and the momentary quiet wherein everyone considered but then, nearly as immediately, forgot, because the booze was that good, that strong. They'd seen Paris. They'd seen Rome. They'd seen the *Mona Lisa* and *Whistler's Mother,* for chrissakes. There was a mood of accomplishment and authority. Del Paige floated about the lobby as if on air, as if a feather re-lofted by the current of one conversation after another. He schmoozed and danced and vaulted about that last night with the best of them, with the heaviest of the drinkers. He'd been spared the Roman contagion. He'd heeded the warning about the water . . .

The next morning, they rose—the partygoers and the merely unwell—and finished their final bits of packing. There were last-minute purchases to squeeze into already overfull luggage (that boar-hair brush with the silver-tipped handle! those Laguiole steak knives with the razor-thin blades!), but there were also—from room to room, tourist to tourist, couple to couple, individually and together—so many scraps of paper to be dealt with. There were names on the papers, numbers, fanciful utterances, and now they were being tallied, smoothed one by one into small flat stacks throughout the hotel—

Danced until three, full moon, feel like a newlywed
Brown sugar to make a red sauce
One part bitter, two parts sweet . . .
Delilah: 01-45-34546
Mark my words: next summer, purple everything!
Meet me at midnight; don't tell Kay. Signed, You Know Who!
Tell Stewart: Buy Coke; Buy Gold
Je suis le roi de Denmark et j'aime manger les fraises!

The scraps were meaningless, except to their owners. They were reminders, promises, recipes, epiphanies. They had been tucked all month into pockets, slipped into wallets, sandwiched between books' pages, and now it was time for all to collect, to gather, to assess and reassess and pack neatly into an interior pouch of a valise or an attaché case or possibly even a hat box, where—if the plane hadn't been mere hours away from catching fire, smoldering, sizzling angrily and hotly against the chilly Parisian air—they would eventually have been forgotten by all but one or two, to be found years later: by a daughter, by a husband, by a maid preparing to pack up her employer for the next overseas voyage.

Nearly to the person, the Americans were dragging on the morning of departure. In the lobby, around 9 a.m., there was an air not of frantic hurry but of devil-may-care. Wives lounged in sunglasses and complained of headaches; husbands sucked on cigars and indulged in shots of clam juice and vodka. The Bentleys alone, with cafés au lait and croissants in hand, appeared unfazed by the effects either of the toxic water or the merriment the night before. Only Mrs. Bentley and her mother would be boarding the chartered jet that morning. Mr. Bentley would be taking a commercial flight a few hours later. Their boys were at home, waiting for them, and so they would not risk flying together. Though it seemed a performative superstition, possibly even macabre, it was one they both tolerated and even revered. It was a matter of practicality, responsibility. If a plane crashed, the boys would still have one parent. And their boys were everything to them, and so they flew apart, though in every other way they were joined at the hip. It was a marriage not of convenience but of genuine and mutual admiration. Raif Bentley insisted on going to the airport with his wife, though his flight wasn't for another six hours. He wanted to watch, and did, from the window of the café, as his wife and mother-in-law boarded the plane. He watched everyone board that morning, including a young woman called Rita, whom he didn't know personally or even by name, and yet he witnessed as she, too, walked across the tarmac and climbed the stairs to the aircraft somewhere in the middle of the pack.

Rita, for her part, took the assigned window seat with a small flourish, aware of a bustle of nerves in her stomach. The night before she'd written another letter. She'd written it after the farewell gala, after several glasses of champagne. She'd sealed the letter without rereading it in a fit of — of what? A fit of passion, a fit of youth, a fit of *joie de vivre* and insouciance. "Bully," she'd said to herself before pulling back the covers. "Bully, why not?" She popped a little piece of chocolate between her lips and turned off the lights, falling asleep with the soft candy pressed by her tongue to the roof of her mouth.

In the morning, the letter was still there, on the bedside table. If not for the tangible proof, she might have forgotten she'd ever written it. But there it was. She was most amused with herself. Between tidying and packing—the curling iron she'd brought, not remembering also to bring the conversion attachment, the postcards she'd collected (like a tourist, but who cares? *Call it what it is,* she'd always believed, *and never regret it*)—she picked up the letter, looked again at its sealed back, then dropped it in the trash can. "Silly, silly," she said to herself. "Silly girl."

Still, thirty minutes later, after her luggage was successfully buckled and she'd acquiesced herself into the dreaded winter coat she'd been obliged all May to wear, just as she was about to call for the bellboy to take down her bags and add them to those of the other Atlantans, she allowed herself a brief glance at the trash can. There was the letter, unmarred and unopened. "But I meant every word," she said, again aloud, though truly she remembered not a single thing she'd written. She plucked it from the top of the trash, tucked it into the breast pocket of her coat, and rang for the boy.

On the plane, watching the others find their seats and dispatch their jackets to the stewardess for safe keeping, she was aware most alertly of the envelope that seemed to beat against her chest with a pulse all its own. A woman behind her, thickly accented with the syrup of the South, sang, "Here we go into the pale blue yonder." And then louder, *"Here we go into the pale blue yonder!"* To her seating companion—it was the Pepperdine sisters—she said, "I'm ready to be silly. I'm ready to be really silly. If it isn't fun, then what's the point?" Her sister said, "Your hair looks great." "No. It's awful," said the chanteuse. "No, no!" said the sister. "I like it. I like it." The women howled. It would be a long flight.

When the stewardess made another pass down the aisle, Rita coughed. To herself, she whispered, "Damn it all, why not?" To the stewardess—lovely, French, haughty, Rita thought her sublime—she said, "Can you post this before takeoff? Would you mind too terribly?"

The stewardess, looking already at the next wave of Americans preparing to find their seats and remove their blazers, said, "*Oui. Mais, oui.* Of course."

Rita sat back and closed her eyes, a marvelous wave of simultaneous relief and panic washing over her still-drunk brain. If only she could remember what she'd written.

The stewardess, whose name was Camille, put the letter in the pocket of her apron. She meant to leave it before takeoff with one of the uniformed pageboys who regularly traversed the tarmac taking last-minute requests from captains for items forgotten in the terminal. But as she leaned back into her seat—the plane beginning to taxi—she realized the letter was still in her pocket. *Ça ne fait rien,* she thought. *Je vais le poster moi-même quand je retournerai chez moi.*

She closed her eyes, the engines roared, and at the coordinated universal time of 11:32 a.m. on June 3, 1962, the plane was finally cleared for takeoff. The pilots aligned the aircraft with runway 08, waited exactly six seconds, then applied full thrust. Acceleration, at first, was typical.

By 1,500 meters, the plane had achieved V1, the speed after which a takeoff couldn't safely be aborted, which for this flight had been determined as a knots-indicated airspeed of 147. But this jet, this Boeing 707-328, with the registration numbers F-BHSM, whose first flight ever had been in 1960 and was known by the name *Chateau de Sully*—it not only achieved V1, but then surpassed it.

At forty-eight seconds, the pilot-in-command pulled back on the control column.

The force on the wheel immediately felt off. Instead of smooth, easy pressure, he felt something substantial, something extra and unwanted.

Either the aircraft had been mistrimmed—but how could anyone have missed that?—or there was some sort of jam in the controls. Regardless of cause, both pilots agreed that the pitch of the nose felt low and heavy.

Something was wrong. That much was undeniable.

The pilot-in-command, in spite of having now reached a speed of 179 kt IAS—32 kt beyond V1—made the decision to abort. He must have hoped, by some grace of god, that the runway (though he would have known from training that it wasn't) would be long enough after all for the aircraft to come safely to a stop.

For a period of time between four and six seconds, the jet left the ground. But already the pilots were aborting. Already they were realigning with the runway, returning those ill-prepared tires to the earth, tires that only moments earlier had been traveling fast enough to launch the metal behemoth into the air.

They left the ground; they returned to the ground.

The tires—that heat! that speed!—exploded almost instantly into flames that, to the people who were watching from the terminal, looked like clouds of dust; looked, in fact, like the natural consequence of any 300,000-pound beast attempting to fly. The plane kept moving, now on its belly.

There were only 680 meters of runway left, about 1,300 meters shy of what they might have needed for a successful rejected take-off. Smoke from the torn wheels and from the fire generated by the underbelly's fast drag against the tarmac made its way quickly into the fuselage.

For Camille, the pressure was everywhere and immediate, as though her own body had been submerged suddenly into a pool of water. She saw a plate rattle then lift into the air. She closed her eyes, or maybe they'd been closed for her.

Outside, from the vantage of the terminal, none of this was

immediately evident. The rejected takeoff seemed only a trifle. Witnesses assumed the plane would slow, perform a mannered U-turn, begin preparations for a second attempt . . .

When it didn't stop, when it reached the end of the runway and continued atop the uneven pasture, toward the farmhouses, the trees—how many people saw the dog that ran from the airplane's path, then turned to watch, just as a person might do?

The jet, going 160 kt but now across the rugged terrain, tilted starboard, one wing at a sharp 45 degrees with the earth, the other now being dragged, the other now obliterated by the drag, the other now detached, along with engine no. 2, which eventually broke free completely.

The aircraft moved clear across the road that surrounded the runway then collided into the approach lights. By then it had already started to disintegrate. The fuselage made contact with a farmhouse. The nose came loose.

Finally the bulk of the plane, what you could still call the plane, at its terrible final angle that would be captured in perpetuity first in photographs and then in a painting, came to a stop, some 550 meters beyond the end of the runway. It was still on its extended center line.

In the terminal, people who hadn't been standing now stood.

In the terminal, there was a peculiar moment of silence. The last moment before the obvious sank in, the moment in which those who witnessed the accident had a chance to think—

Surely not
No it couldn't be
But they must be fine
This isn't how a plane crashes
No, no, surely not

Then they saw the fire. They heard the appalling internal explosions. Then there was no more silence. Screaming, crying, panic, yes, but the silence in the terminal and its sweet moment of hope were gone.

The plate was the only detail from the accident that Camille remembered upon waking in a field. There was the plate—rising, falling—then blackness, then—some time later or maybe since the beginning—the thunderous sound of metal and flames and then, later still, and still then in darkness, her eyes not yet open or adjusted, the tinnier, higher cries of Jacqueline and Francoise. The cries came close, then paused, then moved away.

Finally Camille's eyes opened, or maybe the smoke had simply cleared by then. She looked in the direction of the cries—her friends' cries—and she found them, Jacqueline and Francoise, running across a field toward a farmhouse.

"Francoise," she called, and held up her arm, but even from where she sat, she could barely hear her own voice over the roar of the metal and flames. She lowered her hand and, only then, realized that she was still buckled into her seat.

She unclamped the belt and tried to stand, but there was something wrong. Her right leg was bloody, the hose torn, skin from the knee dangling outlandishly to the side. A piece of bone protruded from her shin. She had no chance of standing on her own. She looked instead at the grass by her side.

She thought again of the plate. Already, her memory seemed compromised. Already, no matter how hard she tried to recall the plate rise and fall in real time, already it moved in slow motion. Moments passed, minutes possibly, in which the plate gradually lifted into the air—as if an unseen hand had raised it in display —before crashing back to earth, now in real time, colliding with the sink and shattering to pieces.

Why she did not now think of Marcel, who should have been running through the field with Francoise and Jacqueline, or of Genevieve, who'd been stationed that afternoon in first class, but thought instead of that utterly American woman in the mismatched dress-suit who'd given her the envelope and asked her to post it, she didn't know. But it was that woman, unquestionably still inside the fuselage, who now fully occupied her thoughts.

A sudden panic took hold of Camille and, almost drunkenly, she clawed at the pockets of her apron. The letter was still there.

She took one look at the blackened plane, its mangled wing, the curls of gunmetal-gray smoke spiraling from its engine, and lost consciousness.

Ivan & Lulu

I won't do it," Lulu said. She moved from her vanity back to the bed. "You can't make me. If I have to attend another service, I'll die."

"Think of Raif," said Ivan. "Think how he'll feel if you're not there."

"What about me?" she said.

"We do this to honor our friends."

"I won't honor Nance in this way. She wouldn't like it."

"Think of the boys."

She put a hand to her mouth.

"He wouldn't bring the boys? He wouldn't stoop so low?"

"Of course the boys will be there. It's their mother, their grandmother. They need to grieve."

"They don't need to grieve. They need to play. They need to be outside running and jumping. They need to be children."

"Their mother is gone."

"Don't say it."

"Nance is dead."

"Don't you say it. Don't you dare say that to me. Do you know a letter arrived this morning? *From Nance?*"

"I want you to put your dress on."

"It burns when I touch it."

"Goddamn it, Lulu. I can't miss this service. There are people I have to talk to. I'm the mayor. It's unavoidable that business and pleasure are mixed. You knew this from the beginning."

"You call this pleasure? Memorial service after memorial service after memorial service? I'll go when there are bodies."

"Don't be morbid."

"Ha."

"Don't talk about the bodies."

"How do I even know for sure? Where is the proof?"

"I have seen them, Lulu. I have seen the remains."

"Who's being morbid now?"

"I'll send Alma up to help you get dressed."

"Don't bother Alma. Her nephew is still missing."

"She's our help. That's what we pay her for."

"I don't need any help. I need you to listen. Do you understand that all over this city, letters are arriving? From *them?*"

He walked to their bedroom door and spoke with his back to her. "We're leaving in thirty minutes. I don't have the luxury to indulge your hysteria. It's not just Raif who I have to think about or even his boys. It's the cultural center; it's the museum; it's the PTA and the council members and the Junior League and the clubs and the entire congregations of every white and Negro church in this city. Don't you understand, Lulu? The world—not just the governor, not just the president—the *world* is watching. Right now, I am being watched. You and I and our dear, dear city are being watched. Do you understand? They want to know if we'll ever stand up again. They want to know if this is the beginning of a spiral into the ground, or if we've got fight and life left in us yet. Don't you see, Lulu? Don't you see that? France is talking about sending us a goddamn Rodin, and you're lying in bed like a child."

When she at last responded, she sounded newly calmed. The dullness in her voice disturbed him. "Are you practicing a speech on me?" she asked.

"Your cynicism frightens me, Lulu."

"It's meant to frighten you."

He shivered.

"Are you cold, dear?" she asked. "Shall I hold you?"

"There's no time for that now." He couldn't bring himself to face her. "I'll be downstairs with the children."

Robert

What do you mean you wouldn't know? What do you mean you haven't seen her?"

"I left her. I told you."

"But it makes no sense, Robert. What you're saying makes no sense. You're drunk. You're delusional."

"I am drunk," Robert said. He knocked on the bar for another. "But not delusional."

Robert Tucker had been sitting at this particular bar since morning, since he'd stumbled past it and smelled the fresh Pine-Sol masking last night's booze and had turned, no volition necessary, into the open doorway and taken a seat and ordered the first of who knew how many scotch and milks.

It was P. T. Coleman who was sitting beside him now, asking these questions that felt to Robert as if they were being asked daily but by different people, an endless deluge of the same interrogations.

No matter how deep into Atlanta he went, no matter how often he changed bars, there was always someone new to run into, someone new to beg for an accounting. It occurred to him just then that the trick might be to stay in one place from here on out. Or maybe he'd had that thought before. Maybe he'd had it yesterday and last week, but every morning he forgot, and by the time he remembered, he was already someplace new and there was already someone different asking questions.

Raif Bentley, for one, had found him last week at the downstairs bar at the Ritz. Robert remembered that much for sure. And he remembered thinking after that particular encounter that he needed to curb his frequency at bars with any sort of obvious sophistication. The less swank, the less likely he was to run into someone from his past life. It had taken him at least a week to figure that out. He'd practically been asking for it hanging out at the Ritz with god-awful Ed Noble's god-awful Lenox Square just across the street. Of course Raif and his horrible expression of profound loss had found him there. Raif reeked of loneliness. It was almost too much. It *was* too much. Robert had his own grief to contend with, which he'd been contending with just fine by drinking himself silly. What had Raif been thinking? Being out in public when there were those three boys at home, motherless, grandmother-less boys. It was rude, wasn't it? Walking that amount of grief around in public.

The problem with Raif was that he knew things—more things than most anyway, certainly more things than P. T. Coleman—which meant his questions had a different intensity to them. His were a different set of steak knives altogether that stabbed fresh holes and leaked fresh blood. Raif knew things because he'd seen Lily, first at his own wife's ceremony, or whatever it is they were calling the bodiless funerals, and then at Lily's parents'. Not only had he seen her, he'd taken her to dinner. He'd listened to her story. He'd balled his fists and banged the table. "Damn him," he'd said. "Damn that scoundrel waste of a man." Robert knew this—he knew these words to be exact—because Raif had told him so at the Ritz. "What the hell, man?" Raif had been whispering when he asked this and other questions. Even livid, he had composure. That's something money bought you. Composure regardless of circumstance. "Do you know what Lily told me?"

"I have an idea," Robert had said.

"You walked out."

"Yes."

"Without warning."

"I told her first."

"On the day it happened."

"Yes."

"You haven't seen her."

"Correct."

"You haven't been in contact."

"Correct again."

"You don't know how she is, how the baby is."

"You could tell me."

"You don't know if the baby's been born even."

"Has he?"

"You're unbelievable."

"This whole thing is unbelievable."

"Because some mistress is dead? Some girl barely into her twenties."

"Lily told you about her?"

"She told me you came clean about an affair on the morning of. I told her no. I told her impossible. I told her no friend of mine could be so callous as to confess to something so trite as an affair at a time like this, especially one that couldn't be continued even if you wanted."

"Lily is barely into her twenties."

"She's your wife."

"The mistress has a name."

"I don't want to hear it."

"Then stop talking to me."

"You're saying this to me? To me?" Raif beat at his heart with an open fist. "My wife is *dead*."

"And I'm awfully sorry for your loss."

"Are you looking to get hit? Are you wanting me to punch you?"

"I was wondering the same thing."

"I don't know how you mean that."

"Have a drink with me."

"Did you mean you were thinking you might like to be punched, or did you mean you might like to punch me?"

Robert pulled out the stool next to him. "Both," he said. "I meant it both ways."

Raif shook his head. "You're a bastard."

"I'm not denying that."

The bartender approached.

"Another for me," Robert said. "One just like it for Señor Bentley."

The bartender—he knew who the real boss was—looked at Raif, who nodded. "Just one," he said. Then he sighed resignedly and sat down.

It was true. Robert had left Lily on the day of the crash. He hadn't bothered to clean out the trash can where he'd vomited after hearing the news. He hadn't bothered to pack a suitcase or grab a change of shorts. He'd left his hat on the side table in the foyer. For all he knew, the hat was still there, next to whatever bills had awaited payment that day, whatever correspondence expected reply, whatever calling cards or invitations might have politely requested a response.

Or maybe the hat was gone. Maybe everything of Robert's was gone. If he'd been told that Lily threw it all into the pool, he could have believed it. If he'd been told she dropped it off at an orphanage—his shirts, his pants, his watches and ties—he'd have believed that too. If he'd been told she burned it to smithereens in the front yard for all the neighbors to see? Well, yes, that, too, he would have believed. Since the crash, everything, anything was suddenly believable. But also it wasn't. Because nothing mattered anymore. Because nothing was real. Because life now was just an accumulation of minutes and hours dwindling away under the guise of days and weeks. Life now was merely the passage of time until The End.

The point? That while it was true that Robert had left Lily on the day of the crash, it was untrue that he hadn't seen her. Of course he'd seen her. Like it or not, that baby was his. And a monster he might be — monster, ne'er-do-well, sonofabitch, bastard — but he was still a human being. And he understood that inside his wife's belly was another human being who hadn't asked to come into this world, hadn't asked to be born only to begin the epic countdown of time until the end. That was Robert's doing and Lily's. Of all the people to blame, the baby (not yet born, Robert knew because he'd been spying on Lily big as a house as she watered the ferns and as his car idled behind the giant magnolia beside their neighbor's driveway not twenty-four hours before that day at the Ritz), the baby was not one who could be held accountable. Not yet. No: first he (for in Robert's mind, it was always a *he,* the baby had to be a he) had to come into the world. First he had to grow, become a man, become capable of his own decisions and mistakes, capable of acquiring his own wives and mistresses and blameless children. *Then* he could be blamed. *Until* then, he was still Robert and Lily's. *Until* then, Robert would continue — on mornings he found himself sober enough — to drive up and down Forrest Way, up and down, back and forth, hoping for a quick glance at that belly.

But when he saw the belly, he also saw Lily. And when he saw Lily, he thought of Rita. And when he thought of Rita, all he wanted was a drink. All he wanted was a fist to the jaw. All he wanted was for time to move faster and for night to come and the night after that and the night after that and the night after that until nights stopped coming altogether, until time for him ended. There was suicide, sure. But his ego was too large for that.

"Nance was so good," Robert had said over and over that day at the Ritz, his head spinning with memories he couldn't root in time. It was very possible he slurred his words. He tried to sit up straighter. His tongue felt thick, or maybe it was numb. He couldn't tell.

"Please don't talk about my wife," Raif said.

"She was so decent, so living."

"I'm begging you."

"*Loving.* She was so *loving.*"

"You're pushing me away," said Raif. "Do you know that? You're leaving me no choice but to abandon you here. In this condition. Which is no condition to be in."

Robert smacked his own forehead. "Do you know," he said, "that all I've wanted to tell Lily about for the past year is Rita? And I don't mean that in some gallant way. I don't mean that I've been trying to tell her about the affair, to tell her that I wanted to leave. I didn't. I wasn't going to abandon her, not ever. I'm too big a coward for that."

"I can't listen to this." Raif stood, but he didn't leave; he didn't even turn away.

"What I mean is, I wanted to tell my wife about my girlfriend. I'd go home and I'd think, *That Rita. She's so goddamn funny.* I'd think, *Wouldn't Lily die laughing if I told her what Rita said this afternoon?* I couldn't get Rita off my mind. She's all I thought about. I wanted to talk about her. I wanted to talk about her to Lily because Lily is my best friend. *Was* my best friend." For a moment Robert was quiet. It appeared he'd tapered off finally, come to the end. But suddenly he reanimated. "And the thing about a best friend is that you want to talk to them. You want to tell them what's going on in your life. I wanted to tell Lily. Not because I wanted to hurt her. But because I wanted to share my life with her. And Rita was my life. Do you see? Do you see how terribly knotted up I am?"

Robert slumped suddenly. He put his head in his hands. Was he crying? There were no tears, but his shoulders heaved. He appeared to be struggling for air. Raif hadn't touched him; hadn't offered a single physical reassurance. But when his breathing finally slowed, when his shoulders appeared to have relaxed for good, Raif sat back down. He leaned in close, his mouth very nearly touching Robert's ear.

"When you're ready," Raif said, "I want you to find me. I'll help you. You're digging yourself a hole. You can't see that now, but the hole is already quite deep. It's only getting deeper. When you're ready, when you're able to see what a jackass you've made of yourself and you're ready to get out but think you can't because the hole's so deep, that's when I want you to find me."

Robert jerked away. "I'm not—"

Raif grabbed his elbow.

"I don't care what you think right now." A small amount of spit hit Robert's ear when Raif spoke. "I don't want to talk to you anymore. I don't want to hear you speak when you're on this side of things. I'm telling you, when you're on the other side—which is something you can't conceive of right now—but when you're there, firmly on the other side, and you think there's no way to recover, that's when you come to me. I'll help you. You have my word. That's what a friend does: he gives his word. I'm giving you my word, man. I'll be there when it's time."

Robert thought that, with very little effort, he could nod off. Just close his eyes and forget the day, forget the year, forget this life. Sleep, blissful sleep was mere seconds away; all he had to do was close his eyes.

"Are you listening?"

"I told you—"

"I don't care about that," said Raif. "All I care is that you remember this. Are you capable of remembering this? Think of a hole, as big a hole as your pigeon brain can imagine. When you're in it, when you're seeing it in person, when it's there in front of you, remember me. In the meantime—" Now Raif stood. Now

Raif reached into his pocket, pulled out his billfold, and produced a ten-dollar bill that he placed beneath his empty sweaty tumbler. "In the meantime, stay away from me."

But that was last week and the promised hole, to Robert, was something still theoretical, a fanciful idea given to him by his histrionic former friend. Now, here, sitting beside him was P. T. Coleman, a fuck-up equal in size to Robert, except that Coleman had had the good sense to be born into a fantastic fortune, the size of which guaranteed that—no matter how big the mistake—it was always capable of being swept under a rug. If a rug large enough didn't exist, then his parents had had one made. Except Coleman's parents were dead—gone, like everyone else's it seemed, in the crash.

"Jesus," Coleman was saying now, "that's some story. That's some bloody mess."

"What story?"

Coleman laughed.

Robert wasn't aware he'd been telling a story.

"Do you know they left me everything?" Coleman said. "Can you believe that? The old man's been telling me for years that he was writing me out of the will. I've always half believed it. When I heard the news, when they told me they were gone, the first thing I thought—I'm not ashamed to admit it—but the first thing I thought was that I was officially penniless. I just knew he'd left it all to his queer little sister." Coleman took a drink, though Robert didn't remember him ordering one. "But I was wrong. He left it to me. The houses, the cars, the stocks, the goddamn art collection. You should see the collection. It's— It's so much more than I knew. They were practically living tax free because of the collection. They've got pieces everywhere. Not to mention what's in the houses. I could cry just thinking about it. I could cry just thinking that all I had to do was outlast him. Can you fathom it?"

Robert couldn't fathom it. Nor could he fathom how he was sitting at a bar, still, with P. T. Coleman and how neither of them had gotten kicked out and neither of them had started a fight.

"I'm in a mood," said Robert. He rubbed his temple with his thumbs. There was a chance he might vomit. For more than a week—two weeks? he couldn't be sure; perhaps it had only been a matter of days—it seemed he'd done nothing but vomit and drink. "Apologies in advance."

"We're all in moods. You never need to apologize to me. That's the beauty of me. I'm a sorry-free zone." Coleman leaned in toward Robert's shoulder, as if to inspect something tiny written on his collar. "Is that an ant? Are you covered in ants?"

Robert brushed at his shirt. Nothing was there. "So what will you do?" Robert asked. "What's next?"

"Today?"

"For life. For all your lousy money. What's next?"

"I was in the Bahamas last month. There with three other men, salt-of-the-earth types. Good, decent, fun-loving, god-fearing types. We rented a boat. We took it out every morning at dawn. We did things that teenagers do. We caught fish. We caught at least a few fish. We lived like kings. These were salt-of-the-earth men. Did I already say that? First-class people." He hiccupped. Maybe it was a burp. "We were pigs is the truth. Gluttons for pleasure. We left on a Wednesday. Tony—you know Tony? Nah, his parents weren't on the plane. He's from South Carolina. They've got money, but they don't go wild for the art the way the Atlanta crowd did. Not the point, though. Point is Tony was getting a catheter the following Monday. He'd be done after that. Permanent catheter. As in, Until God Calls Him Home catheter. No more boats. No more bonefish. No more Bahamas. Tony's liver is done, his kidneys too. So I went down. It was his last chance. And through the weekend, all four of us, we lived like teenage kings. I'll take you sometime. I'll fly you down. I've got my license. Of course you didn't know. Why would you have known? Charles Lindbergh made the flight from New York to Paris. Took him thirty-three hours. Famous overnight. That was 1927, the year I was born. You were born in '21? '22? Doesn't matter. He was a prophet, that man was. He knew what was coming. He could see luxury travel, commercial transportation. The jet set didn't exist, but he could see them coming. He was standing on something higher, a ladder, ten ladders, looking out. Man could see the future. He was in Atlanta that October. Month I was born. I take it as an omen. Biggest public gathering in our history at the time. Off topic, I know, except to say that when I fly you to the Bahamas, we'll do Atlanta to Jacksonville. Then another stop in Fort Lauderdale. I have friends there, at the airport. Then it's three hours of low flying and thin blue sky. If you haven't been to Freeport, we can stop there for a night. Worth seeing. And the women . . . But where I want to take you is Little Abaco. There's a fellow, white like us, who grows marijuana and lives in a white castle made from white oyster shells—it's called tabby. He didn't invent it. He'll tell you he did, but he didn't. He has a northern accent. You'd be able to place it. New England somewhere. Boarding school sound, like a Kennedy with marbles in his mouth. He looks like Hemingway. He keeps three women, all darkies, in three different wings of the castle. He has kids with them all. He's plotting to take over the world. He says one of them will be president. He's a crazy sonofabitch—they weren't even born in America; how could they be president?— but I love the man. We're practically brothers. He was the first person to be in touch after the plane went down. He must have gone straight to the wire when he heard. 'I want the Gauguin,' he said. He thinks I'm selling. He thinks because I'm a fuck-up that I am also a fool." Here Coleman finally paused. He looked at the glass in his hands as though it had just sung him the sweetest and saddest ballad in the world. "But I am not a fool, Robert. I think you understand this."

"I only meant to ask about your money."

Coleman snorted and slapped him on the back. Then he stood and, in a manner unsettlingly similar to Raif, in a manner in fact so eerily alike that it made Robert think there might be lessons, or if not lessons then actual genes, responsible for the distinct gestures of the wealthy, Coleman reached into a back pocket and produced a billfold.

He put two tens under his glass.

"That's too much," said Robert. He belched a little. The milk might have been rancid. "That's an obscene amount to put down. Are you looking to be robbed?"

"Come on," said Coleman. He slapped him again on his back, only this time Robert did vomit a little, but the vomit stayed in his mouth and he was able to swallow it down. "What's too much?" said Coleman. "Is too much a thing? Come on. I'll show you what's next for my money. I'll tell you all about it."

"I'm busy." A fly buzzed lazily overhead.

Coleman picked up what was left of Robert's drink—a dwindling ice cube, a splash of cloudy liquid—and sniffed it. "Nah," he said. "You're done being busy with this." He put the glass on the other side of the bar, away from them, as though it were poison. "I've got better stuff at home. Come with me. Let me tell you my plan."

"What kind of stuff?"

"Better."

"Be specific."

Coleman flicked his nostrils with his thumbnail. "Got the picture?"

Robert slipped one of the tens from under Coleman's tumbler. "It's still too much," he said. Then he stood, threw back the last of Coleman's drink, pushed the ten into his own pocket, and said, "What the hell are we waiting for?"

Piedmont

P iedmont Dobbs was one of the 132 eleventh graders who had applied to be among the first Negro students to matriculate into Atlanta's all-white public school system. This was in the month of May, in 1961, nearly a year before the disaster at Orly.

Teachers passed the forms out during second period, which for Piedmont was U.S. history. There were no box fans in their classroom on the third floor. But the windows were open wide, and a breeze from off the playground below drifted up and in, bringing with it the soft scent of fresh mulch and last night's rainstorm.

"Talk to your parents," his teacher had said. "Talk to each other. Think about the pros. Think about the cons."

There'd been giggling from the back row, where the popular girls sat, one of whom was light-skinned and called Lora. Piedmont would be taking her to prom in the coming weeks.

"The world is changing," his teacher said. "This city is changing. You have a chance to be a part of that."

With trembling hands, Piedmont folded the application in two and tucked it delicately between the center pages of his history book.

For nearly seven years, his mother had been dreaming of this moment, ever since the Warren Court handed down its decision.

He was twelve when that happened, and he'd been sitting at the kitchen table with her, the radio between them, when it was announced that *Plessy v. Ferguson* had finally been overturned. His mother just stared at the radio and cried. "This is it," she'd said. "This is the beginning." Piedmont's father had been dead by then for more than two years. "This is the beginning of everything," his mother had said. She rocked and cried, rocked and cried.

Now he was nineteen years old—older than many of his classmates but not the oldest—and he was a junior at Booker T. Washington High School in southwest Atlanta, and here was the application his mother had been waiting for; here was his chance. If he made it, if they picked him to be one of the ten to matriculate, his life would be forever changed. That's what his mother had always said. Those ten students—whoever they might turn out to be—were guaranteed a future of magnificence, of excellence even.

And yet, even as he sat there at his desk, as he listened to the giggling, as he listened to his teacher go on and on, even as he knew he would apply no matter the pros and cons, it nagged at him that his mother had gone to Booker T.; that his father had gone to Booker T.; that Nipsey Russell, who'd been on the *Ed Sullivan Show,* and Martin Luther King, who was suddenly everywhere and everything to everyone—that even they had gone to Booker T. nagged at him. What made Piedmont Dobbs, son of a dead automobile salesman and a decent-but-not-gifted church singer, what made him think he deserved anything more than any of them?

He knew the story of Alveraz Gonsouland, the boy who'd transferred from the Booker T. in Norfolk, Virginia, to Norview High in '59 with sixteen other students. "The Norfolk 17," the papers had called them. Alveraz couldn't deal with the pressure —maybe it was the photographers (there'd been so many, the city had to send in police to thin them out), or maybe it was the white kids. Either way, he'd transferred back to his own Booker T. and would graduate this year with the kids he'd started with.

Piedmont was in tenth grade when Norfolk integrated. He never dreamed Atlanta would do so in time for him to have a chance. There were rumors that the Norfolk 17 had been coached by members of the NAACP to sit together, near exits and in front rows, so they could defend themselves and flee more quickly if attacked. He'd been partly horrified, partly fascinated by such details. Now here it was — his opportunity to be part of history and to matter. That, after all, was what it came down to: his mother and his father, Nipsey Russell and MLK: Booker T. had been good enough for them because no other opportunity had existed. But it did for him. This was his fate. He felt the sureness of it, the rightness of his role as one of The Ten, pulsing just beneath the surface of his skin.

On the news that night, he and his mother listened to the story of Antulio Ortiz, the man who — days earlier — had hijacked a National Airlines flight out of Miami, forcing the pilots to fly to Havana. Everyone onboard, and even the plane, had been allowed by Castro to return the next day. But Ortiz, an electrician from Miami, had stayed. There was new information every day. Tonight they learned that he'd not used his real name to board the flight. Instead, on the manifest, he'd been listed as Mr. Elpir Cofresi, after a nineteenth-century pirate.

"Can you imagine?" his mother said. "Can you even imagine?"

Piedmont couldn't imagine, since he'd never been on a plane, much less seen one up close or in person. The word — *hijack* — filled him with an instinctive sort of terror, but he liked the idea of this man Ortiz and his simple, if disastrous, desire for Havana. Cuba: that was another thing Piedmont couldn't imagine.

His mother stewed greens as Piedmont set the table. Between news stories — up next after the continuing hijack saga was word that President Kennedy's $1.25 minimum wage had passed in the House — his mother would squeeze Piedmont's shoulder and say, "I'm just so proud of you. So proud."

"Ma," he said every time, "I'm not in yet."

"But you will be," she said. "You will be."

She wanted to fill out the application with him, but he'd asked to keep it to himself for a day or two. "I just want to get a sense of my answers on my own," he said. "I just want to make sure I have ideas before getting help from you."

"But you promise you'll let me see it," she said, "before you hand it in?"

"Ma," he said. They were eating by then, the news over and the radio turned off. "I'll let you send it in. You can mail it yourself if it means that much to you."

After dinner, he'd gone to his bedroom. As he did every night, he re-hung the shirt he'd worn that day. He sniffed at the pits —not too bad, plus this one hadn't yet started to yellow. He removed his pants and laid them on top of his twin bed. With an old bristle hairbrush, he went to town on the fabric, brushing from the waistline to the cuffs, paying special attention to the fabric at the knee. It was thinning. He'd need a new pair before the end of summer. But at least they didn't want washing any time soon. Washing, he knew from his mother, weakened the fabric and aged the cloth.

When he was satisfied with their cleanliness, he folded his pants and placed them on the single shelf of his closet above the five shirts that hung below. For pajamas, he wore shorts and an old T-shirt that had once belonged to his father. It was too hot for anything more that night. His bedroom window was open, and the fading light outside was yellow-brown and glinting with the promise of more rain. But he was not so lucky now for a breeze, and his upper lip moistened as soon as he wiped it dry.

Carefully, methodically, he cleared his desk of books and papers until the only thing on it was his lamp (which he would turn on only when it was so dark he could no longer see) and the application he'd been given that day at school. He unfolded the piece of paper, smoothed both sides so the crease was not as pronounced, then sat down at his desk and began.

At prom, several weeks later, on the same day he'd been in-terviewed by the three white committee members who would choose the Atlanta 10, Lora danced with Piedmont twice but no more. She had agreed to go with him because her parents wouldn't let her go with Alfred Thompson, a senior with a bad reputation. Now she was slow dancing with Alfred, and Pied-mont was slumped alone against the wall of the gymnasium. His mother had over-starched his collar, and it itched against his neck. He was scratching beneath the fabric with his index finger when Madelyn Bean appeared by his side.

Madelyn was dark-skinned and tall. Her shoulders were more masculine than most of the other girls and she kept her hair too short for his taste, but she had a nice waistline and she wore her belt cinched tight to accentuate the curve.

Madelyn had also been interviewed by the school board. Pied-mont knew this because he'd seen her with her parents as he was walking in alone.

There was no chance that by talking to Madelyn he might make Lora jealous—his date hadn't looked his way once since that second dance—but it made sense to be friendly since they might end up at the same high school next year.

Madelyn leaned against the wall beside him.

"Who'd you come with?" she said.

"You don't know?"

Madelyn looked down and smiled. "You must have guessed you were just a tool. Everyone knows about Alfred and her."

"Maybe I thought Alfred would have moved on by now."

Madelyn laughed. "Mama says beware the man with so many notches on his belt."

"Guess that makes me a safe bet."

Madelyn turned toward him, her shoulder still resting against the wall. She was nearly his height.

"You want to dance?" she asked.

Piedmont shook his head. "Not really." He said it too quickly and his lack of interest sounded crueler than he intended. "Maybe in a little while," he added.

"I can take a hint," she said. "You don't have to feel sorry for me."

She pushed herself from the wall as if to leave. Piedmont reached for her elbow.

"No," he said. "Stay. I just don't feel like dancing. We can talk, though. I don't mind talking."

She resumed her original position, but now with crossed arms, and instead of facing him, she gazed out at the dance floor. Piedmont did the same.

The music switched from fast to slow, and the lights overhead moved from a yellow filter to red. Everyone looked older, sexier, than they should have. Lora and Alfred especially looked old and sexy. Alfred was holding her close, one knee pressed visibly into the fabric of her dress, he guessed between her legs. Piedmont clenched and unclenched his hands. Of course he'd been just a tool, but part of him—that dreamer side of him who believed, in spite of reason, that if he wished it hard enough someone somewhere would grant the wish—God or whatever—*that* part of him had believed in the possibility that after one dance, Lora wouldn't even remember Alfred's name. But that hadn't happened. And here he was the fool, no one to blame but himself.

"Did they ask you about the bathroom?" Madelyn said. "That was a hoot, I thought."

Piedmont shoved his hands in his pockets.

"The thing about the bathroom," she said, "about what you'd do if there were white kids waiting for you in there?"

He nodded. "Sure, sure. They asked. What'd you say?"

"I told them the girls would probably say hi. I'd say hi back. Then I'd put my lipstick on and leave. What about you?" she asked. "What'd you say?"

"Same. Without the lipstick."

Madelyn giggled.

In fact, what he'd said was "I'd fight. My daddy's dead, but he taught me some before he died. I'm not afraid of anyone." The man who'd asked the question, a psychologist, had smiled and nodded; he'd given no indication that Piedmont's answer was unacceptable. He'd scribbled down a few lines on the notebook in front of him then turned the interview over to the school board committee member, who'd asked him about his mother, about their evening habits, about his favorite subjects.

But now Piedmont understood that everything that came after the bit about the bathroom, all their other questions and all his other answers, didn't matter. It was in that moment—standing next to Madelyn, watching Lora and Alfred slip out the side exit of the gymnasium—in that precise and completely definable and ever memorable moment, when Piedmont knew he wouldn't be chosen to attend one of the all-white high schools in the fall.

He was right.

Five days later, when the rejection letter came, he didn't even open it. His mother did. She cried so that her nose ran and her makeup smeared. "It's my fault," she said. "It's my fault."

"No," he said. "It's mine."

"I've ruined your chances," she said. They were sitting in the kitchen, the discarded letter on the table between them. She put her head in her hands.

"Ma," he said. He put his hand on hers. He was about to tell her about Madelyn, about the conversation they'd had, about his own suggestion of violence as a response to bullying. He was about to tell his mother that he'd known since prom that he wouldn't be accepted, but he didn't get the chance.

"I have to tell you something," she said, pulling her hand away from his. She sat up straight. "You have no business comforting me. I've done something I shouldn't have."

Now Piedmont also sat up and back. There was nothing she could have done—would have done—to ever hurt his chances.

She'd wanted this for him all his life; she'd dreamed of this opportunity. He shook his head.

Her confession was so plain. What she'd done was so insignificant he could spit. On the application, she'd changed his age from nineteen to sixteen. "They must have found out," she said. "I didn't think they'd take you. They'd think you were too old, that's what I thought."

He looked at his mother, her graying hair, her watery eyes. Behind her was the stove, dented and dirty with grease. Next to it was the sink, above which were the shelves, atop which were all the same cans and boxes that every other family on their block had purchased and put away in a similar manner. Beans here, rice there, butter on the counter, greens in the icebox. He'd been so stupid, thinking he was destined for anything more than anyone else. He'd been so unprepared, just like his mother, who was weeping and wailing before him. She'd been equally stupid, equally naïve, believing Piedmont was the future, the way up and out. His mother, his poor, dumb mother, sitting there thinking that his age made any difference at all: he could have been fifteen or forty-five; he didn't stand a chance and never had.

He stood up. "You're right," he said.

"I'm sorry. Oh, sweet boy."

She reached for him.

He stepped back.

"This is all your fault," he said.

"Piedmont—"

"I can't be around you."

"Please," she said. She grabbed again for him. He swatted her away.

"Don't go," she said. "You have to forgive me. You must see I was trying to help."

He went to his bedroom. She didn't follow. He didn't have a plan, but he knew he had to get out. He removed the pillow from its case and shoved inside it a pair of pants, his only other pair of shoes, and all the clean shirts that were hanging.

His mother was standing at the front door. She seemed to be trying to barricade the exit, to block him from what she knew he was about to do.

"I love you," she said. She was crying still, or maybe by then she was whimpering.

He wanted desperately to hold her. He wanted to put his arms around her and pull her in close the way she had with him on the day his daddy died. He wanted to say, "I know you love me, and I love you." He wanted to say, "It's not your fault. It's mine. I've let us both down. I didn't tell you. I couldn't tell you. Forgive me for letting you believe this. Forgive me. You did nothing. It's me. It's my wicked heart that sometimes believes in violence though you have taught me to be better."

He wanted to say all this and more. But he couldn't. Instead, he pushed past her—so easily he nearly crumpled with disbelief—and walked out the door. Behind him, he could hear what most definitely by then was whimpering. He could hear her, over and over again, as he walked down the three flights of stairs and into the dark of the electric night, apologizing.

On the day of the crash, Piedmont was standing behind the counter of the Purple Pigeon on Auburn Avenue, a mop in his hands. On the television above the counter, he watched—along with several white customers—the grainy black-and-white footage of the wreckage. He listened to the gasps of the people on the other side of the bar. A few men stood abruptly and walked out. Piedmont stayed where he was. His first thought—and he felt bad for it after, though that didn't stop him from thinking it in the first place—was that the city had it coming.

Ivan & Lulu

B ut who, dear?"
  "Sit up, Lulu. You'll hear me better if you sit up."
  "Turn the light off," she said. "It's too much."
"The light is off."
"Then close the blind."
"Sit up, Lulu. I'm trying to tell you a story."
"Start over," she said. "Speak more slowly, but also more quietly."
"It's difficult for me to concentrate when you're lying down like that. This isn't healthy. This isn't what we agreed."
"Tell me the story," she said.
"It's just . . . It's nothing. Nothing important."
"But you said Harry Belafonte."
"Yes."
"You said they denied him service."
"Yes."
"And it was his whole party? Whites *and* Negroes?"
"It was."
"Will there be an apology?"
"The diner won't apologize."
"But have you called him?"

"I have."

"That's good, dear. It makes me shiver to think of him enduring such a slight."

"It doesn't reflect well on us. And we're being scrutinized as it is."

"What does the Reverend say?"

"He isn't happy."

"But what does he say?"

"It isn't important."

"But you brought it up. You began the story. It seems as though it must be important."

"Nothing that can't wait until you feel better."

"Did he say something about us?"

"No."

"What, then?"

"He issued a statement."

"What sort of statement?"

"He asked that there be no protests, no sit-ins."

"But, dear, it's Harry Belafonte. They have to protest."

"The Reverend disagrees because of the timing."

"The timing?"

"Because of our loss."

"Our loss?"

"The crash."

"The crash. Yes. Our loss and the crash."

"I shouldn't have said anything. I'll send Alma up with some soup."

"Please close the blind. Please?"

"Yes, Lulu."

"You won't come to bed? You won't hold me for just a little while?"

"It's not yet noon, Lulu."

"Yes. I see."

"I'm closing the blind."

"Yes, thank you, dear."

"I'm closing the door."

"Tell the children to whisper," she said. "I want to sleep."

"Good night, Lulu."

"Good night, dear."

Anastasia

A nastasia Rivers, whose real name was Stacy, was in the middle of her fifth dive of the day—ten feet above the water, the spring of the board still reverberating in her ears, her ass tucked, her toes pointed to the water, every muscle ready to kick the toes, the thighs—delicious thighs, the reason she'd gotten the job in the first place—kick them skyward, ready for the final position of the pike before entering the water cleanly, crisply, as little splash as possible—when she heard the screams from inside the hotel's dining room.

The hotel, a Radisson, was a recent addition to downtown Atlanta, just off Peachtree. Its dining room had floor-to-ceiling windows, sepia-tinted, which protected diners from the sun while providing an unobstructed view of the swimming pool and its professional-length diving board. She'd hoped for work at the Georgian Terrace Hotel, where nearly the entire cast of *Gone with the Wind* had stayed during filming. It would have been an omen, perhaps, portending her future fame, but the Georgian didn't have a pool and Anastasia didn't have the experience they required for cocktailing.

An act of defiance—against whom, precisely, she didn't know since her brother was AWOL and her parents were long gone—

Anastasia dove during dinner hours on Thursdays, Fridays, and Saturdays, and during brunch hours on Saturdays and Sundays. For the gig, she'd beaten out three other girls, all of them still in their teens. The manager, a creep, had hoped for a bikini—red, like the one Dolores Hart wore in the movie poster for *Where the Boys Are*—but Anastasia had convinced him of the impracticality of a two-piece. Perhaps she'd less convinced him than surprised him with her refusal to be duped, something he'd most likely found unladylike but—*those thighs!*—had kept to himself. She compromised with a one-piece, the sides of which had been professionally cut out. She was stunning in the costume and she knew it.

The screams from the dining room occurred mid-dive, three-quarters in. Her finish, her entry into the water, the connection to the surface, was haphazard. Her elbows gave. Her legs failed to complete their extension. The splash was unfortunate. She surfaced, water in her nose, coughing and spitting a mouthful from her lungs.

Her first reaction: embarrassment. She could perform a perfect jackknife with barely a second thought. She hated that diners might have witnessed the sloppy execution. Her brother had once accused her of being a narcissist. She hadn't understood. He showed her a highlighted passage in a book by a man named Freud. She liked neither the word nor its implications. "Not everything is about you, Stacy," he'd said before boarding a train to who knew where. "Sometimes you have to consider the feelings of others." "Anastasia," she'd said. "Call me Anastasia." She'd resented the accusation of narcissist. Were the Hepburns narcissists —Katharine *or* Audrey—simply for wanting more and for going after it? Was Lucille Ball? Was Jean Harlow? No, they were battleaxes. They were talented and had ambition. Maybe Anastasia lacked a particular talent. And maybe her passions—which ran deep—also ran away from her, but still she took issue with this idea of narcissism. Dreamers weren't narcissists. They were visionaries. Besides, if she was a narcissist, then her brother unquestionably was one, too.

By the time she surfaced, coughing, spitting, embarrassment had been replaced by curiosity. She swam to the edge of the pool and gripped the ladder.

There, like a dark cloud hovering over her, was her manager. A fresh towel was draped over his arm. He seemed to be holding it for her, which made no sense. Once he'd gotten it through his thick skull that she wouldn't be putting out the way certain of his waitresses did—pathetic girls who didn't suck in their stomachs in public or brush the loose hairs from their heads before work —he'd left her essentially alone.

Now, though, he was unfolding a towel and holding it open wide, as if he meant to shroud her in it. It was one of the thick beach-sized towels reserved specifically for paying guests. Perhaps he hoped to grope her as he toweled her dry. She remained in the pool.

"Anastasia," he said, "I'm at a loss for words. I'm so sorry."

"Sorry?" she said. "What about?" She let her body drop a little, so that her lips were even with the surface. She blew a few bubbles into the chlorinated water.

"You poor child," said the manager.

Poor, yes. Child, no.

A woman, early fifties, emerged from inside the hotel. Her eyes were bloodshot; her mascara smudged. She approached the manager, took him by the elbow, and gestured toward Anastasia. "Is this the girl?"

Anastasia wondered if it was her turn to be falsely charged with thievery. The female guests had been especially accusatory of the staff in the last few weeks. Whenever another wife left a watch or a pair of earrings in her lover's room, the absence was always pawned off on the help.

But this woman didn't appear antagonistic, quite the contrary.

She put a hand to her chest. It was a gesture—the open palm spread across the place beneath which a heart surely must be—that Anastasia, in just a few days' time, would come to expect, would come to anticipate at her mere entrance into a room.

Her manager was nodding. "Yes," he said. "This is the girl. Her mother *and* her father."

The woman gasped. "Her parents, my brother, so many of our friends . . ." The woman bit down on a knuckle and looked momentarily away. Anastasia thought the gesture divine.

The manager cleared his throat, and the woman was released from whatever reverie had briefly captured her.

They were now both gazing down at Anastasia with such affection—such sympathy and sweetness—that for a split second the girl forgot about the screaming from indoors; forgot that this interruption wasn't standard during her diving sessions.

She was still in the water, still holding on to the ladder and bobbing in the warmth of the early afternoon sun. She felt a deep connection at that moment with her own charm. She removed her swim cap and dunked her whole head beneath the surface. Her hair looked good wet, pulled to the side with a single twist.

She resurfaced and pushed herself from the pool, ignoring her manager's proffered hand. With her legs dangling into the water and her torso turned, she looked up at this mysterious woman—obviously wealthy—and her boss.

She pulled her hair to the side and squeezed out the water. Her thighs were glistening.

"My parents?" she said. "What about them?"

Anastasia's real parents had left her and her brother, twins, under the stone archway of the Baptist Orphanage in Hapeville, Georgia, in 1948. They'd been left with a bandanna full of stale taffy and a suitcase stuffed with the clothes they shared. Before the orphanage, there'd never been a distinction between their sexes. Their parents had cut their hair the same, dressed them the same. On the sidewalk, which in those early days had been made of wood planks, when someone mistook Stacy for a boy, her parents didn't offer a correction. It wasn't until the orphanage that she learned that one was not born a woman but became one.

On the day they'd been abandoned—they were eight that autumn, something Anastasia knew because they aged in accordance with the year: two in '42, five in '45, eight in '48—her mother had affixed a handwritten note to her brother's sweater with a safety pin. Her father instructed them to sit still beneath the portico, chilly in the stone's shade, and wait till they were fetched. Many hours must have passed between being left and being found. The sun moved from one side of the archway to the other. Her brother slept with his head in her lap. When he woke, they switched places and she napped with her cheek against his thigh. They didn't speak in all those hours. They hadn't needed to.

Now Anastasia was twenty-two and living in Atlanta, having made her way from Hapeville, which existed glumly in the shadows of the Atlanta Municipal Airport, a mere seven miles south of the actual metropolis.

"We've just seen it on the television. There's been an accident." It was the woman talking. She knelt down to Anastasia's level. "How terribly sad I am. How terribly confused and sad! Forgive me for sharing this news. But I must." On the woman's ring finger was a bright blue stone. Her pantyhose, which glistened even more than Anastasia's wet thighs, could have been made of silken gold. "It won't hurt less for you to know that I am also suffering. But I am. I, too, am suffering."

Somehow the woman had taken the towel from the manager and, in a single and agile motion, wrapped it around her as though it were a blanket. The woman's hands were on her shoulders. Anastasia felt suddenly like a little girl, as though she were under the most wonderful and useful protection.

"Your parents," the woman said. "The jet. I have to tell you."

"The jet?"

"Yes," she said.

"My parents?"

Above them, she was aware of the manager's murmuring. "She's in shock," he said. "She doesn't understand."

"In Paris," the woman said. "It's everyone. They're all gone. All dead."

"Dead?"

"Yes," the woman said. "Your parents. All of my friends. My brother and his cherished wife." She stood up slowly and looked toward the dining room. She seemed once again lost in thought. "All of them. That's what the television is saying."

Anastasia, who all at once understood, pulled her legs from the water and tightened the towel.

In April, when she auditioned for the job, she'd told the manager and her competition—those three stuck-up girls looking for a cheap chance at rebellion against their humdrum middle-class lives, which was so much less interesting than her own act of defiance, aimed more generally at the world and all its humming human hearts and not simply at a few well-meaning parents in suburbia—well, she'd told them that her parents were among the group of art patrons who would be traveling to Europe to tour the museums. She'd said it in the heat of the moment, an artless lie to shut the teenagers up and elevate her status simply by association. She hadn't seen those girls since the day of the tryouts, and the manager hadn't shown much interest in her boast except to ask every now and then how her parents were enjoying the European weather, which everyone knew had been unseasonably frosty and wet.

It was one of her sloppier lies and she'd regretted it almost immediately, but the diving gig was only for the summer. She assumed her next job—whatever it was—would lead to her inevitable discovery, which would land her in California, maybe New York, where there'd be no risk of being found out as a fraud. And after all, on the mendacity scale, hers was an ultimately harmless lie: what could possibly happen even if she were found out? A slap on the wrist? A *tsk*ing of the tongue?

But that was before. That was before this news.

"Ms. Case is a regular," the manager said. "She's one of our best customers. She's been watching you out here for weeks."

Anastasia owed the Radisson ten more dives that afternoon. She wouldn't be finishing them. What she understood in this moment was that she would never be diving there again. She had no choice but to come clean to this dazzling woman with the mesmerizing blue stone and the shimmering hose. Given the circumstances, given the fact that the imaginary people she'd been pretending were her parents were now dead—and dead along with more than one hundred of Atlanta's most well-known citizens—she would no doubt be fired on the spot. And fired, she assumed, in a most ignominious and embarrassing way.

She stood up. She didn't want to be humiliated while sitting by the side of a pool, as if she were the child and they were the grownups. It was bad enough that she was wearing that stupid bathing costume with its stupid side cutouts.

She opened her mouth, but all that came out was a stammering. "I— I— I—." She could kick herself for sounding so simple, so unprepared, so trapped by her own carelessness.

The woman put an arm around her.

"It was an accident," Anastasia said. She shook the woman off. Her kindness was unbearable.

"Yes," the woman said. "That's right."

"No," she said. "You don't understand."

"You dear child."

The woman reached for Anastasia's hand. She yanked it away. "Don't hurt me," she said. "It was just an accident."

"She's in shock, I tell you," the manager said. "Who should we call?"

"You're not listening," Anastasia said. "There's no one—"

"She must be an only child," said the manager.

The woman's hand went back to her chest. "Of course," she said. "An only child."

"Please," said Anastasia. The woman reached for her hand again. This time, inexplicably, Anastasia didn't pull away, as though her body had discovered an opportunity that her mind was only now tumbling to. "Please," she said again. "Let me explain." But already she felt the explanation slipping away. She felt the desire to be truthful in this moment, like the water on her thighs, begin slowly but naturally to evaporate: how disappointed this woman would be if she learned the truth, how doubly saddened . . . And after all, she seemed to be finding a purpose in her sympathy for Anastasia's plight. This woman had lost real friends. Anastasia could offer real comfort. They could comfort one another. But first she had to correct one misconception.

"I have a brother," she said. "I don't know where he is."

The woman slipped her arm around Anastasia's waist, and Anastasia, she couldn't help it, leaned into her. The woman's skin smelled of lilacs and cherry blossoms, of old age and privilege.

"Darling girl," the woman said. The manager just stood there, relegated now to the role of mere witness. He felt so much already a thing of Anastasia's distant, distant past. "We'll find him together," the woman said. "In the meantime"—Anastasia was aware of being moved forward, being escorted in the direction of the hotel by the woman—"if there's no one else, then it seems, if you'll allow me to be presumptuous, that it would be best if you come with me. I'll take you home. We will weather this storm together." They were moving still, gliding almost, gliding toward the dining room, which they soon floated through—a gorgeous spectacle of grief and generosity to anyone who was looking—on their way to the lobby with its television, which continued to recount the disaster, and then to the driver, who stood uncomplainingly in the lethal Georgia heat, and then to the wonderful house on Tanglewood that surely already awaited them both.

"Would you like this?" said the woman. "Does this sound good to you?"

Their movement was so effortless now.

"Yes," said the girl, without an ounce of reluctance. "Please."

On the day of the crash, Anastasia Rivers believed she'd finally been discovered.

Piedmont

I t wasn't what his mother had imagined for him, just like it wasn't what he'd imagined for himself. Yet facts were facts. And the fact now was that generations of slavery and servitude had been distilled into a single irrefutable moment: Piedmont Dobbs was acting as a chauffeur; he was acting as a chauffeur on a Friday night at approximately 10 p.m., going sixty miles an hour somewhere north of Monroe, Georgia, roughly twenty miles shy of Athens, which was the destination of the two white men who were slumped against themselves in the backseat. Here was one more Negro man—of his own volition and with no shackles necessary—driving a car on behalf of the white man.

The saving grace, as his father would have said if he'd been alive to witness, was the car: a 1960 sea-green Thunderbird convertible with leather so white and clean it reminded Piedmont of teeth and also of a bathroom sink and also of the large serving platter his mother used on Sundays, but only when there was company. The hardtop had been removed from the convertible and the white of the exposed interior practically shone in the night, that was how clean and bright the leather was—as though it had spent the entire day soaking up the sun, and now, the moon the only source of natural light, it was giving back all that energy of the absorbed rays, radiating with the daytime's ridiculous energy.

To the right and to the left, the land was barren. In the day, the red clay would have blazed up and out with wicked heat. But at night, as it was now, it just looked dry and dark. Every few miles a dirt highway cut across Route 29. Piedmont didn't bother slowing down. If he'd turned and followed any of those unpaved roads, he guessed he would have come across shanty-towns the likes of which he'd heard about from kids back home who were unlucky enough to have family out here in the boonies. He'd been told stories of car motors resting in trees, placed at whose whim or with what power — man-made? God-made? — his friends had never wagered to guess or bothered to explain. The babies ran around naked, he'd heard from a boy his age, and Piedmont had closed his eyes and imagined a grassless expanse of run-down, beaten-up farmhouses and tiny black-skinned babies running wild as though they themselves and not the chickens were the pack of animals. Surely his schoolmates had been exaggerating. Surely they'd been pulling his leg, and he, knowing no other life than the one he'd lived with his mother, had been gullible enough to believe them. But that was back then. That was a different life from the one Piedmont was living now.

For the past year, home (he viewed this usage, though instinctive, as a corruption of the word) had been a shared room on the third floor of a funeral home on Decatur Avenue. When he'd quit his mother's apartment, he didn't have a plan. Who knew if he even meant to do more than make a statement by leaving her alone with her thoughts for a few hours and then returning after he, too, had had some time to think, to cool off, to adjust to the disappointment of having a dream — his mother's dream, he now understood, and never really his own — taken from him so cleanly and conclusively.

He'd walked. The night turned from plum-pink to deep purple to black. He walked on. Sweating shirtless toddlers sat on the laps of their mothers, maybe their sisters, and squawked at the heat, at the feeling of their skin against other skin, at the feeling already of what would become lifelong discomfort and disappointment. He walked out of his own neighborhood and into another, then another, then another. He passed parked cars with their pistons and spark plugs sitting on their hoods, passed men who looked like high school boys he'd once looked up to when he was still in middle school, passed women who looked like girls he'd once thought to cultivate crushes on. He walked that night, his pillowcase slung over his shoulder in what must have appeared a childish and dramatic fashion to any real adult watching, until the crowds of colored people thinned and the streets turned empty, and he found himself suddenly at the end of a block with no place farther to walk without turning around and retracing his steps. He looked up. Before him was a large building made of cinder block and painted chalk-white. In black cursive letters above a set of double doors was a sign—*his* sign, Piedmont's sign, the thing he'd been unwittingly waiting for since he left his crying mother and walked out of her house several hours earlier:

WILLIAMS BROS.' FUNERAL HOME & PARLOUR

He'd heard stories when he was in school about gas stations and funeral homes that were run by and for colored people only, and that many of these places—if you could find them—would also put up a traveling Negro, or one who was merely down on his luck, for a night or two. He climbed the stone steps and stood in front of the doors. He looked at his wrist, but he'd forgotten to put on his father's watch before leaving. It must have been close to midnight. He knocked anyway.

As it turned out, there were no Williams brothers alive any-

more. There was only a sister, who went by Miss Carvie, and who
received Piedmont that night with a firm handshake and a promise of a full meal and a safe place to sleep.

She had taken him to a kitchen, and from her icebox she'd
pulled cold chicken and cold biscuits and cold milk. Miss Carvie had not asked Piedmont where he'd come from, as if she'd
known he wouldn't tell the truth or been raised on the same man-
ners as he. Instead she asked, "Are you passing through or settling
down?"

"Hard saying, not knowing," he'd said, which was the truth.

"I have an empty bed," she said. "Two other boys already share
the room. Toilet down the hall. You share that too. No fighting,
no drinking, no women. I go to church on Sunday, but that's not
a requirement. First week is free. After that, I'll ask for help in
any way you can give it. If you can't find work out there, I'll give
you work in here. If you're clean and quiet and decent, then you'll
stay as long as you need." It was a speech she'd delivered a hundred times before, that much was clear.

After he finished his chicken and chased it down with a second glass of cold milk, Miss Carvie led Piedmont up two flights
of stairs and then down a hot and dark hallway that whirred with
the sound of several large box fans. From a pocket of her house-
dress, she pulled a flashlight, turned it on, then opened a door at
the end of the corridor. "Toilet," she said in a whisper, and shone
the light around briefly. She closed the door and moved back toward the stairs. She stopped now at a second door, one he hadn't
seen in the dark. "You'll sleep here," she said, before opening
the door. "Michael and Jeremy are already asleep. Don't fuss or
make noise if you can help it." Quietly, she opened the door. She
beamed the light on the floor just in front of Piedmont's shoes,
then moved it slowly forward and to the right until it hit the foot
of a single bed. The light moved up the wooden leg to a bare mattress and a set of folded sheets. Miss Carvie handed Piedmont the
flashlight. "Hold this," she said. "Keep it trained on me."

He took the light and held it steady. As she made the bed, he looked around. On the other side of the room were two more single beds. These, Piedmont understood, were already occupied, and, squinting, he could see that there were in fact two breathing mounds beneath white sheets and, atop pillows close to the wall, dark brown circles deep in sleep.

Miss Carvie took the flashlight from Piedmont's hand. She shone it once again at the bed. "There you go," she said. "Breakfast in the morning. Dinner at night. We'll talk again at the end of the week."

The flashlight went dark. He felt Miss Carvie's warmth move away and out of the room. He heard the door close ever so softly. For several seconds he stood where he'd been left, his pillowcase by his side, and listened. The boys to his left snored delicately in tandem, something rehearsed—*First you, now you, then you, and you again . . .*—and Piedmont felt something like an ache in his bones, something akin to homesickness, for the siblings he'd never had. He crept to the twin bed that Miss Carvie had made up for him and carefully rested his pillowcase on the floor by his side. He climbed under the sheet, sure he wouldn't be able to sleep, sure that the newness of this place and the sudden image of his mother, alone in her own bed, alone in their apartment and worried sick, would keep him awake all night. But he was wrong. With the heat and the strange boys' snores, he was out cold within minutes.

Now, tonight, he knew he should be angry with himself, with his decision to accept the role of chauffeur, which was disgusting in its obviousness and its preordained predictability: a Negro son of a Negro car mechanic shepherding two down-and-out white men to their desired destination. It amazed Piedmont how incapacitated a man could be—how incapacitated a *white* man could be. Negroes didn't have such luxury. Or anyway he'd personally never known such luxury. But that felt like a judgment, and Piedmont didn't think he was in a place in life where he'd earned the right to be critical of another's choices, especially now that he was no better than a custodian in a white man's club or a chauffeur navigating a white man's car. Perhaps it was this very lack of certainty and conviction that had led him to accept the two men's drunken invitation several hours earlier.

"You, there," one of them had said. It was late. The Purple Pigeon, where he'd found steady work as a janitor, had been nearly empty. Piedmont had already gotten out the mop.

"You, there. Do you know how to drive an automobile?"

He'd stood up straight, an animal instinct to respect the oppressor. "Yes, sir," he'd said. Another animal instinct. He was torn between pride at having been chosen for address, pride in his ability to honestly admit to his ability, and revulsion for his eagerness.

"I wonder, then," said the man, "if you'd very much mind putting down your mop and driving us to Athens. Tonight. Now. This very second, in fact."

Piedmont took in the scene. The man who'd addressed him was sitting upright, but his eyes were droopy. The second man, the one who'd not yet spoken, gripped his head in his hands as though trying to keep his skull from cracking apart. He moaned.

"Young sir," said the first man, "do you have an answer?" His accent morphed from word to word when he spoke, as though he were trying out several possibilities and hadn't yet made up his mind. It reminded Piedmont of a patched-together recording or of the time he and his classmates had performed the Pledge of Allegiance on Parents' Day. They'd recited it from memory one child and one word at a time. "I," said Emilia Johnson, who was first in the long single-file line of second graders. "Pledge," said George Pinckley. "Allegiance," said Piedmont.

And as though it was his turn in line to speak again now, Piedmont answered somehow without thinking, the answer coming from somewhere and maybe even some*one* else. It was as if the experience itself, even as it was happening, in the actual moment of the occurrence, was predestined, forewarned, almost rehearsed in some way. Just as those second graders had rehearsed their words and order again and again in anticipation of their audience. "No, sir," he said, the answer as much a surprise to his own ears as to the stranger who asked for it, "I wouldn't mind."

On other nights since acquiring the job at the Purple Pigeon, Piedmont had put the mop away without notice and left when the floors were clean like it was nothing out of the ordinary. Tonight he did the same and, no boss in sight to contradict, he followed the men outside. On the spot, he seemed to have made the decision that this—this late-night car ride out of Atlanta into a part of the state he'd never been before, though it was fewer than a hundred miles away—this, and not that puerile application for integration, was what he'd been waiting for all his life.

To play the part of the white man's chauffeur? The voice that asked the question belonged to his mother, to her preacher, to his organ instructor, to every teacher at Booker T. he'd ever had.

It's not what you think. It's different somehow.

How, boy?

They saw me. They picked me.

They didn't see you. They saw a colored boy. They saw a sucker who knows how to take an order.

I don't think so.

Do you even know where they're taking you?

It's an adventure.

We'll see how you feel when you're swinging from a tree.

It's not like that anymore.

It's like that more than ever, boy.

Don't call me that.

He says not to call him that! He says he's not a boy! You hear that? Our little Piedmont Dobbs thinks he's all grown up. You hear that? Ooh-wee, he makes me laugh.

Piedmont shook away the voices. They were figments of his imagination, symptoms of his own doubts and fears. But he had no interest in doubt and fear, in entertaining either any longer than he already had. He wanted to live. He wanted to do something different than his parents had done, than his classmates had done. He thought of Lora and Alfred, slow dancing under the sexy red glow of the gymnasium lights nearly a year ago to the day. They'd merely been play-acting as grownups. But here he was a real one, and so he'd said "yes, sir" to the man in the linen blazer. And while "yes, sir" was something that every one of his kind said on a near-hourly basis and therefore was not remotely new or unique, was in fact a state of being, a phrase passed down by blood from one generation to the next, what *was* both new and unique was that he was going sixty, maybe sixty-five—all right, closer to seventy miles an hour, because who was going to stop him?—down a blacktop smooth as silk in a car almost too beautiful to think about, and the yowl of the wind in his ears was nothing short of glorious, something spiritual almost; in fact, downright otherworldly.

The headlights gave him only twenty or so feet of blue-hued road but that was plenty. That was more than he needed. He hadn't been behind a wheel since his father died, but it had come back to him as though it were in his blood, which in some ways it was, since his father had known cars like the back of his own hand.

Piedmont slapped his thigh and whistled. What would his father say now if he could see him? And—who knows?—maybe he could see him. Maybe right then his daddy was looking down from outer space, seeing his son chauffeuring two white men to some rural location for some undisclosed purpose. Maybe that's what his father was looking at right then, and maybe he was thinking that his only boy was a fool, no better than a butler, but alive he'd never once called Piedmont a fool; had never once delivered him the back side of his hand; had never once taken off his belt in threat. And so if he was looking down from space and if happenstance permitted that he was checking in on Piedmont this very minute and not on his mother, who was the only other person his father would bother with, then no doubt what he would be wondering about, like Piedmont himself, regarded not some potential danger but rather the nature of the treasure that must surely lay in store for him on the other end of this dreamlike drive. To another Negro, this opportunity might have been dismissible as mundane, but there was magic in Piedmont's blood. His mother had once said so.

He could have howled at the moon in ecstasy. He might have, too, if it hadn't been for the sudden tap on his shoulder from the man who, at the bar, had been holding his head together with his hands.

What the man's words sounded like — traveling against the hot airstream that blew up from the hood, across and down from the windshield, swirling in and about the open interior — was *ul-ower.* The man said it again, "*Ul-*ower," and pointed this time at the grass on the side of the highway. Piedmont, downshifting from fourth to third to second to first, did as he was told. He pulled over.

The man didn't even open the car door. He just jumped — ditch-side — over his sleeping friend and onto the grass. He doubled over and Piedmont looked away. It wouldn't have been right to watch a stranger — white or Negro — be sick in public. Even if *public* here was nothing more than the side of a deserted highway, a few minutes shy of midnight. Neither did Piedmont turn his head when he heard the passenger's-side door open. It wasn't until the man spoke that he felt it was safe to look.

"Pardon me," said the man, getting into the front seat and shutting the door. "My stomach isn't always so sensitive." He removed a handkerchief from his breast pocket, wiped the sides of his mouth, then stuffed the dirty cloth into his pants. He rooted around beneath his seat and came up with a small metal object. It was a Rayovac Sportsman. The man slid a little switch on the flashlight's side, and the console was lit up by the tiny beam. A moth flew into the light then bounced away. Alive or dead, Piedmont couldn't be sure.

The man turned to Piedmont and raised the light so that it was in his eyes. He squinted. It was not a powerful light. The batteries must have been close to dead.

"What's your name again?"

"Piedmont Dobbs, sir. But you didn't ask me before." He tucked his chin so that the light was on his forehead and out of his eyes. Perhaps he'd been wrong about these men. Perhaps there was something pernicious he'd not caught wind of at the bar, when their inebriation had made them seem vulnerable and non-menacing.

"I didn't?"

"No, sir."

"What about the fellow in the back. Did he ask?"

"No, sir."

"And yet here you are driving his car."

"Yes, sir."

The man clicked off the light. Piedmont rubbed his eyes.

"Extraordinary world, isn't it?"

"I suppose, sir."

"Made up almost entirely of coincidence and chance. Bad luck and good. Fortune and failure. In this way it, life, is fairly predictable. At any given moment, you're either winning or you're losing. I could go on." He righted himself in his seat so that he was no longer facing Piedmont. The Sportsman was still in his lap. "But I won't."

"Yes, sir."

"My own name is Robert Tucker." This man, this Robert Tucker, removed a small vial from an inside pocket of his jacket, held it to his nose, and snorted. "My name, of course, is not nearly so impressive as yours." Now the man held the vial toward Piedmont, who shook his head slightly. He didn't know if he was being made fun of. There was nothing to do either way. "You can call me Robert," he said.

Piedmont took a deep breath; in the air itself, he could taste a mixture of possibility and destiny. He wanted to breathe air like this forever. He wanted to breathe it for the rest of his life, that's how good it felt, as though extra oxygen had been pumped in special for him and his lungs alone. He used to dream about finding whites like these—whites who pretended not to see color. Of course they saw it, but the fact that they were willing to pretend they didn't was a start at least.

Wasn't it?

Was it?

It was!

"Who taught you to drive?" Robert shouted this question against the wind after they pulled back onto the highway, Piedmont going now closer to fifty, fifty-five.

"My father."

"Who taught you to read?"

"My mother."

"Me, too," said Robert, who had angled the seat as far back as he could without ramming his friend's knees. "Mine's dead. Yours?"

"Yep," Piedmont said. "Yes, sir." It wasn't merely that he didn't want to talk about his mother. It was that he didn't even want to think about her. Thinking about her would require that he think about his actions, about the way he'd walked out nearly a year ago and hadn't been in touch since. Thinking about her just got the dubious voices in his head going again, and that was the last thing he wanted with this man now awake beside him.

"You speak well," said Robert.

Piedmont gripped the wheel and sped up slightly.

"That's not a remark about you being a Negro."

"Yes, sir."

"I work in a newsroom," Robert said. "Used to. Maybe still do. I'm on leave, as they say. Point is, I work with kids. Probably close to your age. And it's all howdy-do and gobbledygook. There's new lingo seems like every morning."

"Must not have offered that class at my school," Piedmont said. He could fight if he had to, just like he told that school board committee. If he needed to, he could defend himself against this man and his friend, too.

"Better for it," said Robert.

For several minutes, they were both quiet, the only sounds the working engine and the whistling wind and maybe, if an ear strained itself, this summer's batch of cicadas in the trees to the side of the highway. After a while, Robert turned on the radio and jimmied with the dial, searching for a clear channel. Finally, there was the low moan of a piano, which he isolated then turned up.

A memory flitted about behind Piedmont's eyes. It came in and out of view in a seasick sort of way—seasickness itself something Piedmont didn't know firsthand but something his parents had told him about as a child, explaining their own parents' passage from the familiar to the unknown. In this Ping-Ponging memory, he was eight. His father was beside him. The heat inside the church was stifling. Even the men waved fans in front of their faces. The light, like the memory itself, flickered as the men and women close by swayed: a certain direction, and the sunlight from the high, open windows all but blinded him; the opposite, and he was nearly eclipsed by darkness. He couldn't see her from where he stood many rows back, but he could hear her: his mother's voice rising up above the other singers in the chorus. There was no solo, but he could separate it even then. Closing his eyes, rocking in the heat, he could fold away the other voices and concentrate solely on hers. He didn't know whether or not she was any good then—he was too young to appreciate talent —he only knew that she was his. That voice, singing along with the organ, belonged to him and to his father, and because of that it was beautiful.

"Eyes on the road," said Robert.

Piedmont had allowed the car to drift slightly toward the center. He corrected its course.

The memory went black. He concentrated on the radio. "You like Don Shirley?" asked Piedmont.

"Everybody likes Don Shirley."

Piedmont ruminated on this.

"You know the album where he's sitting at the piano, decked out in the tux, just glowering at the camera?"

"I think so," said Piedmont. In fact, he knew it inside and out, backward and forward. He'd not been the most talented on the organ at church, but he'd been — for a little while at least — the most determined. He'd overheard the preacher once say that Piedmont's hands were a pianist's dream; they stretched a perfect octave.

For his first birthday after his father's death, his mother had given him a portable tabletop Magnus organ. They'd set it up in his bedroom on top of an industrial wire spool. The spool was curved and the edge dug into his forearms when he played, but the splinters never stopped him from practicing. The organ, aside from the apartment itself, was the nicest thing they owned between them. He didn't know where his mother had gotten it or how, and he never asked. In the year since he left home, he thought of his organ every day.

"I wooed my wife with that record. If it weren't for Don Shirley" — Robert gestured toward the backseat — "she'd probably be with that fellow there."

Piedmont looked in the rearview mirror. The other man's chin was against his chest. There was drool on his lapel, or maybe just a leftover stain from a spill earlier in the evening.

"You have a wife?" asked Piedmont.

"You don't think I should?"

"I just—" It was none of his business. He wasn't sure why he'd asked in the first place. "All I mean is this situation—" He lifted a hand from the steering wheel, and the hand, as if attempting to capture the whole of the evening in a single gesture, made a slow circle in the air and then returned to its place on the wheel. "This situation doesn't seem conducive to there being a wife."

"Conducive," said Robert. He gave his own knee a little knock. "I like that." Then he bent over in his seat and again held the vial to his nose. "Nosireebob," he said, coming back up. He didn't offer any to Piedmont this time. "There is certainly nothing conducive about my wife." He wiped at his nose. "Not of late, surely."

Perhaps Piedmont should have accepted the vial when he'd had the chance. Perhaps he'd missed out on his future simply by refusing. "Maybe," he said, "you're on leave from her too."

Robert guffawed. "On leave! From my wife! Yes! Piedmont," he said. The man was suddenly very serious. "You're funny."

"No one's ever told me that before."

"Then your friends lack a sense of humor."

Piedmont thought about Jeremy and Michael. Was *friend* the right word to describe either one of them? They'd not secured regular work as he had. Instead, they helped Miss Carvie at the home and took on odd jobs around the neighborhood. They did this because they wanted the freedom to move about the city as they pleased, taking judo classes with other young Negroes and learning about the Fruit of Islam at a restaurant around the corner.

When, at the end of his first week at the funeral home and sharing the attic room, he came home tired but happy with the news that he'd gotten a job as a janitor at a jazz club on the white side of town, they'd slapped their sides and hollered in indignation. "The well-worn path to servitude," they'd said.

Miss Carvie had shushed them. "Not at my table. No one will accuse him of that at my table." She'd slid an extra piece of fish onto Piedmont's plate. "I'm proud of you," she said. "Looks like you're sticking around."

On the third floor that night, Jeremy and Michael had resumed their taunts. They sat on either side of Piedmont and pressed him for details. They were disappointed in him, they said; but they were also curious about the bar, about the work he'd do. They made fun of him, sure, but there was a tolerance to their ribbing that had at first made him feel like a younger brother and therefore loved, and so he accepted the fun they made, even enjoyed it for the attention that it was. During the days, the three of them existed apart, but at night they ate dinner with Miss Carvie and then retired to the upstairs, where they talked about comic books and the white folks who listened to jazz and the colored folks who could actually play. Sometimes Piedmont would dance around the room in imitation of the customers' bad rhythm. Fridays and Saturdays he worked the late shift, and sometimes Jeremy and Michael would wait for him in the alley and they'd walk home together. They'd tell stories to Piedmont of their adventures outside—the girls they saw, the judo they practiced, the meetings they'd started, just recently, attending.

But a few months back, everything changed. Jeremy and Michael had gone down to Augusta to join up with some picketers at the Delta Minor housing project. Negroes were asking for equal rights at the supermarket where they worked. Jeremy and Michael had gotten wind of the protest, and so when Piedmont left for work one day, they went themselves to Delta Minor. Piedmont was used to keeping his head down at the Purple Pigeon, his eyes trained on the mop. He could lose several hours just listening to the live jazz. That day he'd done the same as ever, not paying attention to the talk of the customers, to the news they brought with them and took away. He was invisible to them and they were invisible to him. This was his excuse anyway for being oblivious to what had happened in Augusta. By the time he got back to the funeral home, Jeremy and Michael were already upstairs. They were agitated, and he listened quietly as they filled him in on the day's events.

What he pieced together that night—and even more in the week to come as the riots and protests continued—was that a bunch of white kids had driven through the housing project throwing stones at Negroes. The white kids hadn't counted on the black kids having guns. But they did have guns, and one white boy took a bullet between the eyes.

Several days passed, and Jeremy and Michael stopped meeting up with Piedmont after his shift. They no longer wanted to talk about jazz or comic books late into the night. Sometimes when Piedmont was in the room, they took to whispering. On one occasion, they straight-up walked out as soon as he walked in.

The truth was, now that he thought of it, Piedmont didn't have any friends—ones with a sense of humor or ones without. He had roommates. He had a boss. He had Miss Carvie, who was essentially a landlady. But he did not have a friend. He couldn't remember a single complete conversation he'd had with another human being since April. It dazed him, this idea that a person could go so many weeks undetected.

In school they'd read *Invisible Man*. Piedmont had been intrigued by it, same as his peers, but he'd felt no special kinship to the unnamed narrator. When his teacher read passionately aloud from it—raising his voice, pounding his desk with a fist—he'd felt a mild embarrassment, as though being asked to watch something that should have remained private.

But now, here, the night pitch-black, blue-black, and the tree frogs screaming bloody murder in the distance and the wind an almost supernatural presence swirling up and around and in them, he wondered if he hadn't, self-consciously, been trying these last several months to re-create another man's experience. He'd lulled himself into near nonexistence until, out of nowhere, this man Robert Tucker and the other who sat behind had seen him.

Had he willed himself into view, wondered Piedmont, or had they?

Ivan & Lulu

"Whose fault was it, Ivan?"

"Why must it be someone's fault?"

"Because it must. Otherwise there is no point."

"There isn't a point, Lulu. Think of Job."

"Good Lord. Are we being tested, then?"

"Forget I said anything about the Bible."

"But where is the lesson?"

"There is no lesson."

"Someone has to pay for this."

"The airline will pay."

"Was the pilot slow?"

"Who told you that?"

"The copilot. I hear he was a little bit off, you know. No wife, no children. There was something off, I tell you. It isn't normal not to have children."

"I'm turning off the lights now. I need to get some sleep."

"Will it bankrupt the insurance companies?"

"Good night, Lulu."

"On the one hand, I would hate for anyone to go broke because of this. On the other, it makes me sick to think of people profiting off the deaths of others."

"Do you want me to sleep in the guest room? I will."

"I hope I never profit off your death."

"Profit is the wrong word."

"What, then?"

"Compensation."

"But that suggests people can be commodified."

"Who taught you that word?"

"I went to school, Ivan. I have an education, same as you."

"People have value."

"Value! You're attaching a price tag to a person's life."

"It's nothing new. We've done it millions of times in the South."

"I feel sick."

"Close your eyes, dear. It's bedtime."

Robert

Half past midnight, Coleman yawned, leaned forward, and tapped the Negro kid on his shoulder. He pointed to a spot in the distance.

"Slow down," said Coleman. "Turn there."

To the west, behind them and going forward, there was now thick black vegetation, a forest of trees and wildlife. But on the east side of the highway, maybe a half mile in front of them, at the spot on the right where Coleman had pointed, yellow lights twinkled sporadically.

"What is this place?"

The moonlight was strong, but there was a layer of low, thin clouds, and through a brief break in the tree line, Robert couldn't make out much more than a field with two long parallel rows of red lights. "Some sort of research facility? Is this government?"

"You asked me what's next," said Coleman. He had angled himself from the backseat so that he was now situated between the two of them, his chest nearly parallel with theirs in the front. The smell of alcohol was overpowering. Robert entertained a moment of shame. It passed quickly, nearly nonexistent.

"This is what's next." Coleman squeezed Robert's shoulder. "See those trees?" He was talking now to Piedmont. "That space between them?" As if on cue, the headlights illuminated another, smaller break in the foliage and what appeared to be a mailbox and the beginning of a narrow gravel drive. "Turn there."

Piedmont slowed. The drive was long and dark. Dogwoods on either side grew into one another overhead. The car inched forward.

Coleman inhaled deeply through his nose. "I love this smell."

"Chicken shit and scotch?" asked Robert.

"Country," said Coleman. "God's country."

Before them, where the gravel drive became a kind of round-about, there now appeared an enormous two-story Greek revival surrounded by tall Grecian columns.

"Christ," whispered Robert, suddenly all accidental reverence. "Is this yours?" Beneath the tires, small rocks crunched and moaned and occasionally pinged sideways in the dark.

"Park there," said Coleman.

Piedmont, who'd formerly appeared a pretty cool customer, at least to Robert's mind, now seemed nervous, agitated. He was licking his lower lip with his tongue. If the place brought to mind the Klan for Robert, which it nearly immediately did, then no doubt it had done the same for the kid. And if the idea of the Klan gave even Robert, a white, middle-aged, presumably affluent man, the heebie-jeebies, then Piedmont was likely berserk with fear. Two white men asked him to drive them out of the city and into the middle of the country in the middle of the night? What had he been thinking saying yes? What, for that matter, had Robert been thinking in hitching himself to a ride whose final destination was a mystery even to him?

Something Robert never told Lily, something he didn't think she needed to know: once, just after their engagement, when cocktail party after cocktail party after cocktail party had been thrown in their honor, he'd sneaked away from the festivities and into her godfather's office. He needed a breather, a moment away from the winks and the tongue clucking and the slaps on the back. He also needed a cigarette, which was why he'd planted himself at her godfather's desk and why he'd given himself permission to root through the man's drawers. He was practically family, he reasoned, or would be soon enough.

What Robert found didn't excite him for its curiosity or his lack of preparation. What he found scared him. Beneath a clamshell jewel box, the type of thing inside which you might store an emergency pair of cufflinks, there was a well-worn piece of paper, the size of a Diner's Club card. This particular piece of paper was also proof of membership. But this card certified that its bearer, Lily's godfather, had been found worthy of advancement in the mysteries of Klankraft. Those words precisely. There was her godfather's name and there was his signature and there, at the paper's top, were the ornately printed words:

INVISIBLE EMPIRE
KNIGHTS OF THE KU KLUX KLAN

Robert was no young gun. He'd been around the block. By then, he'd been a newspaperman for nearly two decades. He knew evil existed. Even so, that little card with Lily's godfather's name on it, the care with which the calligraphy had been recorded, the pride the print suggested, and above all the language — *advancement in the mysteries of Klankraft* — terrified him for the sudden knowledge of his own proximity to evil.

Robert looked again at Piedmont, whose discomfort appeared only to have intensified, as though he'd been watching Robert's thoughts play out like some chilling scene from a movie.

In the backseat, Coleman stood, then hopped over the door in a single bound.

"Are we expected?" asked Robert, who was still seated on the passenger's side. "It's nearly one."

"I don't think I should be here," said Piedmont. He'd killed the headlights and was looking forward into the windshield at . . . At what? His future? His doom?

"Kid, you're fine. You wait in the car. Robert, you come with me." Coleman opened the passenger's-side door. "Let's honky-tonk. Out."

Robert got out. His knees cracked. His back did too.

"Come on, Big Daddy. Let's see what's shaking."

"Stop doing that," said Robert.

"What? What am I doing?"

"Stop talking like some hot rod."

"Don't have a cow," said Coleman. He slapped Robert on the back, hard. Robert turned to him, his right hand in a fist. It was possible he'd had enough. He couldn't tell. But Coleman raised his hands so that they were parallel with his shoulders. His palms were open, his fingers spread wide. "I'm sorry, I'm sorry. I forgot: no more hitting. Really. I'm sorry. No more."

Before Robert could respond—before he could decide even how he might have responded—a second-floor porch light turned on, illuminating the haint blue of its ceiling. The two men looked up. So did Piedmont, but they weren't paying attention to him. And now a screen door on the second floor was pushed open, and what emerged was a relatively normal-looking young man, save for the long white dressing gown he was wearing. To Robert, it almost seemed he was playing a part.

"Who's that?" said the man. "Who's there?"

"He has a gun," whispered Piedmont.

Robert looked at the kid, his hands gripping the wheel at ten and two, his eyes glued to the figure above them. Then he looked again at the gowned man.

Yes, it was true.

At the man's side, a long-barreled shotgun hung from his right hand.

"Jesus," said Robert. "What is this?"

Coleman cupped his hands together, leaned back, and made three yelps in quick succession. Then he righted himself and said, "Put the weapon down, you bastard. It's me."

The man stepped forward toward the edge of the porch, the gun still in his hand, but now he rested it on the railing in a casual way.

"Coleman?"

Behind the man, the screen door opened again, this time only partway. This figure, shorter, more slender, didn't come forward; instead it loitered in the small opening between the door frame and the screen.

The man turned. "Back inside," he said. The figure, which now Robert could see was a woman, a very young woman, and a Negro, moved back into the darkness from which she'd come. The screen door was once again closed. To the small group below, in his driveway, the man said, "You're early."

"I got my times mixed up," called Coleman.

"It's nearly midnight."

"It's past midnight, in fact," said Coleman. "Can we do it now? I'm wide awake."

The man shook his head. With his free hand—the hand not holding the shotgun—he rubbed his eyes. "Sure, sure," he said. "Let me put some pants on first."

He turned to go inside, and Robert was about to ask Coleman yet again what he'd gotten them into, but then the man came suddenly back to the railing of the porch. He raised the shotgun and pointed it first at the car, where Piedmont sat, then at Robert, and finally at Coleman. He took his time with each aim, as though truly considering a shot. Then he spoke, the gun still trained on Coleman, "You have the money?"

Coleman walked to the rear of the Thunderbird. From the trunk he removed a leather briefcase and held it high above his head. "Yeah," he said. "I have the money."

The man angled the gun so that it was now aimed at a distant tree line. He fired. Robert flinched at the sound, but it was the sound that followed—the abrupt quiet, the ensuing and immediate silence from the night's wild that only moments before had been hollering with life—that sent shivers down Robert's spine.

Ivan & Lulu

W hat is it, Ivan? What is it?"
"What? Who's there?"
"You screamed, Ivan. In your sleep. You were hav-
ing a nightmare."

"Nonsense."

"You were making an horrendous burbling sound. *Burble-bur-
ble-burble.* I couldn't bear it."

"I wasn't having a nightmare. I wasn't even dreaming. I'd remember."

"I'm telling you the truth."

"In the future, truth or no, please don't wake me."

"It was horrible—the noise you were making. Where are you
going?"

"To the guest room."

"Please don't go. I'm frightened."

"You've left me no choice. I need my sleep, Lulu. I leave for
Paris in the morning."

"Again?"

"You know this, dear."

"I'm so frightened."

"I'm closing the door behind me. Please don't talk anymore. The children will hear you. We mustn't scare the children."

"But, oh," she whispered to herself once she'd heard the door shut softly behind him. "But, oh, I am so, so frightened."

Piedmont

P iedmont couldn't quite believe what had happened, what *was* happening. The man called Coleman had opened a briefcase filled with bills. He'd separated five twenties and handed them to Piedmont. "For your time and discretion."

"He's joshing," said the man called Robert. "There's nothing here that merits discretion."

Piedmont had never held a twenty-dollar bill, much less five of them.

They'd been standing outside a large metal warehouse, what the third man — the one with the shotgun, who'd identified him- self simply as Burt — had called a hangar. Piedmont had driven the three white men across a field to this hangar. He'd cut the en- gine, as instructed, and gotten out just as they had. He'd watched with a sort of child's disbelief as a large metal door had been pushed open and as enormous and powerful lights inside had been switched on.

In front of them was a real-live airplane.

"You're not going to ask for this back, are you?" Coleman ad- dressed Burt. "You're not going to see the nose lift and have some pang of regret?"

"I want it off my property," Burt said.

It had taken a few minutes for Piedmont to knot together the threads, but he'd finally figured out that this man with the air-plane had lost his parents in the crash. Apparently so had Cole-man. The world seemed all at once too small and too large — too small because here were two men whose parents had both died in the same space at the same time in the same exact manner; too large because here was an airplane and more money than he'd ever seen before.

Coleman held out the briefcase. Burt reached for it but then stopped. "The other offer still stands," he said.

"Come off it, man."

"I'd be giving you the plane and a briefcase filled with *my* cash instead."

"I don't want your money. Your money's bad. Your money's tainted."

"My money is the same as yours."

"Incorrect," said Coleman.

"Fungible is the word," said Burt. "Doesn't matter where it came from — oil, cotton, Coca-Cola — when it goes into the bank, it all gets mixed together. You never know where your hundred-dollar bill has been. You don't know what it's bought or sold. You just take it because a hundred is a hundred is a hundred."

"Wrong," said Coleman. "Your old man and my old man came by their fortunes differently."

"You think there's not a plantation in your past? Not a single slave?" Burt cut his eyes at Piedmont, who focused on the shiny white linoleum of the warehouse floor.

"I'm not naïve," said Coleman. "I'm not an outright idiot. But I do believe in choice. I do believe we can comport ourselves differently moving forward."

At this Burt let out a sour snort. "Nothing moral in your aspect is what I hear. Save your high-horse talk for someone who's buying."

Again Coleman held out the briefcase. "Take it or leave it," he said. "The Gauguin isn't for sale."

"Fine," said Burt, accepting the satchel. "But I want this bird out of my sight tonight."

"You got it, pal." Coleman ducked under a wing of the plane and took into account the various components of the aircraft. "You got your landing gear," he said, kicking at a small tire. "You got your trim tab and your flaps. You've got your stabilizer and your elevator. The fuselage." He ran his hand down the rear end of the plane when he said this word. "She's a beauty, Burt. I'll treat her nice."

"You're a nut for wanting her." Burt had backed away to a wall panel of light switches. He appeared allergic to the thing, maybe even frightened.

"We think about life differently," said Coleman. He opened the door, stuck his head inside, sniffed the air. "You think that because your pop died in the air that you will too." He waited. Burt offered no contradiction. "On the other hand, I think, well, my old man died in the sky, therefore I'm safe from here to eternity."

Piedmont stayed long enough to watch the propellers start. Once they were moving, the blades no longer looked straight. They looked instead like scythes spinning around and around and around. The motor sounded like the hum of a giant bee.

He left the minute Robert and Coleman climbed inside and shut the door. As badly as he wanted to see them take flight, he was nervous about Burt, about that gun, about how he might behave once the other two men were gone and it was just him, a colored boy on a white man's property in northern Georgia at nearly two the morning. Negroes had been lynched for less. That Chicago kid, Emmett Till, had been lynched for winking at a woman in Mississippi. That was in '55, seven years ago. He, Piedmont, had been the same age as Emmett when it happened. It was weeks before he could again sleep through the night.

No, sir, Piedmont had no intention of sticking around. He got back into the Thunderbird, tucked two twenties into each sock, slid the fifth into his front pocket, then backed away from the hangar and drove straight across the field.

Before he'd gotten into the airplane, Coleman had scribbled down an address on a piece of paper and handed it to Piedmont. "Do you know this street?"

"I do," he said.

"You can leave the car there. Put the keys on top of the rear left tire."

"Just leave the keys out in the open like that?"

"You going to tell anyone?"

"No, sir."

Coleman extended his hand. Piedmont shook it. "Pleasure doing business with you," Coleman said.

Robert had taken in the exchange from a periphery. He'd said nothing until the end, until Piedmont was about to get back into the car.

"That's it?" Robert said. "You're sending him with an address and a hundred dollars?"

"Should I give him more?"

"Give me that paper." Robert stuck out a hand. Piedmont removed the slip from his pocket and handed it over.

Robert wrote something down on the flip side. Then he handed it back. "That's my full name and my phone number. Anything goes wrong, you get into any trouble, you call me. Or you have the people who give you trouble call me. You understand?"

"Yes, sir," said Piedmont. He didn't look at the paper. He simply returned it to his pocket. "But I won't get into trouble, sir."

He got in the car and turned on the headlights. For a moment, it might have looked like a game of chicken between the sea-green Thunderbird, its top down, and the single-engine airplane, its bright lights staring straight ahead in possible challenge. But Piedmont put the gear into reverse, and the car began moving slowly backward across the field. When the plane started to taxi, Piedmont cut the wheel in the shape of a U, switched into first, and looked once more in the rearview—first at the plane, gaining speed away from him, then at the solo man, now just a black shadow of a figure, standing beneath the powerful glare of the hangar's fluorescents.

When the tires hit gravel, he turned, and when the gravel gave way to asphalt, he turned again. As he pulled onto the highway and pushed into the accelerator, he heard the hum of the giant bumblebee overhead.

He looked up.

There it was: his first airplane ever and now not simply in person but in flight above him. He wondered if Jeremy and Michael would believe him. He wondered if he would tell them. Piedmont held a hand up, a silly gesture. They wouldn't be looking at him. Or maybe they would. Maybe right then, immediately above him, they were looking down, wondering not only at their own strange place in the sky but also at the strange place they'd put the Negro kid they'd known only a handful of hours.

He waved again, a feeling of—of what?—of triumph in his guts, in his chest, at the very tip of his skull. As if on cue, perhaps actually in signal, the plane banked right, leveled, banked right again, then moved up, away, and beyond. Its lights were there when he looked, but gone when he looked again. The hum vanished shortly after the plane.

It was just Piedmont now, just Piedmont and the Thunderbird's headlights and those ghostly white wee-hour moths kamikaze-ing against the windshield and the crickets—a crescendo of crickets from all sides. He moved into fourth gear, pushed the odometer to seventy, and settled back against the cool white leather.

This, this right here, was what it was all about.

Donald & Timmy

Earlier in the night Donald Glazer and Timmy Rovers responded to a call in nearby Gratis. The call was unimportant, one of routine annoyance to the two officers. Same husband, same wife, same threats. The couple had been drinking whiskey since noon. Husband claimed, as he always did, that the wife had sassed him—his words exactly: ". . . sassing me since noontime." He'd given her a good smack across the face. Wife, as was her tendency, was outside, broom in hand, yodeling at the top of her lungs, when the cops pulled up. Neighbors, also as per usual, didn't so much mind the yodeling as what it did to their mutts. Entire cul-de-sac worth of trailers was lit up with baying, yelping curs. Graveyard shift played their regular parts: took the whiskey from the husband's hands and the broom from the wife's. Got them both back inside with threats of arrest. "One more sound, Betty," they'd said. "One more peep and we take you in. Same with you, Ron. We get another call like this, and it's likely you'll be evicted. Shut it, we said. The both of you."

By the time the squad car was back on 29, tucked beautifully behind two live oaks just past a bend in the highway, it was close to 2 a.m., the coffee in their thermoses was cold, and they were both cranky as all get-out.

Donald heard the convertible before he saw it. Timmy nearly

spit out his coffee when it sped by. The driver—a pitch-black cutout against the startlingly bright interior—was so comfortable, so relaxed, that his left elbow was actually cocked and resting on the door frame.

The cops' reaction was cartoonish in its obviousness. In their excitement to follow, to make sense of, to be in hot pursuit in a manner they'd only ever seen on television or read about in the funnies or heard enacted on radio shows, they spoke in partial sentences:

"Was that—?"

"Did you—?"

"It couldn't have—"

"But it must have—"

"In this neck—?"

"Must be some kind of crazy—"

"Stolen too—"

"Most definitely stolen—"

Did they pause to consider any possibility other than this?

"What do you say, then?"

No. They didn't. It was a complete failure of imagination.

"I say let's get him."

Robert

Is that a cloud?"

"We're at fifteen thousand feet."

They'd been in the air for nearly a half-hour, bouncing up and down in the dark of the night.

"Is that a cloud?"

They were flying now through a godly sort of mist—godly because it had come from nowhere and was unasked for and unwanted but suddenly all encompassing, not to mention scary as hell.

"Want to see something?" said Coleman.

The headlights of the little plane gave the mist a milky yellow glow. Robert was holding on to some sort of instrument panel in front of him. It felt loose in his hands.

"Open your window," said Coleman. "Just turn that lever there and pop it on out."

"I'm not opening the window."

Coleman made a popping sound with his lips, then another and another. Then he turned away from Robert and popped his own window open.

Cold air pummeled Robert's face. "Can you do that? Are you allowed to do that?"

"Natural a/c," said Coleman. "God's air-conditioning unit.

Before you know it, the entire South will be air conditioned. My old man called me an imbecile—his favorite word for me—anytime I talked about air conditioning. 'It's too expensive,' he said. 'It's unnecessary,' he said. 'The hoi polloi won't put their money in it,' he said. 'They don't even know they're hot. They don't know they're uncomfortable unless we tell them they are.' Exactly my point. Someone *will* tell them they're uncomfortable. And the Joneses will keep keeping up with the Joneses, and soon every house, every building in this state will be ice-cold in the summer simply by flicking a switch. Mark my words. Put your money in a/c."

"I'm not hot. I'm very cold already."

"I can pop the door too," Coleman said. "They teach you during training."

"I'm good," said Robert. "No door." There was a possibility, Robert now realized, that he might die on this flight. The odds of coincidence didn't negate the possibility. He'd read in the *New York Times,* not two weeks ago, that one woman who'd died in the crash had been married to a man who'd died nearly twenty years earlier in an airplane crash all his own. Improbable didn't mean impossible. How they'd gotten that story instead of the *AJC,* he didn't know. He was, as he'd told the Negro kid, lately out of the loop.

"Watch this," said Coleman.

Robert followed the movement of his pilot's right hand. What he was seeing didn't make sense. What he was seeing was all wrong. Coleman's hand was on the ignition key. Why did airplanes have ignition keys in the first place? Did jets have keys? Did the 707 have a key?

Coleman turned the key counterclockwise.

"What the hell are you doing?" said Robert. "What the hell are you doing?"

The hum of the propellers—previously so loud that the two

men had been shouting their conversation—sputtered. Next the propellers themselves—not just their noise—slowed down.

"Turn it on," said Robert. He gripped the instrument panel in front of him—whatever it was—more tightly. "Turn it on."

The plane seemed to pause in midair. They were somehow, unbelievably, still parallel with the ground.

The initial drop was sudden—ten feet, maybe twenty, good god, it could have been fifty. It delivered to Robert's gut a sensation similar to being on a boat in high seas. He'd been on a boat in high seas—in something like fifteen-foot waves—off the coast of Mexico a few summers back. He'd been marlin fishing with Lily and her parents. Lily had vomited onto her own skirt when the boat smacked against the water after the first real drop. Robert had put his arms around her. He'd whispered, "It's okay. We're okay." And it had been okay. They'd gotten back to shore, changed their clothes, and clinked martinis in honor of being alive. Robert thought maybe this was okay too, this funny and unexpected drop from one level to another level in the sky. But now the plane, woefully quiet, was turning. He felt certain it was turning. The nose was falling. They were no longer parallel with the earth, but perpendicular. The headlights shone into the clouds.

The plane, and them in it, was diving.

"Oh Jesus," said Robert.

He was about to die. They were both about to die in that shitty little airplane in the middle of nowhere in the middle of the night. Any minute they'd hit land and it would all be over. One minute here, the next minute gone.

He put his hands on the dash in front of him and pushed as hard as he could. He clenched shut his eyes. He told himself he'd feel nothing. He said it aloud, "Nothing." He repeated it again and again. "Nothing. Nothing. Nothing."

Then there was a noise.

A noise like a car engine.

Perhaps he was dreaming. Perhaps he was back home in his house on Forrest Way and what he was hearing was the sound of the lawn mowers out back. It was Sunday morning. The lawn crew was already out there, starting too early like they did when they were about to ask for more money. A flimsy bribe they pulled every few months. When it was your turn, it was your turn. They kept a list and crossed off names.

But this wasn't a dream because now there was laughing and the laughing belonged to P. T. Coleman, who it turned out was a suicidal lunatic and also a murderer. No wonder his father had wanted to disown him.

The laughing turned louder and an engine somewhere turned over and suddenly—*poof!*—the propellers roared back to life, and Robert felt himself, his person, but also the plane, being righted. There was a great pressure on his bowels, in his knees, around his shoulders, as Coleman pulled the nose of the plane up, up, up.

Just like that they were back in the mist.

"That," said P. T. Coleman, "is what you call a free fall." He slapped Robert on the knee. "You're a cool cat. One cool, cool cat. Let's land this little lady and get a goddamn drink on the double."

Robert's armpits were wet. His shirt was drenched all the way down to his elbows and sides. He felt certain now that Coleman wasn't just a loose cannon; he was a masochistic maniac; he was more monster than he was man; he was a dangerous association in ways he'd never previously imagined. All this was eminently true. But also eminently true was that Robert—shivering in the dewy night air that was blowing in from the still-open window to his left—felt alive. He thought of the baby—*his* baby—fluttering, twirling, spinning with life, a corkscrew of energy just waiting to live! He felt clear-eyed and clear-headed, and above all he felt—yes, yes, yes—he felt that it was imperative, absolutely imperative, that he find his way back to Lily, the one true love of his life.

Ivan & Lulu

L
ulu, do you know what time it is? The Parisians are waiting."

"It's morning, isn't it? Haven't I timed this correctly?"

"But it must be the middle of the night there. Are the children all right? Where are they?"

"They're asleep, dear."

"But then why are you calling? What is it? What's wrong?"

"I had a dream."

"Lulu, I'm here on business. You understand? They want to make a donation, a kind of loan to Atlanta as a way to show their sympathy. They're talking about *Whistler's Mother*."

"What about the Rodin?"

"The Rodin is a definite."

"You were dead."

"Come again?"

"In my dream, you were dead."

"I'm very much alive."

"But in my dream, you were gone. You were burning and screaming."

"You have to stop this, my love."

"Two prisoners escaped from Alcatraz."

"Is this why you're calling?"

"Johnny wants a comic book, something about a 'spider man.' He says his friends are talking about it, but I think it will give him nightmares."

"I'll be home in two days."

"There's something else."

"I thought as much. Spit it out. I have meetings. I'm not trying to be cruel. Please just tell me."

"It's Pete."

"Is he sick?"

"He's not sick. It's something he said."

"What did he say?"

"It's something he and Johnny did together, but it's Pete who said it."

"Please stop this, Lulu. Stop speaking in circles."

"They said something to Alma."

"To Alma?"

"The maid!"

"I know who Alma is, dear. She's been with us since the boys were born. Tell me what happened."

"You see, it rained very hard the night you left."

"Yes?"

"You see, there was mud all over the backyard."

"Go on."

"You see, it must have been Johnny's idea because he's oldest, but it was Pete who said it to her."

"I'm having such a difficult time following, Lulu."

"They covered themselves in mud, you see. They went out back, and they rubbed mud all up and down their arms and legs, all over their faces."

"They did what?"

"And then Pete said—he couldn't have known, of course he couldn't have—but Pete came inside and he said to Alma, 'Now I'm Negro like you.'"

"Sweet Jesus."

"He was in tears afterward. Alma started crying, too. She feels terrible for making the boys cry, obviously. But she's also very hurt. As is Pete. He thought he was doing something kind for her. She's been so sad lately, so distant. Ever since her nephew went missing. Did you know he's still gone? He walked right out the front door of his own mother's house one day, and they haven't seen him since. He would have graduated from high school by now. Anyway, Pete and Johnny both thought they were doing something kind. They love her. You know this."

"Oh dear God."

"She knows they love her."

"Has she spoken to anyone about this?"

"Of course not. Is that your first concern?"

"It is definitely one concern."

"*Whistler's Mother*, you said?"

"Yes. That's what I've been hearing."

"I like that one very much."

Lily

Lily Tucker was upstairs packing when the phone rang. She was in a guest room, the one that would have eventually become the baby's room but was now a storage area for boxes.

Since the last round of memorials — funerals wouldn't be held for months, not until the bodies were returned to the States — and since the revelation of the true condition of her parents' finances, she'd stopped answering the phone. She wouldn't have answered it now except for the fact that it was well past midnight, and nobody called after midnight unless it was an emergency, a word that signaled to Lily very little these days. It had to be Robert, calling finally to check on her after fifteen days away. Calling — irony of ironies — on Father's Day.

She took a seat on the edge of the stripped mattress, near the bedside table, atop which the telephone sat. The baby kicked. She ignored it.

It filled Lily with a sick sort of glee — the opportunity to tell Robert that his abrupt and pathetic departure was the least of her worries. They were broke, that was news. The house she thought her parents had given them? It belonged to the bank now, as did the family compound at Lake Lanier. Her parents had been living off the principal of her inheritance for years, having apparently plowed through their own trust funds ages ago.

Where had it gone, this money? After all, their friends had been able to live within reason off dividends and interest; why hadn't the same been true for her parents?

The answer, she'd been learning, was in their excess, their extravagance. There wasn't just one strand of pearls; there were three. There wasn't just one Rolex watch; there were half a dozen. There weren't just the houses in Atlanta—hers and theirs—there were the cabins at Lake Lanier. And, for a while, there'd even been a penthouse on the Upper West Side, but they'd sold that several years ago: something else Lily learned only after her parents' death. Plus there were the memberships at Capitol City *and* Cherokee. To think now about last year's birthday gift—a check for ten thousand dollars from her parents just because they wanted to, just because she was their little girl and their pride and joy and because it made them feel good to share, to be magnanimous in general—to think now about that check and how it had very likely come straight from the principal of a trust in *her* name, left to her by *her* grandparents, a gift separate from the one they'd left to her mother—this knowledge made her tremble from her toes to her fingers. It made her eardrums vibrate in amazement. This—*all this! all this! all this!*—was the real news, and with it, Lily was capable of reducing herself to mad fits of laughter whenever she thought about it long enough, whenever she thought, for instance, of her birthday and the way she'd folded herself into her mother's arms, her father's arms, thanking them both through tears for their unrelenting generosity always and always still.

But the fact that Robert, whom she'd once considered the man of her dreams, had left her?

When she was seven months pregnant?

Because he was in love with a dead girl?

These were mere drips in a bucket.

The phone rang again. She slipped off her earring, a pear-shaped emerald surrounded by diamonds, before picking up the handset.

"Robert," she said. She would need to sell the jewelry sooner than later, the pieces that were still in the home safe. The ones in safe-deposit boxes had already been reclaimed.

"Collect call," a man's voice said.

"I'll accept the charges. Robert?"

"This is the Atlanta Police Department."

Instinctively, Lily's hand made a fist around the earring.

For a split second, she thought he was dead. No. She *knew* he was dead. Was it pain she felt in that instant? Was it regret? Or was it pure unadulterated pleasure? She would never know.

"We have a collect call for Robert Tucker."

"Excuse me?"

"We have a collect call for Mr. Robert Tucker."

Lily opened her hand. The tip of the emerald had punctured her palm. A small drop of blood was blooming at the center of her lifeline.

"This is his wife," Lily said. She thought she might retch.

For two weeks she'd been fielding visits from her friends, women who, for years and years now, had been on the same upward social trajectory as she—doted-on daughter to pampered debutante to adored wife to soon-to-be mother. And in some ways they were on the same trajectory still, the lot of them having suddenly become orphans together in a single, devastating plunge. Martha and Polly and Agatha and Jane, all of them the best of friends and now pitifully grieving daughters. They'd meant to raise their children together, not bury their parents at the same time. The reversal was surreal. Lily might have taken comfort in their friendship, in their meatloaf casseroles and shepherd's pies that they brought over in pairs (never unaccompanied), but for the fact that there were two commonalities she no

longer shared: money and marriage. They could swear up and
down all they wanted that nothing had changed, that she was
still one of them and always would be, but when they left her
house, each returned to a home where a husband waited, maybe
even a newborn. When they left her house, she was alone. There
was no husband to talk to, no first child of her own to comfort
her.

On Polly and Martha's last visit, Lily had paused in the hallway to overhear their whispers. She'd been returning from the
kitchen with lemonades, a duty that formerly would have fallen
to Pearl, but she'd had to let Pearl go.

"I do feel sorry for her," Polly had said. "Maybe if there was
still money. But broke and with a baby, she'll never find another
husband. Men don't want what another has cast away."

Martha spotted Lily first. She'd placed a hand on Polly's forearm as a signal, but Polly—who hadn't even bothered to remove
her gloves—had not immediately caught on.

"Do you think it smells a little rank in here?" Polly asked, still
in a hushed tone. "A little musty? John says it's our duty to care
for her, but if she won't care for herself, I don't see why we should
keep trying. Why should she get all the attention? It isn't right."
Her voice had turned high, plaintive.

It wasn't until Martha *squeezed* Polly's arm—Lily saw this too,
this tensing of fingers around fabric—that she finally stopped
talking.

With great care and deliberation, and trying at all costs not
to give in to the shaking she could feel like the early onset of an
earthquake in the pit of her stomach, Lily put down the lemonades. She smiled as sweetly as she could—an effort that might
have made her appear mildly demented—and told them both
to leave.

Martha moved toward her. "Dear heart," she said. "Sit with us.
Mourn with us. We're sisters in this tragedy." But Lily wouldn't
be comforted and she wouldn't be touched. The shaking had

made its way up from her belly—so full already with the baby that wouldn't stop growing—all the way to her head, which she shook now, tightly, furiously. "Get out," she said, "get out, get out, get out."

Polly, who'd always been considered second prettiest after Lily, said in a dramatic little huff, "You don't have to ask me twice," then stormed quickly out of the room.

For a moment, Martha remained. "Dear heart," she again said.

"No," said Lily. "Don't talk to me. Don't feel sorry for me. Don't pity me."

"I don't feel sorry for you," Martha said. "I'm worried about you."

"Don't be that way either."

Martha shrugged, then she sighed. "Polly doesn't speak for the rest of us. You know that."

Lily's head was still shaking. She had crossed her arms over her chest, and now she was clutching at her breasts as though they were her unborn baby or maybe as though she herself was. "Don't you dare come back here," Lily was saying. "Don't any of you dare come back here to gawk at the freak."

From somewhere beyond the front door, Polly called Martha's name.

"Go," said Lily. "Go on."

"I lost my parents, too," Martha said. "So did Polly."

"I know that. You don't think I know that?"

"People grieve differently."

"Are you an expert? Who are you? An expert? Since when?"

Martha shrugged again. "Herbert and I are here for you," she said. "Call if you need anything."

"I need you to leave."

"If you need a ride to the doctor's—"

"My doctor still makes house calls."

"Yes," Martha said. "Yes, of course." She slipped one hand then the other into her gloves. "I'm leaving now."

Only after Martha had left the parlor, then exited the foyer, then closed the front door behind her, had Lily crumpled onto the love seat and cried herself to sleep. That was three days ago and, so far, Martha hadn't come back. None of them had.

On the other end of the telephone line, Lily heard the policeman's voice say, "The wife accepts the charges. Bring him in."

An hour later Lily was standing in front of a young Negro with a bloodied lip and swollen eye. The boy's shirt was untucked. He stood at a strange slant, as though protecting an unseen bruise somewhere in his midsection. Two officers loomed behind him in the foyer of the house Lily expected to be leaving in a matter of weeks.

"Explain this to me again," she said. She was fully dressed, though it was now well past four in the morning.

"Your husband gave me his number," said the teenager.

One of the officers kneed him in the leg from behind. "We told you to stop talking." The taller of the two officers said this; there was a large cyst at the tip of his nose.

"But you see," said Lily, gesturing with her open palm, exposing the tiny bandage she'd placed at its center, "it's only this boy who can explain things. You must let him talk if he's going to explain."

The boy said nothing.

"It's like we told you," the cystic officer said. "He claims the car belongs to you—"

"No," said the Negro. He braced himself. When no kick came, he continued. "It belongs to a friend of Mr. Tucker. But they were together when they hired me."

"A friend?"

"Coleman," the Negro said. "Coleman something, ma'am. I couldn't tell if it was a first name."

As he spoke, Lily studied his face, his bloodied and as-yet-untended lip and eye. She held up her hand and pointed at the bandage on her palm. "I've hurt myself, too," she said. "Though I suspect my phrasing's a bit off. I suspect *you* didn't precisely hurt yourself."

Lily turned and walked to the living room window. She made her way without urgency. She imagined the three of them watching—her movements that of a shadow cast from a rain cloud overhead. Cupping her face to the glass, she could very easily make out P. T. Coleman's 1960 Ford Thunderbird, its top down. Unmistakable. A beautiful automobile. She'd had sex with him once—before she was a married woman, but after the engagement to Robert—in the backseat. Even from the window, she could see the dent from where he'd once hit a dog. She couldn't believe he hadn't yet had it repaired. There was a time when, with little effort, she could picture quite easily what her life might have been if she'd chosen Coleman. Now, seven months pregnant, all she could conjure were phantoms—memories of memories of memories . . . When she thought of Coleman, she wasn't sure if the image in her mind's eye was of him or of her father or someone else. Perhaps, after all, it was Robert she was seeing. She couldn't be certain. Only what was immediately in front of her was now identifiable; she felt confident only in what she could touch. Everything else was air.

She returned to the foyer and addressed the Negro directly.

"You say my husband gave you his telephone number?"

"Yes."

She looked at the officers then back at the boy.

"You say he and Coleman hired you to return the car to Atlanta?"

"Yes."

"You say that you drove them to an airport?"

"Yes and no, ma'am."

The shorter of the two officers shoved the boy. He stumbled. "Don't be clever," the officer said. "Give her an answer."

"You will refrain—" Lily opened her hand again. She rubbed

her palm with her thumb. The wound was so fresh, yet already it seemed a compulsion to acknowledge it had already formed. "You will refrain from touching the boy again while you are in my house, on my property."

The officer of the unfortunate blemish snorted.

"Explain," she said. She was looking again at the teenager, who was taller than either officer. Why, she wondered, had he let himself be beaten by two such unremarkable goons? Even as she asked herself the question, she felt ashamed at the obviousness of the answer. She added, "Please."

"It was a large field," he said, "with a kind of street made of grass."

He spread out his hands as if smoothing a sheet or performing a glissando across the keys of a piano. She followed the flight of his fingers; she could practically hear their music.

"A runway," said Lily. She felt suddenly dizzy, warm-headed, woozy. At the periphery of her brain's vision, she detected yet another phantom memory. If she turned to look, it would only jump away.

"I've never seen anything like it in my life," the Negro said. He paused, perhaps not believing he wouldn't again be hit. "But then, I'd never seen an airplane up close either. Not before tonight."

Lily nodded.

"You can go now," she said abruptly. She walked to the front door and opened it.

Outside, the cicadas vibrated, a thick chest-rattling call from the outdoors. Somewhere, a few streets down, an owl hooted in the night.

She held out her hand. "The keys to the Thunderbird, please."

The taller officer put his hand in his pocket but didn't then remove it. "If you aren't pressing charges, then he's no longer our responsibility." He jangled the keys against the inside fabric of his pants. Lily regarded the noise. Next to the pocket was his bulge;

she imagined something wizened, something more yellow than pink, something small. Perhaps there was another cyst there, too. "We won't take him with us," the man was saying. "You have to press charges if you want him to leave." His hand was still in his pocket, his demeanor unnecessarily smug. He seemed to believe that in delivering this final bit of news—such insignificant news, another minuscule drop in the crater-sized bucket—he'd somehow won, that he'd somehow dominated her in her own domain.

Lily looked again at the bloodied face, the heavy-lidded eyes of the Negro. This was, she saw now, more a young man than a boy. Above his lip was a hint of stubble. He'd been shaving at least a year, maybe closer to two. She'd pegged him initially as a teen, but now she saw that he was very likely in his twenties, her own age perhaps, which made him indisputably a man. A man, then, and yet what could he do to her that hadn't already been done? What additional indignity might he attempt?

"What's your name?" she said.

"My name is Piedmont."

She couldn't help it. She smiled. "As in the park? Piedmont Park?"

"Yes, ma'am." He looked at her shoulder when he spoke, as though eye contact would have been too difficult. She guessed he was embarrassed by his name. She wondered at this. Recently she was embarrassed by so many aspects of her own—the association that her surname had with Robert, but also, unexpectedly, newly, the mortification caused by her maiden name, as well. How wonderful to have a designation that might affiliate you to a place, to a large and beautiful expanse of earth, rather than to something so terrible as a mere person.

His focus on her shoulder remained so singular that she finally regarded it herself. When nothing amiss was there, she turned to see what beyond might have caught his attention. The chandelier's glow glinted off the lid of her grandmother's baby grand.

She looked again at Piedmont, at his hands—unmistakably, she realized with a start, those of a pianist.

"I have to ask. Do you—" She wanted to distinguish herself from the officers. "Do you play?"

He raised his chin.

Their eyes caught for only a second, but in that tiny moment it seemed she could read his irises, read their plea. *Do not ask me a question like that. Do not ask me in front of these men.*

Discrete images presented themselves in Lily's mind, like Polaroids shared at a garden party: Thelonious Monk on a music bench, a late-night street in Delaware, a billy club, a badge, knuckles so swollen they couldn't bend into a fist. She'd never seen any actual photos, of course, but she'd heard the story. And maybe now what she was picturing was somehow accurate. Maybe her imagination was capable of calling up something she'd never seen but only ever thought about. Or maybe the images were all wrong. Maybe it wasn't Thelonious Monk, but again her father. And maybe it wasn't a swollen pair of knuckles but a baby swaddled in blue. Or maybe the face in the image didn't belong to Monk or to her father; maybe it belonged to the trumpet player in London, the first man to steal her heart, though she'd known him for only a few hours. In London on her nineteenth birthday, unaccompanied by her parents, she'd gone to a club where she slow danced with a woman. Afterward, she smoked a marijuana cigarette and, her brain gloriously loose from the drug, she kissed a Negro trumpet player behind the stage. A burgundy velvet curtain had been the only boundary between privacy and publicity. Behind that curtain, the air thick and close with sweat and smoke, she'd let the trumpeter slip his hand beneath the waistline of her skirt. He started at the back, unzipping the garment only enough to allow his hand access, and then he moved it sideways and around—so slowly! such wonderful agony in his precision! —until his hand was on top of her little mound. He paused long enough only to be granted permission, then pushed aside the fabric and entered with a single finger. It was her first experience with actual ecstasy. To this day, she considered that solo and singular event—a secret from everyone but the musician himself— as the day she took possession of her body as a woman.

When Lily spoke again, it was not to the officers but to her bandage, which she now looked at but didn't touch. "Piedmont, as he is called," she said, "may stay here."

"That's not a good idea, ma'am." It was the short one who offered this morsel of wisdom, and Lily couldn't help wondering whether this was her earthly punishment: to be again and again contradicted and second-guessed by average and uninformed men.

"We have a guesthouse," she said.

"Are there locks on the doors?" It was the one with the nose again. He sniffed the air suspiciously. "Locks on the windows?"

She ignored him and looked instead at Piedmont, her brows furrowed in a kind of unhinged and abrupt delight. "Are you strong?" she asked. "Can you help lift? I need to bring the upstairs down."

"The upstairs down?" Piedmont asked.

"So to speak," she said. "I'm moving. There are boxes. Could you help me?"

Piedmont nodded, though he seemed unsure.

She held out her hand again to the officer, who this time gave her the car keys. They were barely on the other side of the threshold when she closed and locked the front door, shutting out the so-called authorities and shutting in this stranger. She felt a stranger herself.

"I'm sorry," Lily said—her first words alone with this Negro, with this Piedmont who was named for a park—"about the misunderstanding."

She looked again at his hands. "But now tell me," she said, "since we're alone finally, do you play?"

Piedmont

"Where did you come from?" the woman asked, and Piedmont thought, *What a question!* Surely she didn't mean from which block or which mother or which congregation or which homeroom . . . Piedmont wasn't a fool. And yet these questions that the white folks asked seemed outlandish in their—what?—in their privilege? their straightforwardness? their unabashed directness? His own mother would have blushed in shame if she'd heard him be so blunt.

She didn't wait for a reply, which was good since Piedmont still didn't know how to answer. Instead, she moved away from him, turned around, and walked into a darkened room of the house and said, only as she was already leaving, "Follow me, please."

He did as he was told, following her through at least two separate and unlit rooms before she came to a stop in what felt like the very back of the house. Here, she turned on a single overhead light, and he saw he was in a kitchen. A kitchen that, save for its size, wasn't all that dissimilar from Carvie's or his mother's, which he hadn't seen in more than a year.

She pulled out a chair. "Sit," she said. "Please."

He sat.

A clock in another room chimed five. It was the earliest he could ever remember being awake without first having gone to bed. He yawned. In his other life — the life he'd been living since leaving his mother's apartment — he'd be home asleep by now.

Piedmont was startled by a cold hand on his forearm. It was the white lady's. "I'm sorry," he said.

"Dear lord," she said. "Stop apologizing. You must be dead tired."

He nodded.

"I'll let you sleep," she said, "but first you have to allow me to clean you up."

He saw now that on the table in front of him was a small bowl of sudsy water. In the woman's hand was a washcloth. She held it up. "May I?" she asked.

Never in Piedmont's life, not once before this night, had he been touched by a white woman. He feared it might change him, as a human touch supposedly changed forever the smell of a baby bird, making the hatchling unknown to and undesired by its own mother. With deep discomfort, he watched the woman dunk the cloth into the bowl and wring it out. The drops, still white and clean for now, returned to the surface and disappeared.

His face burned where the soap made contact with his open wound. She wiped at his forehead. He could feel she was being gentle, trying to be gentle, but it made his stomach turn to imagine his skin being pulled and the blood running freely.

She dunked the cloth again, and this time when she twisted it, the water that returned to the bowl was pink and bubbly. He thought he might be sick. He closed his eyes. When he felt the sting against his lip, he turned away instinctively. With her free hand, she took hold of his chin. He didn't wince again but neither did he open his eyes. He was scared to. He was scared to see her face so close to his.

Who he thought of at that moment surprised him. He should have been thinking of Miss Carvie, comparing that woman's kindness to this one's. He should maybe even have been thinking of his mother, whose touch he knew so well he would have known it in the dark, known it like the touch of his own hand against his face. But no, he wasn't thinking of either of those women; he was thinking of Jeremy and Michael, thinking of them awake upstairs on the third floor of the funeral home, the window open wide, their arms stretched long outside to hide the smoke from their cigarettes. No doubt they'd have stayed up, the radio playing low, the lamp between their beds turned high, waiting for Piedmont's return from work, wondering at his first deviation from routine since he'd gotten the job and gotten to know them.

Even before Jeremy and Michael, Piedmont had been aware of certain movements. He'd studied civil rights in high school. Of course, he'd dropped out by the time protesters marched down Broad Street in Albany, but he'd seen the photos in the paper. He'd once gotten his hands on a copy of the *Southern Patriot* that someone had left rolled up in a toilet stall in the men's room at the Purple Pigeon. He'd unfurled it but hadn't dared open its pages. The couple who published it had been arrested by the House Un-American Activities Committee. Piedmont didn't know what, if any, the ramifications might be if he were caught with such a thing. Could possession alone get him arrested? Was it illegal or just frowned upon? So he'd furled the thing back up and left it where he'd found it, wedged between a toilet basin and the rear wall. Later that same night, he'd returned to mop the floors after closing and it was gone. Maybe it had been placed there deliberately, a surreptitious handing off, or maybe his boss had seen it and tossed it.

Whenever Michael and Jeremy talked about the meetings they attended, Piedmont would wonder about his own responsibility with regard to the Negro Cause. He wondered if it was okay to sit back, keep his head down, and wait for whatever improvements those around him might acquire on his behalf. He wondered if he even believed a better future was possible. He sometimes actively tried his hand at cynicism. But the truth was he dreamed often — not daydreamed, but nighttime dreamed — about a different type of life, not just for him, but for all Negroes. He sometimes woke up with his heart racing and his chest sticky with sweat to a feeling of urgency but also of futility. It was like trying for a word, feeling it on the tip of your tongue, nearly snatching it back from the corner of your mind where it had formerly been forgotten, and then realizing—suddenly, sadly—that you hadn't lost it irretrievably, but that it was never there at all. The word you wanted so badly did not even exist. This was what Piedmont felt whenever he awoke from such a dream.

And so it was Jeremy and Michael and their burgeoning activism and also this vague fantasy of a different kind of life that Piedmont was thinking about as the white woman cleaned his wounds and the soapy warm water turned cold and dark with his blood. He thought about what Jeremy and Michael would say if they could see him now, his left eye swollen unevenly, his lower lip torn in two places. They wouldn't be gentle with him as this woman was, as surely Miss Carvie would have been too. They would have been angered, outraged. Since the stonings and subsequent shootings at Delta Minor, their moods had changed. A week after the incident with the picketers, a Negro in California, thousands of miles away, had been murdered by white cops, and Michael had said—at the dinner table and in front of Miss Carvie, which was unlike him—that this was what the movement had been waiting for, an act so egregious, so outrageous, that the cause would surge with support, that even bystanders would turn indignant. "Our voices will be heard," he said. He'd hit the table with such fury that a fork had been knocked to the floor. "If we have to pummel their ears with our fists, we will. If we don't stop them now, they'll only keep killing us. We'll never be free if we don't fight for our lives." Piedmont had been moved when Michael said this. He felt the surge in his own bloodstream. But he was also frightened by the idea of action. He wasn't sure that violence was the right response to violence. "My daddy taught me to fight," he'd said to those school board members. He'd said it because he wanted to sound strong. He wanted to sound confident. He wanted them to think he could defend himself if necessary. But the truth was his daddy hadn't taught him to fight—his mother wouldn't have allowed it. Her preacher taught kindness and compassion. From childhood, he'd known always to turn the other cheek. And he thought of that phrase again when he heard Michael talking about the man in Los Angeles, but he also knew that the Bible was filled not with true anecdotes but with parables. And so when Michael talked and as he heard the phrase in his head, he didn't see a cheek turning but a body. And to himself alone he wondered how many bodies could be turned, how many more Negroes could be killed, pushed to the side of the road, forgotten about, until perhaps violence *was* the only option. Maybe this was what they had come to. Maybe Michael was right. But Piedmont was still scared, and in his most honest moments, he was able to admit (but then only to himself) that the kind of change he hoped for—because he did hope for change—would come about *for* him, without his personal efforts, without risking his own skin.

What frightened him now, sitting at this white lady's kitchen table, was knowing that Michael and Jeremy, when they did see him and the state of his face, as well as whatever hideous bruise was no doubt spreading across his rib cage like some sort of fast-growing mold, would desire action. They wouldn't be content to sit back and do nothing. They would want to find the white men who had done this; they would want to take revenge, to do to them what had been done to Piedmont only worse, only more so. But this—and this realization was happening to him live, as the woman tended to his face—wasn't possible. Because what they wanted wasn't simply to punish those police officers in LA or those types of county cops who'd beaten up Piedmont, what they wanted ("they" being not just Michael and Jeremy but also many of the do-gooders and cause leaders and even some of the freedom fighters) was to humiliate them. But they (now the other "they," the ones who fought to keep people like Piedmont and Jeremy and Michael separated and down) would never be humiliated, not on any grand or national level. Individually, here and there, the White Man could occasionally be brought low. Yes. Of course. But what Jeremy and Michael and much of their crowd wanted was something global. And maybe even Piedmont wanted that, too. Certainly he did. But he understood, sitting there with that woman's fingers gently applying Vaseline to his lips and forehead, that humiliation like that would never be possible. It was Us against Them, Coloreds against Whites, and the Whites had won. They'd trained an entire nation to believe, at a pre-birth bone-building level so ingrained in the country's genetics it would never go away, that the Colored Man was inferior to the White Man, forever and for all time, amen.

Piedmont was suddenly exhausted.

"Oh," said the white woman. "Oh, dear. I must let you sleep. You poor thing."

"Thank you." He stammered out the words. "For your kindness. I've stayed too long. Thank you." Piedmont scooted back in his chair and stood. He was uncertain about which way to move. There were three doors, he saw now. One that appeared to lead outside, to the backyard presumably, and two others that filtered back into the house. He'd been so done in, so discombobulated, that he wasn't sure now which door he'd come through to get here.

"Where should I—?" he started. "How do I—?"

The white woman also stood. She seemed to understand his confusion in spite of his inability to explain.

"Piedmont," she said. "May I call you Piedmont?"

He nodded.

"It's close to daybreak," she said. "Would you consider staying here? As I said, there's a guesthouse out back. You'd have as much privacy as you pleased. When you feel up for it, you can help me with some modest lifting. It simply wouldn't be decent —not decent at all—to let you leave in this condition. I know it isn't truly my husband's fault, not truly, but he and Coleman are responsible for putting you in this position in the first place, and you did manage to usher the car to safety in spite of those terrible men, and, oh, will you please just say yes so that I can stop my silly rambling? I do feel very silly and very culpable, and, oh, please just tell me you'll let me fix this as best I can? Of course, if you must get home, then you must get home. There are people who are worried about you, no doubt. Of course. I hadn't even thought. Oh dear. Forgive me? Oh dear. Please tell me what you'd like to do . . ."

Piedmont's head buzzed with sleepiness. His cheek and chin ached anew. His ribs felt wobbly with pain. He thought of his bed on the third floor of the Williams Bros.' Funeral Home. Even if he managed to sneak in unseen by Miss Carvie, Michael and Jeremy would see him. They would see his face; demand to hear the story. What they would hear—what he would never be able to keep from them, though he might wish to, about the indignities done to him by two white police officers from the middle of nowhere, the money they'd stolen from him—would incense them. They'd demand immediate revenge. And maybe they'd be right to, but the truth—the whole truth and nothing but—was that at this moment Piedmont wanted only to sleep. He wanted a bed to lie down on and a pillow on which to rest his head. He wanted to close his eyes and drift away, drift back to one of his dreams about an Atlanta that had never yet existed but one day might. He wanted to forget, for a little while, for even just a few hours, the state of his body, the confusion in his mind. And so to the white lady whose open face looked up at him in complete curiosity and kindness, he said, "Yes."

He said, "I'd like to sleep now. And I thank you for your generosity in advance. I can help with the boxes. With whatever you need. There's no one who's worrying over me. I can stay as long or as short as you'd like. But first, yes, I'd very much like to sleep if there is room."

The way she beamed up at him, at his ridiculous acceptance of her preposterous offer, was truly a wonder. Such a wonder, in fact, that when she took his hand—a white lady holding his hand!—he didn't even flinch. He simply let himself be led out the back door, across the luminous green of the backyard, around the perimeter of a real-live private swimming pool, to a single-story building inside which was a bed, where he lay down, alone, in what could rightly be called a fugue state, and slept.

Anastasia

Anastasia Rivers was sitting up in bed. It was midday. The curtains were pulled and the windows wide open. The fan overhead was on high speed. Genie Case's house had central air conditioning, had been tricked out completely a few years earlier, but Anastasia liked to sit with the windows open and smoke cigarettes in bed.

The horsy aroma of nicotine mixed with the honeysuckle outside brought on the periphery of a memory from ages ago, a crescent of a recollection she would never recapture but that she knew came from her youth and those peculiar pre-orphanage days when she'd lived as an itinerant with her parents and brother. There was so much from that period that would remain forgotten, but this particular combination of aromatics never failed to retrieve a specific and pleasant sensation of butterflies, excitement, and the possibility of minor danger.

She heard, from the back patio below, the splashes of her brother and his friend Tito, a peculiar little man of indeterminate race. They were playing Marco Polo and drinking rum from halved coconuts. She knew this detail—halved coconuts and rum—not because she'd bothered looking out her window that afternoon, but because this had been their routine for many days now, ever since they'd arrived via train, all the way from California. It was Father's Day by the time they finally showed up.

Genie Case had given Anastasia both car and driver on the afternoon of her brother's arrival. She, Genie, had instructed Anastasia to take the young men for lunch at the Ritz on her tab. "I'll call ahead," Genie had said. "There will be a bottle of champagne waiting for you at the table. Twins! Reunited after so many years. It pleases me to be able to do this for you." This conversation had occurred not two weeks into Anastasia's residency at the Case house, but already she was annoyed by Genie's generosity, by her presumption that Anastasia would do exactly as told: the driver, the Ritz, the bottle of champagne. At first it had startled her, the manner in which a person, though physically absent, could still exercise control over another person. Now it simply weighed her down and filled her with a constant sort of dread at the mere prospect of waking, of moving about the house, of being discovered and then instructed how and where to be.

The generosity came, as all things did, Anastasia understood, at a price, which was why she was able to be vexed by the prospect, say, of a free meal. It wasn't actually free. Nothing was.

How Anastasia had come to be seduced by Genie, a woman three decades her senior, still confounded the young woman. She could puzzle through the timeline, stack the series of events in a chronological pile, and still she couldn't make total sense of things.

There was the afternoon at the Radisson, when Genie had cloaked her in a monogrammed towel and steered her through the restaurant and throngs of gawkers. There was the hazy drive through downtown, past the cathedrals and the duck pond and the high-rises that had only just gone up. There was the turn down a driveway with a canopy of such lush overgrowth that Anastasia assumed for a moment that they'd left the city, that they were no longer in Atlanta proper or even one of its suburbs. The few times she'd tried to talk on that drive, Genie, who was sitting in the back with Anastasia, had put a hand on her knee. "Hush up, dear," the older woman kept saying. "You poor thing. *Shhh.*" So Anastasia had hushed up, and she'd allowed Genie's driver (again at the older woman's insistence) to carry her up a magnificent set of marble stairs. She'd leaned her head back into those giant arms and gazed up not at the driver's face but instead at the chandelier, so bright, so high, so expansive that it had a hypnotizing effect, and Anastasia, who might until then have been playing at being tired, at being overwhelmed, at being the bereft daughter of two of the disaster's victims, truly was all of a sudden.

Her eyelids turned heavy, her breathing shallow. Genie and the driver tucked her in, still in the red one-piece with the sides professionally cut out, to a bed on the second floor of that miraculous mansion. She remembered the blinds being pulled and the sunlit room taking on a haunted copper hue. A vaporizer had been plugged in or turned on because she could hear its watery hum and feel the faintest of mists flutter across her cheeks, nose, lips. She remembered all this even now. How long she slept she didn't know, but when she woke, it was a new day and the blinds had been opened and Anastasia was wearing not the bathing costume but a silk dressing gown the color of flesh—who had changed her?—and on a bedside table was a glass of fresh-squeezed orange juice and half a grapefruit with the meat already separated from its skin and a note that read, simply, *Rest up. Take a dip. I'll be back midweek. We'll make proper friends then. xoxo Genie*

Anastasia had done as instructed. She'd rested up, taken several dips, allowed herself to be pampered and fed by a large colored woman called Henrietta. Occasionally she caught the driver, a former football player who went simply by Fred, watching her. She thought nothing of it—all part of the package, she assumed, whatever the package was. Anastasia had additionally taken those several days to do two very important things: (1) locate her brother (through a series of maddening phone calls and Western Unions) and (2) get her story straight.

Her story, which she told to Genie several nights later, went like this: She and her brother had been abandoned in Hapeville in 1948, which was true. They'd been adopted several days later by an older couple who'd never been able to conceive themselves, which was untrue. This couple, the Merryvales, had provided the twins with a near fairy-tale existence for several years: home schooling them, spoiling them rotten, giving them all the unconditional love they'd never gotten from their own parents. The twins' only complaint ever was the seclusion in which the Merryvales lived; a small ranch in the distant and dreary hills of Stone Mountain was their home. The aging couple was close to only one other family, whom the four of them would visit for several weeks each summer at a cabin on Lake Lanier. This was the Smith family. Anastasia had chosen this family from the manifest printed in the *AJC* because of the blandness of their name and because there'd been no special articles about them or their connections.

"The Smith family," Genie had gasped when Anastasia said the name.

"You knew them," said Anastasia. This was on the night of Genie's return. Her heart had beaten wildly. Of course she'd prepared herself for the possibility that Genie might be familiar with them, but now that the actuality was upon her, she was newly nervous. She felt unsure of her skills, unprepared to continue convincingly.

Henrietta, as if on cue, entered the room and set down two small glasses of sherry. They were in the blue parlor on the first floor. It was dark out. Anastasia and Genie were both dressed in nightgowns, as though in the midst of a luxurious sleepover.

Her hand trembling, Anastasia accepted the sherry. She drank it too quickly, and a small drop splashed onto the silk of her gown.

"Child," said Genie. She took the empty glass from Anastasia. "Do not fret for me. I didn't know them. Not personally. But I know who they are. Who they *were*. I know they were on the plane."

The heat in Anastasia's cheeks lightened. "Oh," she said. "I thought maybe—" She looked down in an effort to hide the slightest of smiles; she couldn't believe her good fortune. "I hoped you *had* known them. They were lovely people. Lovely people! And when the Merryvales passed away—"

"The Merryvales are dead?" Again Genie gasped, this time one hand going to her chest and the other gripping the fingers of Anastasia's hand.

The girl nodded. "Yes," she said, the sorrow of all the world weighing her down in that instant. "It is a very sad story. I was orphaned twice already and now, with the crash, a third time. You see, first my parents abandoned us. And surely the Merryvales never would have intentionally left us alone, but they died in a wretched automobile accident when we were only seventeen. If it weren't for the Smiths' continued care, we would have been completely on our own. And you must understand: we were never allowed to speak of their generosity. They had children of their own, you see. But they had always been fond of my brother and me, and we'd always been fond of them. When my brother decided to move to California, it was the Smiths who made his trip possible. I always felt terribly uncomfortable with the idea of accepting their money, and so, with the exception of a room they paid for until I turned twenty-one, I took nothing they offered. Only their love." As she talked, small tears pushed their way up from her eye ducts to the edge of her lids, where they teetered delicately against the crystalline lenses of her eyeballs for a moment before spilling down the skin of her cheeks. "The truth then," Anastasia said through sniffles, in quiet awe of her own performance. "It wasn't my real mother and father who died. I don't even know who my real mother and father are. But the only other people to ever care for my brother and me are gone now, too. I'm sorry if you feel misled. I understand if you want me to leave."

"Dear girl, dear girl." Genie allowed her hand to drift from Anastasia's fingers to her forearm. Now she stroked back and forth from the girl's wrist to her elbow. "You are so lovely," she said, "and I am so alone. We will mourn our friends together."

"You mustn't tell anyone who I am," said Anastasia. "You mustn't tell anyone about the Smiths."

"Lie down," said Genie. She pulled the girl delicately toward her, and Anastasia—sensing there was no choice but also feeling no desire to resist, feeling instead a great deal of relief and even power in her own beauty and persuasion—allowed her head to be placed on Genie's thigh. "Sweet, sweet girl," whispered Genie.

"But what will you say when people ask who I am?"

Genie raked her fingers through Anastasia's long brown hair. *"Shhh,"* she whispered. "Don't fret, sweet child. No one will ask."

"But they will."

"No," said Genie. "I promise. They won't."

"But why not? Why wouldn't people want to know who I am?"

"People will want to know you," the old woman said. "They will want to know who you are. And we will tell them you are Anastasia. We will tell them you are my companion, my friend, my very dear new confidante. I found you at my darkest hour. We will tell them this, and it's the truth. But where you came from is none of their business." Genie ran a pinkie along the curved edge of Anastasia's ear. "You'll see," she said. "You'll see how people know better than to ask questions."

Anastasia fell asleep that night on the sofa, her cheek pressed sweetly into the silk of the old woman's nightgown. In the morning, it was settled that Anastasia would stay and that the twins

would be reunited, and in the two weeks that followed, as Anastasia waited for Billy, who now went by Skylar—Skylar! such
a flamboyant choice! she couldn't help but admire his pluck!
—to make his way from California back to Atlanta, Anastasia
learned that Genie was right. None of her crowd asked questions. At each party to which she was taken, she was introduced,
fawned over, petted, moved about, admired, kissed, hugged . . .
But she was never asked to explain where she came from. She was
never obliged to offer her origin story. When the plane crash was
talked about—and it was, often—Genie's friends did glance in
her direction. They moved their hands to their hearts in a sort of
unstoppable show of empathy. But they never asked questions.
They never said who they thought she really was. Only once, and
then very late at night, after a dream so shocking it had startled
her awake, did she wonder at the convenience of this lack of curiosity, as though Genie Case's friends had somehow experienced
someone like Anastasia before.

They fell into a routine quickly. Mornings, Anastasia was
awakened by Henrietta with a tray of fresh fruit and a cup of
black coffee. From downstairs would come sounds of a house
already alive with work being done and plans being made. The
telephone usually started ringing around 10 a.m. Genie's parrot
squawked in response. Orvil, as he was called, could sing all the
words of "Jesus Loves Me," and sometimes when the doorbell
rang, he would begin a knock-knock joke but never finish. To
Anastasia, in the course of two short weeks, these noises came
to signify wealth, eccentricity, freedom from boredom and a life
spent trying only ever to pay one's bills.

By 11 most mornings, Anastasia would be poolside with a stack
of photography books and exhibition materials that had been cu-
rated closely by Genie, who seemed determined to educate the
girl, refine her ways, elevate her conversation. Anastasia wanted
these things. She wanted to be refined. She craved sophistication and dignity. But like a child who longs to play guitar but

has no capacity for or interest in self-discipline or callused fingers, Anastasia merely skimmed the pages. She preferred pamphlets saved from past exhibitions to textbooks about art because they were thinner and weighed less and therefore didn't leave red marks on her skin where she rested them against her thighs. Here and there, she might pause and marvel over a particular painting or photograph. But it was never a brushstroke or the angle of light or the conscientious choice an artist had made that struck her. Usually it was some similarity she detected between the subject and herself—the worried brow of the young woman in Ruth Orkin's *American Girl in Italy;* the distracted expression of the nymphet to the far right in Helen Levitt's *Girls Dancing Above 96th Street Near 1st Avenue A;* the beautifully grieving eyes of the *Woman with white gloves and a pocket book, N.Y.C.* by Diane Arbus.

For several days Anastasia was quite taken with Arbus's work. She was mesmerized by the ugliness of *Stripper with bare breasts sitting in her dressing room, Atlantic City, N.J.* If she turned away from the page, she found herself almost immediately turning back. Surely it was not Genie Case's intention, but when Anastasia looked at this stripper—the oddball and tacky half-sleeves she wore, the suggestion of stupidity in the pout of her mouth, the unfortunate roll of fat around the stomach—she couldn't help but think that she, Anastasia, would make such a finer model for this photographer. She might not yet have the air of distinction that Genie and her friends seemed to inhabit without effort, but she did have an undeniable brightness to her eye. Her figure was unusually symmetrical. Her chin was defiant in its natural arrogance. She was, quite simply, as her own brother had once pointed out, statuesque.

During those late morning and early afternoon hours by the pool, while she waited for Genie to finish her phone calls and more business-related appointments, Anastasia would lean her head back, close her eyes, and imagine the titles for all the photographs that hadn't yet been taken of her— *Girl at side of pool in a red bikini, Girl in sandals staring at diving board, Girl with painted toes eating grapefruit, Girl with cigarette in swim cap.*

Genie usually appeared midafternoon in an ankle-length caftan made of linen or thin muslin. She liked to lie in the sun next to Anastasia, but she didn't like to expose so much skin. Genie was trim and even tidy for her age, but it wasn't fat that troubled the old woman. "Wrinkles," she once said. "They are the devil's way of laughing at us. We get wiser and wiser as we age, but to balance out that wisdom and keep us in our place, we also get uglier and uglier, more and more shriveled." She would sometimes stop talking midsentence, absorbed suddenly by the back side of her hand. When her conversation at last continued, it was never to resume where she'd left off but to lament in some new way the opacity of her skin, the prominence of her veins. "Look," she might say, pinching up or kneading together her flesh. "Look. It's vulgar what aging does to a person. It's downright crass."

Visitors usually began arriving at Genie's house around cocktail hour, which in her blue parlor might be as early as three or four and never later than five. There were two types of visitors, as far as Anastasia could tell—business and social, the latter of which could be additionally divided into the categories of fun or not fun. The not-fun visitors were the ones who came to mourn. They came to bemoan the loss of Genie's brother, who had apparently been a stalwart, upstanding, venerable, adored, important, and blah-blah-blah member of society. His wife, also newly dead, had been the same. These guests of Genie's were not merely annoying to Anastasia for the doom and gloom they brought with them, but for the doom and gloom they left behind when they finally took their leave, usually late at night, after a mundane dinner during which talk was only ever of the past. When they left, it was Anastasia who had to listen to Genie cry. It was Anastasia who had to hold the woman's hand with its unfortunate veins and its doughy texture. It was Anastasia who, at the old woman's insistence, sat by her bedside while she cried herself to sleep.

She preferred the boisterous visitors, the ones who brought cases of wine, sometimes vials of drugs. They brought presents from places they'd been. One man ushered them all to his car, which was parked out front, in the back of which was a large cage, inside of which was a lion cub. He'd gotten it on safari, he told Genie. "Let her lick your palm," he said. "That's right. Hold out your hand. Not inside the gate. Yes, just there. You see? I dare your spirits not to be lifted by a licking kitten. It's science. It's been proven." Genie had extended her arm through the rolled-down window. She'd allowed the cub—so young still its eyes were droopy, or maybe it was drugged—to lick her open palm. And the man had been right. Her spirits had improved. She'd opened a jeroboam of something French and old that night and several extra bottles of champagne. Anastasia had flitted about from corner to corner, guest to guest. Any time she moved, it seemed her elbow was taken hold of, and she was pulled in some new and exciting direction by some new and exciting person. "Look at her chin," someone might say, and hold up her head as though it were an object separate from her person. "You can't fake a chin like that. It's in the breeding." "My god," someone else might say, "she could be Egyptian royalty, the nose." "Not Egyptian at all," from yet another. "Greek maybe. Something patrician for sure."

Anastasia lived for nights like these when bedtime usually wasn't until sunup, and she was never expected to comfort, console, or commiserate with Genie's untimely and tragic loss.

The dynamic they established during those initial two weeks and during that revolving door of visitors—of gaiety some nights and anguish others—was disrupted the night before Anastasia's brother finally arrived. There'd been an unusual visitor that day, one who (or so it seemed to Anastasia) was both expected and unexpected, both welcome and unwelcome, both business and social. He wore a somber brown suit and brought the doleful respects of someone who'd once been close to the recently departed. Genie had been flustered by this visitor, though he hadn't seemed unkind. "I'll be dining out tonight," she told Anastasia. "Without you. It's business and it's private and you're very good to understand." Anastasia didn't understand, but she also didn't mind the idea of an evening alone. She was giddy with the knowledge that she would be reunited with her brother in fewer than twenty-four hours.

For dinner that night she ate a small bowl of apples and cottage cheese prepared by Henrietta. She was in bed by eight o'clock, asleep by nine. In the enchanting hour between wakefulness and rest, Anastasia replayed bits of her childhood and of their years at the orphanage. Just before the twins turned eighteen, Billy and the other upperclassmen had managed to procure a few cans of beer and a bottle of scotch. In the boys' ward, they'd drunk until they were rolling around on the floor in fits of laughter. Someone had swiped a copy of the 1955 January issue of *Playboy* with Bettie Page (kneeling on a carpet of white shag, her ass firmly planted on her toes) as centerfold. In her left hand dangled a simple silver ornament that covered the *hint* of the idea of what they called, at the orphanage, the Secret No-No Place. She was winking, which must have been what drove most of the boys crazy, like she was winking specifically at them. And she was wearing a little red Santa cap with its fuzzy tip pulled to the side. What killed them—most of them, Anastasia had been given more details than she wished—was that she could have been their mother. There was something so wholesome, so welcoming about that wink, about the open-mouthed smile. (The open mouth, this had driven them nuts as well. All the things they could imagine putting in that mouth . . . Another bit of information Anastasia hadn't needed.) The issue was close to three years old, and the image was one they were all more than familiar with. But it was something else entirely to have the copy in their possession for so many hours, to be able to pore over every detail as they drank and danced and told stories not of what they'd done—sexually—but of what they would someday somewhere somehow to someone do. At some point, Billy passed out, and the other boys—these kids who he'd assumed were his friends—decided it would be a good idea to shave him. They pulled off his pants, lathered up his pubic hair, and brought the razor to his skin. The problem—and Anastasia knew about this, knew about all of it, because they'd elected one among them as leader and supreme bearer of burdensome and non-essential news and tasked him with the unhappy job of delivering the anecdote directly to her the next day in the schoolyard—was that he enjoyed it. That's how Peter (or Frank or Stanley or Malcolm or whatever his name was) had said it, "He enjoyed it. Very much. We think maybe he might . . . You know." Anastasia had laughed. Inside she'd felt a sort of sinking sickness knowing that Billy had made himself vulnerable, had allowed himself to be made fun of, had put them both in the awkward position of possibly being pitied by these dumb boys, whose pity she didn't care one whit about. But outwardly she was wise enough to laugh.

"Enjoyed it?" she said. "He was asleep. You said so yourself. You'd have enjoyed it, too, I suspect."

"Your brother's a pansy. I'll tell everyone."

Had Anastasia, then still Stacy, truly cared that this creep might rat out her brother? Had she even thought him capable of following through on his threat? Ramifications were known to go both ways at the Hapeville orphanage. Snitching didn't always produce the desired effects. Plus he'd have had to explain the circumstances—the booze, the magazine, the prank itself. All of which would have landed the other boys in their own hot water. And with a conjectured erection the only proof that her brother might be a homosexual, she must have understood that the kid's threat to tattle was more than likely empty.

But if that was the case—and it was, it must have been—then

why did she go with him to the chicken coop on the east side of the orphanage's compound and why did she let him unzip his pants and why did she let him put her hand on his own erection and why, further, did she leave it there as he pumped it back and forth until a sticky white product spat out, a surprise, it seemed, to them both?

Depending on her mood, she was sometimes willing to admit the answers to these questions and sometimes not. The truth was she'd allowed herself to be bribed as much out of boredom as for consideration for her brother. The truth was she'd been disappointed first by the *look* of the kid's Thinking Stick—what she and the other girls had dubbed the male member because *penis* was just too ridiculous a word—and then by the fact that he hadn't even tried to put it inside her. Nothing but her hand had been violated; he'd not attempted to gain access to her panties. He hadn't even grazed her sweatered breast with his hand. The entire experience was one of disappointment and disillusionment. When it was over, the kid stuffed himself back into his pants and took his leave from the chicken coop with an embarrassing kind of sigh. This expulsion of air—this sigh that proclaimed not only accomplishment but also satisfaction—filled Anastasia with such grief, imagining the dull life he would no doubt live, wherein moments such as this might actually bring him pleasure, that the only thing she could think to do was shove her own hand between the waistline of her skirt and her bare skin and bring herself to climax. That was the first time she'd exchanged access to her body for something she wanted or thought she wanted. It had happened more than a few times in the years between, never with men she didn't find attractive and, until Genie Case, until the night before Billy reappeared, never with a woman.

Somewhere in her orphanage reveries—part prurient, part sentimental—Anastasia had drifted off to asleep, but just after midnight she'd awakened with a start. There'd been a sound, a sound so lucid, so clear that, even asleep, she'd had a sort of awareness that it was coming from without the dream, not within. The dream itself? Barely relevant, as nighttime dreams rarely were. But there'd been a sort of clawing, and her brain had tried to incorporate it into the sleepy scenery as a sort of offstage sound effect, a sort of premonition of the next act to come, but it hadn't worked. She'd awakened almost immediately, raising herself onto her elbows and lifting the eye mask to her forehead. What was it? A cat's claws against tree bark? The room was quiet. She waited. Again she heard it, but this time it seemed to be coming not from outside the windows as she'd first suspected but from somewhere inside, and not simply inside the house, but inside the room, her room.

She clutched the top sheet to her chest, feeling instantly dramatic and therefore somewhat divine.

Yes, the sound was coming from someplace close to her bedroom door, which—her eyes now adjusted—she saw was open by about a foot. A spray of muted light fell from the third-floor chandelier, which was nightly left illuminated.

She pushed herself up farther, so that she was now nearly sitting up in bed. She looked to the right. There was nothing to see. She looked to the left. Nothing there either, other than the dusty-rose carpet that continued into the balcony hallway outside her room. At the foot of her mattress, a place she could not see without getting out of bed or crawling to its end, the sound now came to a stop.

"Hello?" she whispered, her breath shallow, her heart fluttering. "Who's there?"

Enough light was allowed by the open door that she could all too clearly see the hand when it rose up from the base of her bed and grabbed hold of the footboard. Reflexively, Anastasia dug her heels into the mattress and shoved herself back against the headboard. She grabbed her knees, trying to make herself as small as possible, trying to increase the space between the hand and her body. "God, god, god," she said. This was it. She'd known this day would come.

There'd been a nun (everyone called her a nun, though her qualifications were murky, one of the side effects of childhood and gullibility) at the orphanage who'd taken a certain pleasure in the acquisition and distribution of such ghastly news as, say, the Lonely Hearts Killers — Raymond Martinez Fernandez and Martha Jule Beck — who'd killed a dozen or so women in the late '40s. Nighttime stories in the upper girls' ward were as likely to be about a naughty princess who learned her lesson the hard way as they were to be about the Glamour Girl Slayer Harvey Glatman, who posed as a photographer in order to rape and kill women, or Albert Fish, who didn't just rape his victims (usually children, the nun assured them) but also ate them. And of course there were the Texarkana Moonlight Murders, made somewhat more alluring than they should have been by the 1942 movie *Phantom Killer,* the poster of which the nun had once unrolled and shown to the girls just before bed. Plus there was *Psycho,* a movie Anastasia had seen with her own two eyes, meaning she knew about sociopaths. It didn't surprise her that she would be targeted; she was *so* much better looking than Janet Leigh, and glamour attracted envy, which was often accompanied by anger, ire, the desire to take away what another person was not only born with but additionally knew how to cultivate. But it disappointed Anastasia — as she sat up with alarm, the sheet to her chest — that it might happen so soon, before she had a chance to blossom with true discovery, to bask not just in Genie Case's attention but also in true and widespread fame. She wanted to wear it — fame, recognition — like a skin. She didn't want to possess it like a certain type of woman possessed a fur coat, something that could be removed (it was impossible not to think of *All About Eve* when she thought about fame), but as a biological piece of herself.

"Who's there?" she said, imagining Grace Kelly's quiet and

maddening hysteria in *Dial M for Murder*. "I can't *stand* it." The fact that she couldn't herself decide if the hysteria she heard in her voice was performed or legitimate only intensified her dread.

Next to the first hand another soon appeared.

She heard her name, not being said so much as slurred.

Then she heard the question, desperate, pleading: "Why don't you *like* me?"

At this, Anastasia pushed herself onto her knees, prairie-dog style, and looked over the edge of the bed.

There was Genie, drunk, pathetic, her hands hooked to the footboard, her arms extended, her head dangling weakly between them as though pilloried. The sight of Genie in such a position — puny, needy — filled Anastasia with quiet indignation. She imagined grabbing hold of the old woman's hair, raising her head up so that she was facing Anastasia eye to eye, and then spitting right onto the face of that cloying and raggedy woman. Where had this violent fantasy come from? Anastasia didn't know, but she realized suddenly that whatever anger she was feeling now had been simmering for many days and had finally come to a boil. She should have been sleeping. Her brother was slated to arrive midmorning. Her eyes would be a mess from lack of sleep, and it would all be Genie's fault.

"What can I do," Genie was saying to the carpet, the voice whiny with alcohol, "to make you like me?"

On so many nights before this one, Anastasia had sat on the edge of Genie's bed as the older woman had fallen asleep. She knew now what was expected of her — at least she thought she knew what was expected of her — and so she climbed off the bed (spitting wasn't an option if she wanted to stay) and took a seat on the carpet by her side. "Here," she said, relaxing Genie's fists, guiding her shoulders down and her head toward her lap. She patted her thigh. "Put your head here. That's right. Yes. Now quiet down and stop your silly nonsense. Of course I like you."

"Oh," said Genie wetly. "Oh, I am so glad. I'm so glad you like me." She began, very quietly, to weep. Her shoulders jerked in sadness.

"What's wrong?" said Anastasia. "What happened? What did that man want? Did he hurt you? Was he mean to you?"

"It isn't his fault," she said. "It isn't his fault at all."

"What isn't his fault?"

Genie's cheek was now resting against the top of Anastasia's thigh, her face turned toward Anastasia's stomach. Her hand, Genie's hand, was around Anastasia's lower back. "I should have known my brother wouldn't do as he'd promised. I should have known my brother would have forgotten all about me."

"What about your brother?"

"He wants the Gauguin."

"Your brother?" Perhaps the old woman had fallen asleep. She sounded delusional. Her brother and the other hundred or so were dead, burned to bits, in fact. She shivered just thinking about it, thinking about *them* and their bodies and the smell of so much burning hair.

"Not my brother." Genie whistled her response. A bit of spittle landed on Anastasia's leg. "*Him.* That man. My dining companion. *He* wants the Gauguin." Her soft tears had turned to steady sobs.

Anastasia brushed her fingertips through Genie's short bob. Every day since her arrival, there'd been some discussion of the Gauguin. Any visitor, no matter how seemingly intimate to the woman and her house, how seemingly familiar already with the painting, was shown this particular piece of art. In only two weeks, Anastasia had seen it so many times, she'd lost count. It was housed in the first-floor drawing room, whose shutters were always angled down to block out the sun and whose French doors were always kept locked as if to keep out potential thieves. But who, Anastasia wondered whenever she saw it, whenever she heard Genie's guests inhale sharply or exclaim in delight at its supposed magnificence, would want to steal such a painting? Its colors were ugly, its subject even uglier.

"Who cares if he wants the Gauguin? It's yours."

"But it isn't mine," Genie said. She wiped at her eyes and nose with her free hand. Then, instead of returning it to its place beneath her chin where'd she'd previously had it tucked, she rested it open-palmed on the fabric that covered Anastasia's upper thigh. Anastasia regarded the hand. Genie's eye, the one the girl could see from above, was closed.

"Whose is it, then?"

"That's my point," said Genie. "Precisely my point. It is supposed to be mine. Every bit of it. Not just the Gauguin, but all of it. It was all meant for me. Instead it belongs to him."

"Your dining companion?"

"Of course not," Genie said. Now her eye opened and she turned her face sharply toward the ceiling, toward Anastasia. "It belongs to my brother's son, that feckless ne'er-do-well."

"You have a nephew?" In all the mournful visits paid to Genie, she'd never once heard of, much less been introduced to, a nephew.

Genie closed her eyes again. She was done with this conversation. She rubbed her cheek in slow circles against the skin of Anastasia's leg, just above her knee.

Anastasia watched.

Next the older woman slid the open palm from above the fabric of the girl's nightgown to underneath it.

Anastasia watched this too.

It was almost like being in a movie, the camera's point of view uncomfortably close (she was thinking of Janet Leigh again) the way she watched, from a kind of psychic remove, as Genie—keeping her eyes shut now, as if unsealing them might betray her intentions and allow Anastasia to object—opened her mouth and began gently biting Anastasia's inner thigh.

She continued watching until Genie's fingers found the elastic hem of Anastasia's underpants and tugged until the girl had no choice but to tilt her ass first one way and then the other in order to accommodate their removal.

After that, Anastasia looked away and let the old woman do as she pleased.

The next day Billy and his little friend arrived. Every night since—there had been five so far—Genie had waited until the house was quiet, which was sometimes not until three or four in the morning, before creeping into Anastasia's bedroom and re-peating her transgression.

What occurred to Anastasia now, as she sat up in bed smoking, listening to Billy and Tito call "Marco" then "Polo" then "Marco" once again, picturing them with their coconut halves filled with rum, was that Genie had deliberately saved her solicitation until her brother's imminent arrival. Anastasia was no longer simply beholden for herself. She was beholden now for Billy and even for his friend.

Her anger, formerly a boil, now bubbled hotly over its edge.

Ivan & Lulu

B ut I heard you, dear."
   "You heard wrong."
   "You said something about the FBI."
"Lulu, I've talked to you about the eavesdropping."
"But something about Sammy?"
"Who, Lulu?"
"Sammy Yorty? In LA? Has he done something wrong?"
"He hasn't done anything wrong."
"Something about that poor boy Ronald Stokes?"
"Ronald Stokes was a man, not a boy."
"Something about a lynching?"
"He wasn't lynched. He was killed by police officers."
"Why did they say lynched, then?"
"Who said lynched? Who have you been talking to?"
"Nobody," she said. "Everybody."
"You aren't making sense, Lulu. Perhaps you should go back to bed."
"But you told me to stay away from the bedroom. You said at least five hours."
"I know what I said."
"Did that man out in California really say what they're saying he said?"

"You're talking in circles again."

"Did he say this is the work of God?"

"The work of God?"

"This," she said. She looked up at the ceiling and tried to hold back tears. "The accident. The crash. He said it was God's work."

"Have you been in my office?"

"Of course not."

"Have you been listening to my calls?"

"Of course not, dear."

"That would be an egregious offense, Lulu."

"Yes, dear. I know, dear."

Skylar

Skylar took the train in from Los Angeles. He'd been out there living his version of inescapable paranoia, writing screenplays without plots and swimming laps by the dozen, when he got the call. The odds that he'd die in his own crash were terrifically small, and yet he was haunted by Joseph Heller's novel, which had been published only the year before but which he'd read straight through three times already. Paranoia excused you from nothing. That's what he learned from Heller. And so he'd purchased a first-class train ticket and another for his friend Tito, who may or may not have been a prostitute before hooking up with Skylar, and the two of them trained together straight across the United States—2,000-plus miles through Phoenix, Tucson, El Paso, San Antonio, Houston, New Orleans, straight into Atlanta—on the dime of some rich lady they'd never even met.

In LA, he'd been paranoid, just as history and current culture had prepared him to be—the fate of Alan Turing, the murder of that sad sap British schoolteacher who'd dared to wear a wig and whose name nobody ever remembered, the lavender scare, Harry Hay's Mattachine Society—the stories were always in the wind, always on the tip of the tongue. There was always something to be made nervous by; if not history, then news of some formerly unimaginable violence in an alley or a bathroom or a bus station that required he be constantly on guard. Fit in, assimilate. It was a mantra; it was his mantra. House parties were the only safe places. From day one, he avoided clubs like the plague. Clubs got raided, houses too, but only when you weren't discreet, and Skylar had learned to be discreet. He'd learned that lesson early, from those days in the orphanage, and it was how and why he was still alive. He was discreet and he was paranoid. He popped pills, traveled in pairs, carried a knife—which he'd brandished one time in an alley near Cooper's Do-nuts on Main Street, though he couldn't be sure now if that was a dream or an intense high or possibly someone else's memory.

He'd been paranoid and good at it, and look what it had gotten him: a telephone call in the middle of the night. Nothing necessarily new about that except it wouldn't stop ringing, and so he'd gotten up to answer it himself, which meant that Tito was out for the night and probably for the morning and maybe even for the next few days. Tito was indiscreet but he was also Skylar's weakness, and Skylar had given up trying to change him. His time, Tito's time, on this earth was limited. Skylar believed that. And so he took the good with the bad and tried to remind himself that he could only worry on his own behalf. To worry on someone else's was extra jaw grinding that produced nothing but blunted teeth and the ache of ineffectiveness.

The night the call came, Skylar's silk robe hung haphazardly from his shoulders though he'd been alone all evening, no one brought home as a temporary replacement for Tito (not Skylar's style, far too risky), and yet still there was the desire to look right just in case, just in case it was his turn for the paranoia to be justified, for a mug shot, to be the victim of the latest crime. He'd taken the stairs—three flights!—with grace and dander—a resplendent combination of the two (or so he imagined), which he was brave enough to indulge in only because he was in his own home.

The only phone was mounted to a wall in the kitchen, and he made his way that night with no haste at all—kimono hanging so precipitously from his golden shoulders that its position might have seemed, to an unseen audience, maintained by glue or tape—and still, minutes after it had started, it was ringing.

He was disappointed. Missing a call meant imagining who it might have been, and in Skylar's view there was always so much more promise in what might have been than what was.

"Moshi moshi," he said, his mouth dry, his voice hoarse.

"Billy?"

"Moshi moshi," he said again, either because he was still stoned from before bed or possibly still asleep or maybe just confused but definitely 100 percent unwilling in that moment to believe, because what good could believing do at a time like this, since what he was hearing was impossible. The impossible was his sister, his twin, which this voice obviously couldn't belong to even as it did, because how on earth could she have found him?

"Billy?" she said again.

And his own voice sounded as impossible as the voice he was hearing, because his own voice was speaking now, even though he was positive he'd asked his brain not to speak. He was positive that he'd told his brain to tell his hand to hang up the phone even as he heard himself saying, "Stacy? Is that you? Are you all right? How did you find me?"

And Stacy was already responding—though he was still quite certain this was nothing more than a dream—she was saying, "Billy, I need you. I've gotten myself into something. I need your help. You have to come now. I'm in a mess, Billy, and I need you. I'm in a jam. Can you come immediately?"

He hadn't been back to Georgia since the day he left, which meant he hadn't seen his sister in something like four years. When he told her, the day he left, that he was gay ("homophile" was the word he'd used), she said—and this was something he'd never forget in part because he still didn't know how he felt about it—

"Of course you are. You're a pervert. You think I didn't know?" He'd felt so close to her at the moment (of course she knew!), but also still angry, still cheated by the fact that she wasn't and he was. He was leaving not because he wanted to leave but because he was frightened of always comparing himself to her, always using her image to gauge his own.

Of course, he'd told none of this backstory to his friends in LA. To his friends in LA, he was an orphan. To his friends in LA, he was from a different city every week. Lying was an eccentricity he wore like an accessory, like a used bracelet or a new bandanna. He told stories and he was good at it, and so nobody cared what the truth was as long as he was entertaining.

But who he'd been in LA didn't matter anymore because he was returning once again to Atlanta, to play the part of grieving sibling, to reap the rewards as long as he could stomach it of his sister's curious arrangement.

Robert

Coleman was driving a Benz, one he'd imported himself on a trip to Germany. Robert was in the backseat, lying down, his knees bent in order to accommodate his long frame. His eyes were closed. When he complained of carsickness the first time, Coleman had handed him a flask. He'd tossed it onto the floorboard. "No more booze," said Robert. "At least not when the sun's still shining." When he complained the second time, only a few minutes later, Coleman had pulled over and instructed him to get in the back. He'd obeyed. Now they were speeding down the expressway on their way to yet another one of Coleman's meetings.

Robert put his hands flat on his face and breathed in deeply. He could smell the funk of cigarettes in his pinkies, but also whatever scented soap he'd been using since staying at Coleman's. It reminded him, the soap not the funk, of Lily. It was last December; they didn't yet know for sure that she was pregnant, but they both had their suspicions. They'd been like giddy teenagers since Thanksgiving. Rita had broken it off with Robert in early November—something she'd done every couple months since the sneaking around started. She hated herself, that's what she'd always say. She didn't want to be one of *those* women. There were

millions of other men, unattached men, men more decent than
Robert. Robert represented the middle, the status quo. He was a
dime a dozen. Usually she'd work herself into a fit when she delivered the End It All speech, as he'd come to think of it. Tears
—tiny perfect beads—would pop from the inside corners of her
eyes. He'd try to concentrate. He'd nod his head in agreement.
He'd turn his lips down, furrow his brow, and work desperately
hard to listen. But all he could do was watch those popping tears
land on the apples of her cheeks and wonder how long it would
be this time before she talked herself back into the affair.

But in November, after she'd broken it off yet again, Robert,
feeling confident it was only a hiatus and likely a short one at
that, had flung himself back into his marriage. He'd been missing
Lily. He'd been feeling bad himself. And he was soon reminded of
the million reasons he'd married her to begin with. For one, she
was smart as hell. Sure, she'd been born into money and therefore
received a stellar education. But the kind of smarts she had—the
sensitivity to really *fathom* a person, a situation, to see not just
the story someone was telling but also the one he wasn't—those
smarts weren't something you learned in school. Lily was perceptive. The most perceptive woman he'd ever met. Except when it
came to him. When it came to him, she was a pushover, she was
butter, she was a puddle of warm goo. For a long time, he'd liked
the way he turned her silly with love; that he, not some boarding
school brat or Harvard man, was the one who'd won her heart.
On their first date, he'd driven her to a basement jazz bar. Two
songs in, he'd stood, taken her hand, and led her to the center
of the tiny dance floor. He pulled her in tightly, his hand on the
small of her back. Her face in his neck, her breath hot against his
skin, they danced the next three or four songs without interruption. When they finally sat back down, her hand still in his, she
turned to him, her eyes wide, her face at first revealing nothing,
and said, "My god, you're a man, aren't you? A real-live man. I've

heard about you. I've read about you. I've never before met one of you. I'm afraid I'm a bit of a goner." For the first time in his life, he imagined what it might be like to propose, to drop to one knee, to make a go of it with another person. Their courtship was fast, steamy, intense. What she admired about him, what she pointed out whenever he questioned her choice of a poor geezer like him, was the fact that he was a first-generation self-made man. That was her phrase: first-generation self-made man. "Don't self-made men have fortunes?" he'd say. "I don't have a fortune." "But look at you," she'd say. "Look at what you've done and who you are and where you came from. You're a natural leader. Just look at the way McGill leans on you. You're some kind of magnet. I've never seen a man be so respected by other men. You're an alpha. Even my father admires you." This admiration caused in him his own admiration for her and the fact that she belonged to the cookie-cutter crowd but was able to look beyond it, outside it, to distinguish in him a quality and type of masculinity that she valued not simply because it was different but because to her it was also substantial. "You're the type of man who wins wars, who builds countries," she once said to him. She'd made him feel like a king.

Around the time Rita came into his life, Lily had started talking about babies, which had made him feel palpably less like a king. Which had made him feel like a means to an end, in fact. Maybe he was revising history. Maybe this was the story he told himself having met Rita, having entertained the idea of Rita— entertained the idea of her flesh, her scent, her touch, her fingers running across his bare shoulders, for example. Maybe. Or maybe both stories were true, in the same way a person could be telling one story that he wanted heard and another story he didn't mean to be heard. Both were true—the audible one and the quiet one. Just sometimes when you listened, you could hear them both and sometimes you couldn't. So he told himself a story in which Lily made him unhappy, perhaps had been making him unhappy for a spell. And it was this story that he listened to most keenly when Rita was nearby. It was this story he listened to when he finally kissed Rita in the stairwell at the *AJC* and then kissed her again and then moved her hand to the erection beneath his trousers, and she, to his great surprise and utter delight, did not shudder or pull back but instead gently and with great deliberateness ran her thumb up and down, up and down the fabric in such a way that he thought he might be brought to completion then and there.

None of which was the point. The point was he'd been missing Lily and the power of her attention, her affection. Rita ended things in November and that very evening he brought home a bouquet of tulips for his wife. She'd taken them in her hands, assessed the flowers seriously for a minute or two, then looked up at him — those eyes! that gaze! that magnificent mind! — and said, without a trace of anger, "You're back." Later that night, her head on his naked shoulder, her hair in gentle disarray against his cheek, he listened to her light snore and thought about those words — *you're back*. How much did she know, he wondered. Did she suspect another woman? Or had she simply intuited an emotional hiatus from their marriage? Did she think it was merely what happened when two people had been intimate long enough that the butterflies had worn off? He tried to imagine a scenario in which he told Lily about Rita — not to hurt her but to be open with her in a way he believed she deserved — but he couldn't work up the courage (was that the right word? surely not) and so he didn't tell her. He didn't tell her until the day of the crash. His confession when it finally happened had nothing to do with courage either, but courage (the windows to the Benz open wide and the air flowing in ripe with the smell of linden and honeysuckle) was something he now craved — courage to start over, courage to stop feeling sorry for himself, courage to tell Lily he was sorry. But courage wasn't acquired simply by wanting it (thank you, L. Frank Baum), and Robert wouldn't belittle Lily's intelligence by presenting himself to her thusly. First, he needed to right himself, and before that, he needed to figure out what such a concept even looked like.

Coleman put the car into park then swiveled in his seat so that he could observe Robert from above.

"Can you muster this? Should I leave you in the Benz? Or do you want to come with me?"

"Where are we?"

"The Pink Chateau."

"Bullshit."

"Sit up and see for yourself."

Robert sat up. His knees cracked. What Coleman said was true. They were parked in front of an enormous mansion built entirely of pink marble, known in Atlanta society as the Pink Chateau. A family by the name of Whitney had leveled the original home in the '40s and had this monstrosity built in its place. Robert had only ever seen photos.

"What's your business with the Whitneys?"

"The Whitneys aren't here. They won't be back until the Fourth."

"If they're not here, then why are we?"

"It's where this fellow we're meeting stays when he's in town."

"Do the Whitneys have a daughter?"

"There's a daughter. Sure. But as I say, none of the family is here."

"Who's this fellow we're meeting and what does he want?"

"He wants the Gauguin."

"Everybody wants the Gauguin, though I have yet to *see* the Gauguin. Prove its existence. Reveal the masterpiece."

"It's at my aunt's house," he said. "The poor queer. I've given her through the end of the year to find another place to live."

"Why aren't we meeting at your aunt's?"

"She's sensitive. Let's leave it at that."

"Why are you kicking her out of her house? How can you even do that?"

"Because it's mine now," Coleman said.

"But you already have a house."

"Her house actually belonged to my father," he said. "He'll roll over in his grave when I take possession. That's an image I like to think about—the old man rolling over in his grave."

"That's your father you're talking about. The man is dead. There's no need to be cruel to his memory. It's unnecessary. And why punish your aunt?"

"I like you better when you're high."

"I want to be sober."

"Are you coming or staying in the car?"

"It's ninety degrees."

"Then straighten up. Let's do this."

Coleman opened the front door and stepped out. He opened Robert's door, too. "Out," he said.

"Sure," said Robert. "Sure. I'm coming."

"For fun," said Coleman as Robert climbed out of the back-seat, "if this fellow names a figure, add a couple thousand and pretend you're interested."

"What do I get out of it?"

"Do some knee bends," said Coleman. "You look like crap."

Robert did a few jumping jacks and shook his head quickly back and forth. His mouth was cottony, his wrists shaky. His body needed booze, but he didn't want to give in. "So you *are* selling," Robert said. He squeezed one earlobe, then the other. It was something Lily had sometimes done for him when he complained of headaches after work. It didn't help now.

"No," said Coleman. "Not actively. Not actually. I'm not selling the Gauguin. What I'm selling today is dreams. These men want to dream of owning it. I'm here to provide that possibility."

"Hell of an idea."

"Everyone's doing it. Look at the Soviets. Look at Cuba. Those missiles they just approved—unanimous vote, by the way— they're not real. Yes, they're *real,* but they'll never be used. It's the *dream* of detonation that the Soviets are selling. And they're sell- ing that dream to us, whether or not we're in the market to buy."

"You're a crazy man," said Robert. "You know that."

"I'm a genius," Coleman said. "When I die, they'll chop off my head and study my brain. They'll wonder how I could see so many connections."

"Who's going to chop off your head?"

"Scientists—at Carnegie, maybe Emory or Johns Hopkins. Hell, Stanford can have me if they can get me on ice quick enough. It's in my will. I'm donating my insides for the better- ment of mankind."

As Coleman talked, they made their way down a pebblestone path toward the marble monstrosity. There were flowing stone fountains on either side of the mansion; in the center of one was a mermaid, arms raised skyward, breasts perky and glistening. She was posed to suggest the beginning of ascent, the moment just before she might eject herself from the water for some epic arc that would eventually return her to the sea.

A man in a light brown suit emerged from the front door. He regarded Coleman and Robert. Then he regarded the statue that had momentarily stolen their attention.

"There's a girl staying with your aunt who is the spitting im- age," said the man. He moved down a short series of steps in their direction and gestured to the mermaid. "Have you seen her? She's exquisite. The likeness is uncanny."

"You've been to my aunt's?" said Coleman. "You didn't say you'd be stopping by my aunt's."

The man in the light brown suit extended his hand. Coleman took it but didn't immediately let go. "You shouldn't be talking to her," said Coleman. "She isn't in charge. She's authorized to make zero decisions or gestures or donations. Zero as in nada. I'll stand by nothing she might have insinuated or promised."

The man cleared his throat. "Who's your friend?"

"He goes by Robert." Coleman let go of the man's hand at last. "He's a crazy sonofabitch. Swam across Lake Michigan and back last summer. One hundred miles. We'll call him an interested party, for the sake of argument. Robert, this is Ed Klein. We'll call him an interested party, too."

Ed Klein held out a hand. Robert shook it. He'd been to Chicago twice. The first time to cover the opening of the Playboy Club in February 1960; the second time, seven months later, to cover the Nixon-Kennedy debate. Not even a toe of Robert's had made contact with Lake Michigan.

"Hell of a handshake," said Ed.

"Had it all my life," said Robert.

To Coleman, Ed said, "Your aunt told me only that you were in charge. She's on your side. The people I represent want to do this properly. They're prepared to dot every i and cross every t. I wanted to see her because her brother, your father, was a close friend. I wanted to extend the same sympathies that I'd like to extend to you now."

"You didn't see the Gauguin, then?"

Ed Klein shrugged then brought his hands together as though in prayer. He shrugged again. "It's a stunning piece," he said. "Why wouldn't I have asked to see it when it's a single set of French doors away."

Sweat beads formed and ran down Robert's back beneath his shirt. He licked his lips. "Would it be impolite to ask that we move this conversation inside?" asked Robert. He cleared his throat. "I could use a glass of water."

"Excellent idea," said Ed Klein. He clapped Robert on the shoulder, steering him around the side of the house. "I can do you one better. Nina's made a bit of a stink about Coleman's visit.

There are refreshments in the pool house. There's also air conditioning. Do you like air conditioning? I love it; love the smell. We'll be more comfortable there."

With Coleman following behind, Robert allowed himself to be guided down a wide slate path that snaked its way to the property's backyard. On the far side of a white-bottomed pool—with a set of marble stairs leading straight into its clear blue water— was a square brick cottage covered in ivy, completely unlike the pink mansion it stood behind.

"One of the oldest structures in Atlanta," said Ed Klein. "The only part of the property that was preserved. I try to see it whenever I pass through. The Whitneys are good enough to let me stay when I'm in town."

Robert stopped abruptly. "Wait," he said. "Isn't this where . . ."

"Yes," said Ed Klein.

"Every year on the Fourth," said Coleman.

"What? No. Wasn't there a lynching here? A mass lynching?" asked Robert. "In the thirties? A whole family?"

"Technically it did happen on the property," said Ed, "but the tree no longer stands."

"Jesus," said Robert. "McGill covered that story. He was here. I've seen the photographs. This building . . ." He moved almost in a trance, maybe it was the heat, maybe it was the discomfort of sobriety, toward the small brick house. "It was in the pictures. I remember . . ." He looked around for—for what? Evidence? A place in the ground where the tree once stood? He didn't know.

Ed Klein coughed. "Have you ever been to one of their parties?"

"Independence Day," said Coleman. "Every year on the nose I'm here. Traffic shuts down for a mile in both directions. I'd say I have no idea how they get away with it, but—" He rubbed his middle finger against his thumb. "But I know *exactly* how they get away with it." Coleman was pleased with himself. "Have you ever been? I don't remember you being here last year."

"No," said Robert, still shaken and shaking. It would have been ludicrous to say aloud, but he thought he could feel them—the ghosts, the dead, the people who'd been brought here to live and work and die as slaves. "Lily never wanted to come. There's a daughter. I'm sure of it now. Same age. They didn't get along."

Coleman slapped Robert on the back. Bile lifted then fell in his throat.

"Don't worry, old chap," said Coleman. "As I said, the whole lot of them are in the Islands for the month. You won't be knocking elbows with them today. At ease, soldier."

"You stay well informed," said Ed Klein.

"I consider it one of my many talents," said Coleman.

Ed reached the cottage first. He opened its small front door. The air conditioning was immediate and divine.

"I feel faint," said Robert.

Ed Klein smiled at this, as though what had been said was a joke of some kind. He raised a hand and beckoned them to enter the single room—its ceiling soaring—that was decked out with gold and crystal furnishings, all of which shimmered, from top to bottom, like the tips of waves under a high summer sun.

"Gentlemen," said Ed. "Let's talk money."

Lily

When the phone rang on the morning of June 23, which was a Saturday, Lily Tucker was already awake but still in bed. She'd been talking aloud again.

Lately, at odd moments, as if coming to from a stupor, she found herself addressing the baby. She would stop herself immediately, midsentence if necessary, troubled by her motivation to converse with an unborn child. More disconcerting still was the fact that what she invariably discovered herself talking about—*who* she discovered herself talking about—was Robert. Just now, for instance, with the phone's initial ring, she'd been describing to the baby—unwittingly!—Robert's face, its high cheekbones, the devilish hints of a smile that seemed always to lurk in their steep shadows. "It is a fine jawline," she had been saying. "A very fine jawline and you'll see—" But here the phone had rung and she'd caught herself—she'd come to, as it were—and she'd stopped before she could embarrass herself by saying more.

The ringing was coming from the kitchen; she'd had every other extension in the house disconnected. Lily rubbed her belly and listened. After ten rings it went silent.

Not even eight in the morning, and already the sun hit the windows above her bed with a bright orange glare. Birds somewhere high were *chirp-chirp-chirp*ing their approval of the day's beginning. She felt immediately lonely. She rolled onto her side. The baby kicked; the phone rang again. She made no fast move to answer it. In her condition, there were no fast moves. Instead there existed slow, decisive gestures that occurred only after she'd thought them through ahead of time, which was what she did now, just as the phone stopped ringing for a second time: *And now I will roll onto my back. And after that I will bend my knees as best I can. And after that I will slide my bare feet across the sheet ever so slowly until my toes have reached the edge of the bed. And after that I will sigh. And after that I will inch my lower back toward my heels. And after that I will push up onto my forearms and, first left foot and then right, I will make contact with the floor and—finally—I will stand.*

On her feet at last, with one hand under her stomach and the other on the arm of the sofa for stability, the phone began ringing for a third time.

As she made her way to the kitchen, she tried to recall the loneliness she'd experienced only seconds before, but already its intensity was floating away because already she was thinking about Piedmont, the young Negro who had been staying in her guesthouse for nearly one week now.

By the time the phone started ringing for a fourth time, she was standing in front of the icebox feeling queasy. She'd nearly forgotten about the telephone and that its high-pitch cry was what had called her to the kitchen in the first place.

There were a million pieces of news she might have been prepared for or could have guessed at, if she'd wanted, as she picked up the receiver. The fact that another jet had crashed, not a month after the Orly disaster, was not one of them.

Her knees buckled. She fell forward, her palms hitting the linoleum hard. There was a pain in her side so acute, so immediate, she thought maybe the baby had gotten hold of something —the end of a lung, an inch of her intestine—and crushed it in its fist.

From the earpiece of the receiver, which dangled now from its wall mount, she could hear Martha saying her name. She pulled herself up, using the edge of the countertop, and then gathered the cord until the phone was in her hand.

"Thank you," she said breathily. "Thank you for the news. I have to go now."

She hung up before Martha could say more.

It wasn't sadness that had sent her to her knees—that's not what she would call this sensation: the bony pyramid of her nose wasn't burning; she did not feel on the cusp of tears. What it was, what it must have been, was shock. She had simply not thought it possible that another jet—another 707, in fact, and this one also operated by Air France—would crash so soon, in the same month even. The probability felt off, the likelihood (and here she nearly snickered) unlikely. Martha had said it went down the day before, in the West Indies, while trying to land. She'd said it was bad weather, that there were no survivors, not even a stewardess or a pilot. But by then Lily was already on her knees, her palms already smarting against the cold floor. She wasn't interested in the particulars. She was confused that Martha had called her; that Martha had thought this news was somehow necessary to share. Did it lessen their losses? Was that what Martha was thinking? Did another hodgepodge of adult children who'd been suddenly left without parents, on an island a mere 1,800 miles away, make their plight any less absurd?

Lily didn't think so. She didn't think so at all.

The Black Forest cuckoo clock in the hallway struck eight.

"Damn," she said, looking at her bare feet, at the silly floral hemline of her ridiculous nightgown. "Damn, damn." Last night she'd invited Piedmont to come over at 8:30 for breakfast and afterward to have a turn at the baby grand. But she'd dillydallied in bed, babbling on about Robert's face to the baby, and time had slipped away until Martha's insipid phone call with its even more

insipid news and now here she was, barefoot and completely unprepared for company.

Why had she invited Piedmont to play her grandmother's
piano? Because Raif Bentley had visited her unannounced the
day before. He'd made her an offer she knew better than to re-
fuse, and as a result, after he left, she found she was feeling both
generous and uneasy—a little unhinged really—and she'd done
the only thing she could think of to dispel some of her nervous
energy: she'd walked across the backyard to her pool house and
knocked on its front door.

"You asked if you could be of some additional use," she'd said
to Piedmont. Days earlier he'd moved several boxes from the upstairs of the main house to the downstairs, a chore that had taken
him less than an hour.

"Yes, ma'am?"

"It's Lily," she said. "Please."

"Lily," he said. He looked at his feet. He was standing in the
doorway, she on the WELCOME mat.

"The piano needs playing," she said.

He frowned. "Ma'am?"

"Lily," she said again. "Please!"

"Yes," he said. "I'll try."

"What I mean is, what I was hoping was, if you'd play me
something . . ." Her hand circled her belly. "If you'd play *us* something. The baby's been kicking, and I'm on strict orders not to go
anywhere, nearly house arrest it feels like to me, and there's a little
club I'd go to if I were allowed or if my husband were here, but
I'm in no shape on my own and so . . . Am I making any sense?"

He nodded.

"I don't mean to intrude. And I surely don't mean to suggest
you might not already be busy, but if you were, for instance, free
tomorrow, which is a Saturday, then I'd be delighted to make you
breakfast—" When she saw his face drop, she corrected herself.

"Make *us* breakfast and then perhaps you could play for me? If it isn't too much trouble."

He looked down again. She thought she detected a rush of pink at the tops of his cheeks. "Yes, ma'am," he said to the ground. "Lily," he corrected. "Yes, Lily."

When he looked up, he was smiling. It was a large, earnest, natural smile and—perhaps merely because of this or perhaps because Raif had eliminated some of her immediate stressors with his visit and unexpected offer—she, too, smiled.

"Eight thirty, then," she'd said, and he'd nodded.

Raif's offer was a simple one. He'd finally heard her news—her parents' news really: that they'd left Lily destitute, broke, that the house wasn't hers, that she would soon be moving out—and he'd rushed immediately over. Yes, they'd had dinner together after the crash, Raif had held her by the arm at his own wife's memorial, but Lily had not let on to him about the money. All she had allowed of her private life was that Robert was gone. It was Polly Granville, who'd stopped him in the hallway at Westminster after he'd dropped the boys in their respective homerooms and who'd asked, with no attempt to hide her amusement, whether or not Raif had heard about Lily's situation. He assumed she meant Robert, but what she added to the story had devastated him. He'd gotten directly into his car and driven straight to Forrest Way, not bothering even to say goodbye to Polly.

"Forgive me," he'd stammered from the front the porch once Lily had opened the door. "I should have phoned. Forgive me. But this is urgent."

She'd let him in, of course. They were old friends. She'd been close not just with Nance, but with Raif, with the boys. His own loss had rocked her to her core. The idea of those three boys suddenly without their mother . . . It was too much. It was simply too much.

"Why is P. T. Coleman's Thunderbird in your driveway?"

"You've come to ask me this?"

"Of course not," he said. He was flustered—flushed and flustered. "But it's curious. Is he here? God, I hope he isn't here. I don't care for that man."

"It's a bit of a story," she said. "He isn't here. You needn't worry about that. But if there's something on your mind, you'll likely prefer to skip the explanation for P. T.'s car. It's lengthy."

"Forget the Thunderbird. Just tell me. Is it true?"

They were standing now in the foyer, where just the week before Lily had stood in the middle of the night with Piedmont and the two uniformed goons.

The skin beneath Raif's eyes was bruised and tender. It was true what they said: you could spot from a mile away a man who lacked a woman. He looked noticeably less well now than at Nance's memorial.

"Is what true?" She touched his arm.

He jerked it away.

Then he put his fingers to his temple, closed his eyes, and shook his head. "I'm sorry," he said. "I just— It's important that I be able to concentrate. When you touch me like that— When *anyone* touches me like that, I think of Nance."

"You haven't hurt my feelings. You mustn't worry about hurting my feelings, about hurting anyone's feelings . . ."

Raif, as if his irises had only now adjusted to being indoors and away from the glare of the sun, began slowly to look around him. Lily watched him take in the changes to her home, the one he and Nance used to visit with such frequency for bridge games, dinner parties, Sunday breakfasts, Easters. She watched too as he walked from the foyer to the dining room and then into the kitchen. He came back to the foyer, looked at her, then moved in the opposite direction toward Robert's office. She followed him.

"Please," she said. "Please, don't."

But it was too late. By the time she'd caught up, he'd opened the office door.

His shoulders slumped.

Still standing behind him, she saw it all as he must have seen it—the unmade pull-out sofa she'd been using as her bed, the filled-up boxes, the scattered papers, the pile of clothes that a person could just make out on the bathroom floor beyond.

"Don't embarrass me," she said. "Please."

He turned around slowly. His hands were shaking, his eyes newly bloodshot. "You must let me help you."

"There's nothing to do," she said. She shrugged. The baby performed what felt like a somersault. She grabbed at her belly. "Help me to the chair," she said. She gestured toward Robert's office chair. "It's the only place I feel comfortable sitting." Raif took an arm and she read the expression on his face. "Not like that, not for sentimentality's sake. For genuine comfort. I can get a good angle here." She sat down. "Thank you."

He unstacked a box and also sat. He looked out the window. The sprinklers were on. "It's all gone?"

"All of it," she said. "Yes. It seems it's been gone for some time."

He nodded, still taking in the lawn and the few cars going by. "You say there's nothing to do."

"That's correct," she said, leaning back in the chair and closing her eyes. How many times had she fallen asleep to the sounds of Raif's voice and Robert's going on late into the night about politics, about the news, about what was fit to print and what wasn't, as she and Nance nodded off on their respective sides of the couch, their stockinged legs intertwined like two high school girls in love? She couldn't begin to count.

"But you're wrong," he said. "I can help. I can help very easily."

She opened her eyes. "If you're about to propose," she said, "you should know I am pregnant."

He smiled, but then almost immediately he began to sob.

"I can't come over there to comfort you," she said. "It simply isn't possible. I'm a beached whale over here, and so you need to stop that crying."

"You're so strong," he said.

"Yes," she said.

"So loyal."

"Yes."

"Stubborn."

"True, too. It's likely why he left me."

"He left because he's a coward."

"He fell in love," she said. "That's something other than being a coward. Being an idiot maybe . . . Being a fool . . . You've told me before what a catch I am, and I won't disagree, Raif. I know I'm a catch." She paused. "*Was* a catch. Will be again once I get this baby on the other side of me. Oh, stop it. Stop crying. Please laugh. I'm trying to cheer you up."

"And that's what's so awful," he said. "That's what's so awful about all of it—the idea of you and me trying to cheer each other up. It isn't right. It isn't fair."

"Who's to say what's right or fair?"

"Listen," he said. He sat up straight, rubbed at his eyes. "Listen to me now. If I offered you a place in my own home, you'd say no. Am I right?"

"You are right."

"And we've never been in love, have we?"

She shook her head.

"No," he said. He looked truly disappointed. "I didn't think we had. It's a shame too, really. The boys adore you. But I've been in love and so have you, and we both know what it feels like— that princely and abysmal feeling—and so we'd both know what we were missing and we'd always be resentful . . ."

"What are you getting at? What's your plan here?"

"It's no secret that I am a wealthy man."

She couldn't help it. She laughed.

"Yes," he said, still quite serious. "We are both aware. It's an absurd fortune, but I've done good things with it—for the city and for the country—while preserving the bulk in order for my sons to have good lives, comfortable lives if they want them."

She nodded.

"I have more than enough to help you now, too," he said.

"I couldn't—"

"Let me finish," he said. "I have more than enough to help you and thirty more just like you, but there is only one you, Lily. There is only you. You know Nance would want you taken care of. In fact"—and now he sat up even straighter, a new idea suddenly having come to him—"and yes, you see, the simple and plain truth is that you must allow me to provide for you. Nance would insist. I'm not doing this for you. Do you see? I'm doing this for Nance. You must let me," he said. "It's of the most extraordinary importance that you let me help you."

On and on he went. Lily leaned back and listened. Leaves of the Tasmanian tree fern out front swayed in an unfelt breeze and shadows of brown and gold tickled the office ceiling. She'd not felt such tranquility in ages. She drifted in and out of the most amazing light sleep that must, at some point, have led to an intense and deep sleep because when she woke, Raif was standing at a far window, the light was in a different corner of the room, and there was a blanket draped over her knees.

She yawned. "I think I might have fallen asleep."

He didn't turn to face her.

"You think I'm so stubborn that I'll say no."

"You are stubborn."

The sun inched down. The room darkened.

"What would Robby say?"

"You oughtn't think about him."

"And yet I do."

"What would he say to my offer?"

"What would he say if I accepted?"

"He would say you are wise."

"He would feel emasculated."

"By me? Look at me. Robert could level me with his left pinkie."

"I wonder."

"What do you say? Will you let me help you?"

From the yard out back, all at once, the crickets came to life.

"What will people think?"

"Do you care what people think?"

"No," she said. "But I do care about Robby."

"He's left you in this bind. He's offering no other solutions, is he?"

"He doesn't know about the money."

"It's a crying shame, his behavior is."

Lily pushed back the tiniest of tears with her knuckles. "I'm not a fool," she said at last. "I have more than myself to think about now. If the offer is real, then I accept. I accept your help with utter gratitude."

"Lily," Raif said. "Lily, where is your phone?" His posture had tightened. His hand was on the windowsill. Something outside had caught his attention.

"What is it? What do you see?"

"There's a man out there," he said. He pointed sharply toward the backyard at the pool house. "A Negro."

Lily sighed. "Yes," she said. "His name is Piedmont Dobbs."

Raif turned abruptly to face her.

"You know him? Does he work here?"

"He's my guest."

"He's staying here?"

"In the pool house."

Raif took another look out the window. "Is he a teenager?"

"No," she said. "Help me up. My foot has fallen asleep."

Raif came to her. "Should I be worried about you?"

"You mean worried about him?"

"I mean worried about the decisions you're making."

"No," she said.

Raif pulled her gently to her feet.

"I have one condition for accepting your help."

"Is the boy to do with the Thunderbird?"

"My god, you're clever."

"But is he connected to P. T.? I don't like it at all if he's connected to P. T."

"He has no affiliation with Coleman."

"And what do you mean by *condition?* Oughtn't it be *me* asking a condition of *you?*"

"Perhaps," she said. She began walking toward the front door. She was ready to lie down, to take a nice long uninterrupted nap. This, the pink time of night, was her favorite part of the day. "But you won't." She paused. "Will you?"

"You know me too well. What is your condition?"

"Leave me alone," she said. And then, so he would understand she didn't mean it in any cruel or permanent way, she gripped his arm. "For now, until the baby is born. Leave me alone and, if you can, keep them away."

"Them?"

"You know who: Martha and Polly and Agatha and Jane . . . I can't bear it. I can't bear the way they look at me."

"You clump me with them?" Raif didn't pull away, but he did look genuinely hurt.

"Of course I don't," she said. "You have to stay away because otherwise I'll fall in love with you."

"Don't tease me," he said. "You're still in love with Robert. I wouldn't stand a chance."

"Yes," she said. "You're right. I am. And this alone is where I am the fool."

"You think I'll fall in love with you, though. Is that it?"

"See?" she said. "I know you too well, and you know me too well."

"For now," he said. "For now I'll stay away, and I'll do what I can to keep the others away as well. As for the boy—" He looked again toward the office, as though he could see through walls, see through brick, wood, and mortar, and observe young Piedmont

Dobbs where he now stood or sat or perhaps reclined. "You'll be careful?"

"He's harmless."

"Tell me you'll be careful."

"I'll be careful."

He bent and kissed her on the forehead.

"You can start unpacking," he said. "You'll own this house as soon as the paperwork is ready. And you're right, by the way."

"Right about what?"

"I could have loved you."

"Anybody could love anyone. That's what they don't tell you. All you have to do is make yourself available to the possibility."

"I'll think about that," he said.

"I can never repay you."

Raif opened the door and stepped to the other side of the doorway before saying this: "Just keep living. Just promise me you'll keep living."

Lily lingered in the doorway, watching as he backed out onto Forrest Way. She held up her hand but, because of the angle of the setting sun, couldn't be sure that he'd seen. It was then, the evening moving with an unexpected urgency from fuchsia to magenta and toward the inevitable plum-indigo of night, and her stomach vibrating with nerves, that she left her house, walked around to the backyard, and delivered to Piedmont an invitation for breakfast followed by a turn at her grandmother's baby grand piano.

That night, Piedmont having said yes, she found herself overcome by a flattening fatigue. Within minutes of lying down, she was asleep. In the morning she awoke feeling fresh, rested, a burgeoning sense of awe and relief. This home would be hers again, hers and the baby's to share. When she began murmuring to the baby about Robert and the features of his face, it wasn't so much that she'd forgotten about her invitation to Piedmont and the fact that she ought to be up and readying the kitchen for company, as that she'd simply gotten lost in her own mindless reveries of the past.

Now it was 8 a.m., Martha had called with her sickening news, and Piedmont would be over in half an hour. "Damn," she said again aloud. "Get your head on, girlie. Crack some eggs. Melt some butter. Do something." She was about to put on an apron when she realized she was still in her nightgown. "Well, yes," she said. "Sheesh. That's a good point, I suppose. First things first. Put some real clothes on, girlie. Sheesh. Sheesh."

She surprised herself with the alacrity with which she moved just then—not like a lady set to give birth at any minute, but like a person who'd been given a fresh start, a new chance, a do-over on life. By the time Piedmont knocked on the back door, she was dressed and standing at the stove with a bowl of biscuit batter and the butter just beginning to fry.

"Lily," he said as she opened the door.

"That's my name!"

"I practiced all night." He blushed, then smiled. She smiled too. "And a few times this morning."

She motioned him into the kitchen. "It shouldn't be this awkward, should it?"

"What shouldn't be awkward?" He wiped his feet.

"Oh, golly," she said. "*This.* Having company. It seems it shouldn't be so hard."

He nodded. She must have sounded like an idiot, like the privileged white idiot that she was. She longed for a way to show him she was different, to show him she didn't care. But even that thought—that she somehow *was* different from the others and therefore better—was so naïve, she could have almost stomped her feet.

"I brought this." He held up an old encyclopedia. "Not the book," he said. "Inside."

The encyclopedia's heft surprised her. It had been ages since she'd opened an actual book. She placed it on the kitchen table, one end of which was set for two and one end of which was clear.

She sucked in her breath.

Between the pages of the encyclopedia was a perfectly pressed and preserved magnolia flower.

"I didn't pluck it," he said. "It was in the swimming pool."

She stopped herself from admitting that she knew the flower's origin. She'd seen him his first morning on the property—perhaps one could say she'd been spying on him—when he'd walked out onto the covered front porch of the pool house and then just stood there, blinking, watching, thinking. His face was still swollen but already looked better than when he'd shown up bloody and bruised. She'd watched him that morning while standing at the kitchen sink. He'd lit a cigarette and sneezed. She was about to join him, about to greet him officially and in the light of day, perhaps ask for a cigarette as they discussed the dodginess of the previous night, but before she could move, he did. He extinguished the cigarette—only partially smoked—and returned what remained to his shirt pocket. Then he walked to the deep end of the swimming pool. Lily had had to change her position in order to maintain her line of sight.

At the edge of the pool, he bent down and stretched out his arm. She didn't immediately understand. But then she saw that an entire magnolia flower was floating toward the middle, too far for him to reach. She stood there watching, marveling, wondering at his interest, as he made his hand an oar and dipped it into the water and caused waves in his direction until the blossom floated obligingly toward him. He kept the water moving until the magnolia came all the way to the edge of the pool, where it bobbed against the ledge and where he let it continue to bob for several minutes—Lily knew this because she had watched him the whole time—until at last, bored perhaps, he picked it up. He shook it gently, little drops of water splashing onto his pants and shoes, then went promptly back inside the pool house and shut the door.

"Can I pick it up?" she asked.

"Not yet," he said. "It's still drying. Better to keep it pressed another week or two."

She nodded. The kitchen timer buzzed.

"Oh," she said. "The biscuits. Have a seat, will you? We'll eat and then I'll show you the piano."

Over breakfast, she asked him about flower pressing, where he'd learned how, who had taught him. He blushed whenever she asked him not to call her "ma'am," and she observed his smile —it was sweet, with none of the mischief of Robert's lips or, say, the trumpeter's so many years ago in London—with a tinge of melancholia.

In the music room, after biscuits and eggs, they sat side by side at the piano. She raised the fallboard, but he made no move to touch the keys. On the rack was a sheet of Tchaikovsky.

"I've only ever played an organ," he said.

"So you don't know pedals."

He shook his head.

"This has eighty-eight keys and they're weighted," she said. "The organ is shorter, yes?"

"Yes," he said.

"The piano is more fun. Hold out your hands."

He held them out, above the keys, in a perfectly neutral curved position. He was a natural. There was no doubt about it.

"See?" she said. "These will fit your fingers better. The keys are larger. You play by heart? Here. Start here." She rested her own hands on top of his and moved them to the C position.

He was about to play; she could tell: he straightened his fingers and the knuckles cracked. But as soon as his fingertips made contact with the ivory, he pulled them away and moved them instead to either knee. He turned to face her.

"Are you one of them?"

"Will you not play?" she said.

"You are. Aren't you?"

"One of whom?"

"The orphans."

Lily felt her cheeks turning warm. "Where did you get that word?"

"It's what they call you in the papers and on the television."

"I'm a grownup," she said. Why did she feel defensive? He wasn't wrong. But she'd not wanted to talk about herself this morning. She'd not wanted to think about what she'd lost or what had been taken away from her. She wanted to hear music. She wanted to hear about somebody else's life for a change—somebody whose experiences and societal expectations were unilaterally different from hers. "And, anyway, grownups can't be orphans." But the truth was she felt very much like an orphan at that moment and more like a child than a grownup.

"I'm sorry," he said. "I've upset you."

"No," she said. "Well, yes, but also no. I'm upset with the situation—the injustice of it all. I'm not upset with you. Yes. I am one of them. Though to be completely accurate, we aren't all orphans. Not everyone lost both parents. Many of us lost only mothers. I lost both. And several friends."

"I can't imagine." He looked down at the keys when he said this.

"That's because it's unimaginable," she said. Out the window, a woodpecker started up.

"Do you still want me to play?" he said.

"Very much," she said.

From his knees, he raised his hands. Again their position was perfect.

He turned his chin in her direction and then said, not a question but a statement, "You like Don Shirley."

Before she could catch her breath or wrap her mind about what he'd said and how he'd said it—was she imagining things or had his voice dropped just slightly? and was it a trick of the morning sunlight or was there a quality of mischievousness to his profile she'd not previously detected?—his fingers met the keys and suddenly she was listening to an impromptu version of "The Nearness of You." It was as though—it truly was—as though Don Shirley himself were there in the room, playing just for Lily.

What Lily thought about that night, a single sheet atop her body, draped high and falling at a ridiculous angle because of her belly, was not, as she expected, Piedmont or the way, late into the afternoon, outside on the front porch, several cans of beers divided between them, several albums' worth of jazz and blues played and discussed, or the way that she'd laced her fingers between his. Nor did she think about the way he'd lowered his gaze, then his head, then—his head still lowered—raised his eyes so that he could watch her and she could watch him, watch his eyes as she moved her fingers up and down between his, the feeling as sensual as any she'd ever known. They might well have been naked for the intense pang of intimacy it had triggered throughout her body. For many years to come, often at night and especially in the summer, she would think about that day, that afternoon, that particular and unexpected moment. But on the night of, she did not.

On the night of, she thought of Helen Seydel, lovely Helen Seydel. Since the crash, Lily had been successful in her efforts not to think of the letters Helen had sent from Paris, from Florence. Helen's husband had left her the year before; she'd been blindsided by his departure. Her marriage, Helen had believed, was one of the good ones. But he'd left, and poor stupid Lily had had the audacity to pity her. She'd had the audacity to think, *Poor Helen, what did you expect? Everyone knew but you . . .* When Helen booked the trip to Paris alone, Lily had made fun behind her back, as if painting classes and a trip to the Louvre would solve any of Helen's problems. As recently as last month, Lily hadn't felt glad for her friend; she'd felt sorry. *I am ready to begin again,* Helen had written, and Lily had decided that her friend was worse off than before, delusional and unprepared for her life back home as a spinster. No, Lily had not wanted to think about Helen and for good reason.

But Helen's face was in *LIFE* magazine, practically the centerfold, which had turned up in the day's stack of mail, which Lily had made the mistake of sorting through just before bed, after Piedmont, sleepy and drunk, had finally said good night. Now the issue was lying on the floor next to the pullout in Robert's office. She'd been completely caught off-guard by it. There was a photograph of one of Helen's self-portraits—who'd let the cameramen into her house? who'd given them access to Helen's studio?—a beautiful self-portrait that did duty to the face in that it caught less the actual features and more the spirit of the woman. Lily had seen that portrait before; had been in the very same room where the cameramen must have stood; had seen her artist's supplies; had derided their existence . . . But now, in the pages of *LIFE,* those tubes of paint and well-used brushes appeared so obviously full of vitality, of promise. The expression of the self-portrait seemed almost to predict the artist's early demise. Anyone looking at that mouth, its acceptance, its tacit acquiescence to what will and must be—anyone looking also at those eyes, their determination to reject sadness and disappointment—*anyone* would have had the same terrifying thought as Lily: that she knew, she knew, of course she knew.

And so it was Helen who Lily thought about on the night she first held hands with Piedmont. And for a little while, it was also her parents. And for a little while after that, it was the whole lot of them—Agatha's parents and Jane's and Polly's and Martha's—it was the entire 130. How could she not think of them?

Next to the portrait of Helen there'd been the photograph of the wing, its edge a row of jagged burnt teeth. *That image!* If only they understood the effects of that image on those who'd lost someone . . . But they mustn't have known. They mustn't have understood. Because if they had — the newspapers, the television stations — if they had known, then they'd have never shown it in the first place. They'd have burned it the moment it was taken, burned it like the plane and all the people inside.

Coleman

For Coleman, 1962 would always be the year of ants. Not the year of the crash—his parents' or his own. Not the year of "Happy Birthday, Mr. President" or the seven-hour, 22-inning game between New York and Detroit. It wouldn't be the year of the Cuban Missile Crisis or the year of Johnny Carson. It wouldn't even be the year of Robert Tucker or the year he lost, after settling out of court, close to 50 percent of an inheritance he'd only just gotten his hands on, including the beloved Gauguin, which was stolen before he could sell it. Instead, for all time, he would remember that year, that summer in particular, as the summer of ants.

They came in late April, before his parents had even left for Europe. His mother stopped by with a check. It was the last one, she'd told him. His father had found out, was livid. "I need to respect him," she said. "Until you change your ways, Claude's done helping. You're too old to be living like this. It's . . ."

Disgraceful was the word she didn't say. She didn't need to. They both knew. He'd taken the check. Perhaps she had hoped he wouldn't: she was always so grotesquely hopeful. "Next time, next time, next time." It was practically a refrain. *Next time, your father will be less angry. Next time, he won't pull my arm like that. Next time, I'll remember no chives in the salad dressing. Next time, you won't wet the bed and so he won't . . . Well, let's not say he hit you, Cole. Let's not say anything so dire as that. He was too rough. You're right. But let's not use words we don't mean and anyway next time . . .*

He took the check. On her way out—the last time he would see her, though the flight out was close to a month away—she'd stopped. She knelt to inspect the gap between the front door's frame and the carpet. She didn't let her stockinged knee touch the floor. She leaned in closer, then shook her head. Very carefully, with so much grace it made him want to topple her, a direct hit into her shoulder with the heel of his shoe, she stood up. She wiped her hands, one onto the other. "Ants," she said.

"It's fine," he said.

"If you don't take care of them, there will be thousands by the end of summer."

"Thank you, Mother." He had always called her Mother.

That was in April.

By early June, by the time his parents were dead, the ants were everywhere. Out of the corner of his eye, he'd sense the floor was moving. He'd creep closer and discover not the floor, but a steady parade of tiny black ants. When he found them inching across the tile on the first-floor bathroom, he scoured the room with bleach himself. When, several days later, he discovered a slow line of them making their way across the windowsill of the master bedroom, he dropped what he'd been doing and drove straight to the hardware store. "Give me everything," he'd said. "I need a Hiroshima." The couple behind the counter—husband and wife, Greek—hadn't cracked a smile. But they had given him a bottle of something with a frighteningly strong odor. For several days, the ants were gone. He was free of them.

But then, at a traffic light in Buckhead in mid-June—a week or so after news of the crash—he saw a single ant tiptoeing across the outside of the windshield. He watched it make its steady way across the glass. Then he looked back to the place where he'd first spotted it, on the other side of the glass from the rearview mirror. There was another one. He watched this one too. When it was finally out of sight, he looked again at the place on the windshield just beyond the rearview. There, again, was another.

A car behind him honked. The light had turned from red to green. He lurched forward, made it through the intersection, then pulled over and parked not quite parallel with the curb. He looked again, but the ants—for the time being—were gone. What he noticed instead was a well-dressed man stumbling down the sidewalk on the opposite side of the street. He checked his watch. It was 10 a.m. and a Wednesday. The man was drunk. Coleman smiled. He knew this man. This man was an editor at the *Atlanta Journal Constitution.* This man was a friend. This man was someone with whom Coleman could get rip-roaring wasted and not afterward have to worry about consequences or judgments. This man was surely as big a fuck-up as he. This man was Robert Tucker!

He'd gotten out of his Thunderbird and followed him promptly into a bar.

Robert

"Fine," said Robert. "I admit it. I'm worried about her."

"Ha," said Coleman. "I knew it."

They were sitting at a back booth in a dirty yellow diner on Peachtree Battle, drinking strawberry milkshakes. For the past hour, Robert had been trying to convince Coleman it was time to retrieve the Thunderbird, which was parked at the top of the driveway of the house on Forrest Way.

"I thought you didn't want her to see you like this."

"I haven't had a drink in days."

"That can't be accurate. Can it?"

"I want to go home."

"What makes you think she'll take you back?"

It was a good question, one Robert had been mulling over. She would take him back because she still loved him, not because he deserved her. She would take him back because the baby was his. She would take him back because she missed the way he sometimes sidled up from behind and nibbled on her neck while she sliced vegetables for dinner. She *wouldn't* take him back because

he was cowardly

he was unfaithful

he was selfish

he was unreliable

he was . . . himself.

He thought of an aphorism he'd overheard years earlier, before he'd become someone's husband and someone else's lover: "Wherever you go, there you are." That seemed precisely to be Robert's problem. Wherever he went, there he was. And lately, there was his scalawag of a friend as well.

"Plus," Coleman was saying, "with whatever inheritance she has coming her way— Do you know the number? Ballpark? Ignore me. The question is gauche. Unless you want to spill? No? My point being that she has even less incentive to take you back. Am I wrong? She's likely being wined and dined by Atlanta's finest, preggers or no."

"I'm not above slugging you," said Robert. "Lily isn't disloyal. She's incapable."

"Anyone is capable. Haven't you figured that out yet?"

It surprised Robert that he'd failed to consider her fortune. Either this lack of consideration meant true love—that he wasn't and had never been in it for the money—or it meant he was a rube and a total loser and had never been able to see the whole picture or more of the picture than what included him. Possibly it meant all of the above.

"She can have the Thunderbird," Coleman said. "Consider it a baby gift."

"I thought you loved that car," Robert said. "At least let me help you get it back. I owe you that."

"I'll buy a new one. What's money?"

"That's the point," said Robert. He sounded desperate. He *felt* desperate. He hated that he was pleading with P. T. Coleman of all people. "You have money. It's your responsibility to find value elsewhere."

"You're encouraging me to find value in sentiment?"

"I'm encouraging you to get back the Thunderbird, and I'm offering my services."

"In Honduras, for fun, I once fished for tarantulas off the deck of my bungalow using a ball of yarn, a piece of gum, and whatever bug was unlucky enough to get stuck to the end of the line. Relevance? I've never needed someone else's services. But if you want to make an ass of yourself in front of your wife and if you need *my* services, just ask. You don't have to win me over with deception. Do a line with me." Coleman flipped a metal napkin dispenser on its side and poured out a small pile of cocaine.

"I'm off that stuff. I told you."

"More for me," said Coleman. He put his face to the metal surface.

"Wipe your nose," said Robert.

Coleman ran his nose across his sleeve. "Ready when you are," he said.

Twenty minutes later they were parked behind the giant magnolia across the street from the house on Forrest Way, and Coleman couldn't stop laughing. The Tudor was situated on top of a hill, set back from the street by about two hundred yards. At the curb was the mailbox and a sprinkling of tulips. Closer to the house, on either side of the drive, there were smatterings of bright white hydrangea bushes. Behind these were more magnolias and a handful of dogwoods, which lined the interior of the property. Their realtor had warned of blossoms in the pool in the summertime. "The water will never get warm in shade like this, and you won't go a day without skimming the top." But both Lily and Robert had liked the idea of cold water in summer. And on the day when they looked at the house, there'd been blossoms covering the surface and neither had minded. "It's romantic," Lily had said, linking her arm with Robert's. The realtor had shaken his head.

Coleman was laughing, though, not because of the landscaping but because of what they were looking at on the front porch. There, in plain sight, in broad daylight, under the hard glare of the Georgia sun, was Lily. And there, also in plain sight, also in broad daylight, also under the hard glare of the Georgia sun, was the Negro kid they'd paid to drive them to the airfield in Athens and then return the Thunderbird to Coleman's driveway, an assignment he'd clearly failed to complete. The two of them were drinking beers and yammering away like old friends.

"God*damn*," said Coleman, catching his breath. "That is the craziest thing I've ever seen. And I've seen crazy. I've watched a pygmy eat the umbilical cord from a giraffe's calf." Coleman waited a beat, then added, "While it was still connected."

"Please don't talk," Robert said.

"I've swum with a whale shark off the southern coast of Thailand. I've seen a lion and her cubs devour an entire zebra in Zimbabwe. I've reeled in a blue marlin off the coast of Mexico only to have a great white shark jump from the water and eat all but the dorsal and the spear. But I have never in my life seen a woman who looks like Lily drinking a beer with a boy who looks like that, in Atlanta-galactic-Georgia of all places. Kill me now, I say. I have finally seen it all."

"Please," said Robert. "If it's the only favor you ever pay me, please stop."

Coleman put his hand on the inside latch of the Benz and pulled. The door popped open. At the same time, across the way, the Negro kid held up a hand—not in salutation—and Lily (*what, by god, was she doing?*) held up her own hand, and the two of them proceeded to press their palms together as if comparing size.

Coleman started to get out of the car.

"What are you doing?" Robert's heart beat heavily against his chest. A line of sweat broke out across his forehead, another above his lip.

"You said you wanted to see Lily. You said you wanted to get the Thunderbird. Here we are."

Robert's pulse quickened. Perhaps this was the heart attack his doctor had promised, perhaps the stroke he'd always feared. A stroke had rendered his father useless; a heart attack had ended his mother's life. He never should have pushed for this. He never should have allowed Coleman—allowed? My god, he'd begged! —to be this close to his house, to his Lily! He was playing fast and loose with his own health. He was playing fast and loose with his life!

"Close the door," said Robert. "I think I might be having a heart attack. You need to take me to a hospital." He wiped sweat from the back of his neck and regarded his hand. "I'm definitely having a heart attack."

Coleman shut the door. He took Robert's face in his hands. He moved it up and down and side to side like some diabolical optometrist. "Not a heart attack."

"What do you know?" Robert jerked his head away. "You're no doctor." He looked again at the scene on the front porch. Lily's hand was on her mouth; she was covering a smile. "Please," said Robert. "Please let's just get out of here. I'll do anything. Please just take me away from here."

"Anything?"

"My chest is exploding. I need water and a doctor."

"And I need jazz."

"I don't care where you take me," said Robert. "Just step on it. Get me out of here. Goddamn it, P. T. Get me out of here now."

Another twenty minutes later, and they were safely installed atop leather-bound stools in a jazz spot not too far off Ponce de Leon. The walls were dark and the air was cool. Coleman was drinking something thick and sweet. Robert was on his third glass of water. "I want to go home," he said. "I should be with Lily."

"You don't know what you want. You're all over the place. You're worse than a five-year-old. Shut up and listen to the music." At a piano on a small riser in the back of the bar, a Negro was playing a doleful tune. Robert had wooed Lily with music like this. The truth was, he'd wooed Rita with it, too. He put his head in his hands. He didn't want to feel sorry for himself. But he did. He was a sorry sonofabitch and an even sorrier one for knowing it.

"I've been thinking," Coleman said, "and you're right."

"No," Robert said into his palms. "No more from you."

"I should have the Thunderbird for the Fourth. What's the point of fireworks if you don't have a convertible. Truth be told, seeing it made me crave the feel of wind in my hair. I get your point now. About money being only so valuable."

"I can't go back there again. It'll kill me. I won't go back there until I deserve her, until she asks me herself. What was she doing with that kid? Did it look like they were flirting? Did it look like she was giggling? I haven't heard Lily giggle in . . . Good god, what have I done?"

"Hear me out," Coleman said.

The piano man segued into a melancholic rendition of "Somewhere Over the Rainbow." Robert pictured Judy Garland, those awkward pigtails. Her face was so young, her eyes spread far apart like a cow's. But that voice—it contained multitudes. If that's what people meant by God, then maybe he did understand something.

"You want her back," said Coleman. "At least you think you do. Fine. Sure. But you're down-and-out right now and in no condition. An hour ago you thought you were having a heart attack. There's a colored kid getting drunk and playing footsie with your pregnant wife. Great. Agreed. We both understand the situation."

"They weren't playing footsie. Were they playing footsie? I didn't see that. Is that real?"

"An expression. Lily's fooling around with a darkie, wasting time until the baby hatches or until you come groveling. Whichever happens first. I appreciate your dilemma. I appreciate"—Coleman made a fist and beat three times against his chest—"the heaviness. I am not an ogre, my dear friend. What I propose is simple. It's a beginning. It's a First Step in a multifaceted maneuver to reinstate yourself into her life."

Robert grimaced.

"We drive back over. Nope. Hear me out. Listen now. We drive back over. We explain that we've come for the Thunderbird and nothing more. You say hello. You maybe even tell her you miss her. If she's interested—you'll know if she's interested, you'll read her—then you tell her you're sorry. If she isn't ready yet—and I think it's safe to assume that she won't be given the state of affairs (pun intended, apologies)—well, she'll at least know she's on your mind."

"What if the kid is still there?"

"The darkie?"

"His name is Piedmont."

"All the more reason to go back. Let the darkie know you're around. Let him know you're watching, that you're still in the picture, regardless of what Lily has or hasn't intimated." Coleman burped. "See what I mean?"

Sadly, Robert did see what he meant. But he wasn't convinced. "I need water."

"You're boring on water. You've had too much of it. Did you know it's possible to poison yourself by way of over-hydration? I've read the studies."

"Where's the barman?" asked Robert. "I need to think."

"Here." Coleman slid a glass of water in Robert's direction. "Take mine. I don't want it."

In one gulp, Robert drank half the water. He put down the glass and wiped his mouth. The piano man moved into "Moon River." Robert had seen *Breakfast at Tiffany's* first with Lily and then, at a matinee the following week, with Rita. Both women had cried at the business with the cat. He'd comforted each. He closed his eyes and concentrated on the melody. He tried not to

hear the lyrics in his head, which was nearly impossible. He tried
not to think about what a rat bastard he'd been. Also impossible.

He finished the water and pushed the glass, now empty, away.
He was conscious, he realized, for possibly the first time in his
life, of his body's insides. As the water hit each new surface, he
was aware of his tongue, of the triangular fold beneath it, of his
uvula and his hard and soft palates. There, as the water slid down,
obeying gravity, was his palatoglossal arch, his lingual tonsils, his
epiglottis. As the liquid met each surface, the vocabulary came to
him, the anatomy suddenly being made real, made comprehen-
sible in a formerly unfathomable way. He opened and closed his
mouth. He licked his lips. He looked at Coleman, who was grinning. Robert could feel the lobes of his brain lighting up and going dark, lighting up and going dark again: like some mind-con-
trolling game from the future, first his frontal lobe illuminated
itself, then his occipital, his parietal, his temporal, his frontal
again. Around and around, back and forth, his brain came in and
out of the light. "Coleman," he said. He felt his body rising, he
felt weight — the concept of it — leaving his person. "Coleman,
what did you give me? What have you done?"

Coleman clapped his hands together and stood. "Now we're
cooking," he said. "Let's motor. Let's agitate the gravel, burn rub-
ber, flat-out floor it, goose it, lay a patch. Let's pop the clutch.
You with me?"

When Robert's mouth opened, when the words came out,
when language finally found itself, it was as though Coleman was
speaking through him. As if he'd not just been dosed, but dosed
with some aspect of his companion: "Word from the bird," Robert said. "Let's punch it off the line. Let's giddyup. I'm with you."
The words — Coleman's words but from Robert's mouth — came
as effortlessly as if he'd been reading lines from a cue card. "Lead
the way."

They glided single file, the two men, out of the club, up its abbreviated staircase, out into the hot, thick rain forest of the night. They stopped long enough only to light cigarettes and roll up their sleeves. Then they were back in the Mercedes, the windows open, cruising beneath the elevated streetlights of Peachtree Avenue, hitting green light after green light after green light, in the direction — they both knew, though neither had said it aloud — of Coleman's 1960 Ford Thunderbird convertible.

It was late enough now that there was no traffic. Coleman slowed as they approached the driveway of the Tudor on Forrest Way. He turned off the headlights on the Benz and started to pull up the drive.

"What are you doing?" said Robert. "You'll wake her. Just park on the street."

"Fine, fine." Coleman backed out, the lights still off, and pulled the car alongside the curb. For a minute or two, they just sat there, looking at the house. The Thunderbird, thankfully, was still parked out front. Robert wouldn't have to raise the garage door, which jammed at about two feet and always made a terrible racket. It was possible Coleman could simply put the car in neutral, back it down the driveway, and not start the motor until he was safely on the road and out of earshot. But even if the noise did wake Lily, they'd be long gone by the time she made it to the front door. That was how Robert was imagining it anyway.

When Coleman opened his door, Robert put a hand on his knee. "Wait," he said. "You'll be extra careful, right? Quiet as possible? Quiet and quick?"

"I'm a trained assassin," whispered Coleman. "I'm in like Flynn."

"It alarms me," said Robert, removing his hand and looking back up at the Thunderbird, "that you would even make that joke."

Coleman crept quietly from the car, which he left running, presumably to make it easier for Robert to slide into the driver's seat and take the wheel when it was time. But for now Robert stayed put. He did not think it safe to move. There was a feeling in his gut that suggested he might foul himself right there in the car. His stomach growled.

From the passenger's seat, he watched Coleman run, half-bent, up the driveway and crouch next to the convertible. Coleman gave him a thumbs-up then tried the driver's-side door. It didn't open. He looked in Robert's direction. The light from the moon was enough so that Robert could see, or thought he could see, Coleman shrug then slink around to the passenger's side. For a moment, he disappeared.

Several seconds later, when the passenger's door of the Benz opened without warning and Coleman loomed suddenly and un-expectedly above him, Robert nearly cried out in terror.

"Car's locked," whispered Coleman. "No dice. So here's the plan: you give me your keys to the house, I go in the back door quiet as a cat and come out with the keys to the Thunderbird."

Robert was shaking his head. "Absolutely not," he said. "Everything about that is off. No way. Not happening."

"You still keep all the keys in the kitchen? To the right of the sink? Next to the silverware?"

"How do you know that?"

"I'm your friend. I bet she added my keys to the drawer."

"You're not that kind of friend."

"Sure I am."

"Who showed you our drawer of keys?"

"Don't be crazy," Coleman said. "I saw them last year, on the Fourth, at your party."

"We didn't have a party on the Fourth."

"Oh, man, did you ever. Fireworks at sunset? Nude swimming after midnight? Lily was out of control."

"That didn't happen here. That was at the Pink Chateau maybe. And Lily wouldn't have been there. She doesn't like the daughter. I told you. Anyway, we've never thrown a party on the

Fourth. Did Lily show you the key drawer on a different day? Is that how you know? I'm so confused."

"Give me your house keys." Coleman held out his hand. "Fork them over."

"You don't understand," Robert murmured, his heart was racing again. "I think I need medical attention. You've drugged me."

"The keys." Now Coleman jabbed at Robert's chest. Robert swatted at his hand.

"I'm a dead man. You're murdering me."

"I know dead," said Coleman. "You're not dead. My old man is dead. His old lady, too. You're alive as a kangaroo."

Again Robert swatted at Coleman's hand. "Get out of my face." His whisper contained real hysteria. "My house keys are long gone."

"What does that mean?"

"I left them somewhere. I don't know. The Ritz? The Purple Pigeon? The diner? They're gone. I haven't seen them in days, weeks."

Coleman fell slowly back onto the lawn with his knees hiked in front of him and his feet planted on the street. "Damn," he said. "You should have told me." He allowed himself only the briefest moments of defeat, then he pushed himself up and brushed off the seat of his pants. "Plan B, then."

Robert looked up. His stomach growled again, but the sickness had passed. "Plan B?" he asked.

"We break in."

Before Robert could say anything, Coleman was moving back across the dimly lit yard. It was late enough—early enough—that dew was accumulating on the grass. Coleman's shoes made imprints as he scampered away. Robert nearly fell out of the Benz trying to follow him. He caught himself before slamming the door, reached inside, turned off the motor, removed the key, then delicately pushed the door into the frame. He turned and trotted quickly after Coleman.

By the time he'd caught up, at the back door that led to the kitchen, Coleman had the doormat already flipped over and was running his hands across the top step. "Christ," Coleman said. "Christ. No spare key? Who doesn't leave an extra key lying about?"

"For this very reason," Robert whispered, returning the mat to its rightful place. "To protect ourselves against bad guys like you."

"We'll just have to break a window," said Coleman. "This little guy right here." He knocked lightly on the small square pane just above the doorknob.

"Cut it out," said Robert; he snatched Coleman's hand away. "You'll wake her."

"You're right," he said. "Maybe we should just wake her. Why not? What's the big deal? It's your home, after all. And it's my car. You go hide behind the bushes, and I'll stand right here and knock until she lets me in."

"If you think you're going to knock on this door at this time of night," Robert said, "then you're out of your mind. Come on. We'll come back tomorrow. I promise. You and me both. We'll go through the front door together. No more excuses. Just let me be sober, clear-headed. That's all I ask. That's all I want."

"No more excuses?" asked Coleman.

"Cross my heart and hope to die."

"First thing in the morning?"

"As early as you get me here."

"Deal."

As Coleman started to move away from the door, a spotlight hit his face. He held up his forearm to shield his eyes. "Jesus," he said. "The hell?"

The beam moved from Coleman's face to Robert's. He, too, held up his forearm for protection. "Who's there?" said Robert. "Who is that?"

The light suddenly went dark. Then a different light, one just above the back door, snapped to life.

Footsteps approached from the direction of the pool house. Robert's sight was still compromised. He rubbed at his eyes. "Hello?"

Behind him, the back door opened. Robert didn't want to turn around. He didn't want to see her. He didn't want her to see him.

But the voice he heard first didn't belong to Lily. The voice he heard first belonged to the Negro kid who, Robert realized in a stunning moment of clarity, must be staying in their pool house. Lily had put him up there. Of course she had. Coleman had sent the kid off on a fool's errand, and somehow he'd ended up here instead, and Lily—because she was decent and good and the opposite of everything Robert had become—Lily had offered him a place to stay. It both did and didn't make perfect sense. Wherever you go, there you are.

Robert closed his eyes and took a deep breath. With great purposefulness, he turned toward the kitchen door. The light overhead showed everything, more than everything. It showed too much.

Lily had stepped forward so that she was backlit. But even in the shadow, he could see her belly was large as a house. Between last week and today, it seemed to have swelled in size. Or maybe it was merely his proximity to her; maybe it was merely being so close after so many weeks. His instinct was to move toward her. His body, his whole body, seemed to want to take hold of her, to put his arms around her, to put his hands on her stomach and wait for the inevitable and outrageous kicks of life inside. My god, he wanted to hold her!

What he did was stay put. What he did was not move a single muscle.

Did it surprise Robert when Lily chose not to address him first? When she chose not to address Coleman either, but when she addressed, instead, the Negro? Perhaps it did surprise him, but what surprised him even more was the tone of her voice when she spoke. For a moment, he worried that his jaw had gone slack and that his mouth was open.

"Please stay," said Lily, so soft, so sweet, so full of soul. "If you don't mind, Piedmont, stay until they're gone."

By way of an answer, the kid stood still.

Finally Lily faced them. And this simple act—Lily, a few steps above them just beyond the doorway, turning in their direction —was nearly deafening in its effectiveness. That belly! When it moved, the attention of a room—a room, a yard, a world!— moved with it.

To Robert, she merely said, "Yes?"

He swallowed hard. This meeting—offensive, indecent, completely without decorum—was everything he'd hoped to avoid. In his quest to be reunited with his past life, he'd taken one giant step backward, and it was all because of Coleman.

What he wanted to do was drop to his knees. What he wanted to say was that he was sorrier than she'd ever know. "We're here for the keys," he said instead.

"The keys?"

"To Coleman's Thunderbird."

Lily looked at Coleman, who'd dug his hands into his pockets and trained his eyes on the grass at his feet. He looked like some gangly schoolboy who'd been caught peeping through the window of the girls' first-floor bathroom.

"Are you bored?" Lily directed this question at Coleman. "Is that what this is? Have you nothing better to do?"

Coleman didn't respond.

"Just give us the keys and we'll leave," said Robert.

"Yes," said Lily. She smiled suddenly. It was an awful thing to see. "I understand that you, Robby, want the keys to the Thunderbird. What you don't understand is that I mailed them to Coleman last week. The day after you turned Piedmont into a target by asking him to drive what might as well be a brand-new convertible with a flashing neon sign that says ARREST ME back to Atlanta while you—is this really true? While you *flew* around in some airplane in the middle of the night?" She raised her hand. "Don't answer. I don't care. But Coleman has the keys. There's nothing I can do for you." She stepped back, so that she was now immediately under the outdoor light. Her face, which had been backlit and difficult to see, was now lighted from overhead. Her nose stretched out in a funny way, and her mouth was pulled too far to one side. But even in the grotesque lighting, he could see her eyes were bright and clear. She looked once again beyond the men, at Piedmont. "Unless you want to come inside for milk," she said, "I think we ought to get some sleep now."

It was outrageous, yes? The fact that Lily was inviting a Negro into her home in the middle of the night?

"Thank you," Piedmont said. "But I'm tired. If it's okay, I'll skip the milk."

"Another time," said Lily. She smiled, something different than what she'd shown Robert. Then she opened the door, walked inside, and turned off the light.

Outside, the three men stood motionless for several seconds. Light from the moon reflected off the surface of the pool, and all around the perimeter of the property, atop the even blades of blue grass, there was a pale afterglow.

Without asking, without saying good night or goodbye, Piedmont turned and walked slowly across the yard. He did not use his flashlight. At the pool house, he paused, looked up at the sky, back toward the two men, then—without any ceremony or explanation—he walked inside the pool house and shut the door behind him.

Robert couldn't bring himself to look at Coleman. He was afraid that eye contact, even in the dark of the night, would be too much. He'd slug him. He'd push him into the deep end. He'd dive in after and hold him down. The ire he felt was propelled by humiliation, confusion. He felt like an animal. He felt like a dog who'd been kicked but didn't know why. He felt completely without language.

He turned and walked away from Coleman, around the side of the house, past the dogwoods, under the magnolias, skirting the hydrangeas, back in the direction he'd come five or ten or fifteen minutes earlier. It—time—continued to elude him, surprise him. In seemingly unimaginably small moments, the story—his story—kept changing, kept turning, kept being something other than what it had been a measly few seconds before.

Beneath his shoes, the grass folded against itself, flattening wetly into the soil. At the Mercedes, which was still there—because, why wouldn't it be?—he stopped. He didn't have to get in. He knew that. He could simply walk away. He could travel the sidewalks until morning or until he came to a halfway house or a hospital or maybe just a clean and cheap motel. He could do anything he wanted, including disappear forever. But what he did was so predictable he could spit: he opened the passenger's door and got in.

"Man, listen," said Coleman, after he'd also climbed in. "The keys to the Thunderbird are at my place. I was just having a little fun. I'll pick the car up tomorrow. I'll have someone else drive me. You won't be involved at all. I'm sorry. I didn't think—"

"It doesn't matter," said Robert.

Coleman nodded. "Whatever you say." He turned the key and the ignition roared to life. "You want a drink?"

"I want a bed," said Robert, "and a pillow and a set of ice-cold sheets."

"Sure," said Coleman. "Sure. You got it."

"One more thing."

"Name it."

"If you dose me again, I'll murder you myself."

Ivan & Lulu

I've been thinking, dear. The crash in May? It was a warning . . ."

"What crash in May, Lulu?"

"The other crash—when the Dow Jones fell."

"I don't remember talking to you about that."

"But, dear, just because we don't talk about something doesn't mean I don't know."

"Of course, Lulu. Is Alma downstairs? Is she with the children?"

"The children are back in school, Ivan."

"It's seven a.m., Lulu. It's summer. School isn't back in session. It's too early."

"Is it? It is. You're right. I must have looked at my watch wrong."

"Have you seen them this morning? Do you know that they're awake yet?"

"If it's seven, then they must be."

"Please go see if Alma is with them."

"Yes, but first I have to finish what I was saying. Do you remember what I was saying?"

"Is that a question or an accusation?"

"I was telling you about the crash. The precursor? The Dow

Jones fell 5.7 percent. You remember? Two and a half hours after the market closed, the ticker finally finished reporting, that's how bad the losses were. They say it was the second-largest point decline on record."

"I don't understand why you care about this, Lulu. I feel this isn't a healthy use of your time."

"But what is a healthy use of my time?"

"The children."

"But they're only children."

"They need to get ready for school. You should check on them now."

"But let me finish. It's important I tell you. I believe that the Flash Crash—did you know that's what they're calling it?—was a kind of heralding of the Orly disaster. Do you know that Donna and Jake wanted to come home early? And if they had come home early, do you know that they'd still be alive?"

"That isn't healthy, Lulu. That isn't healthy thinking at all, and your logic is all wrong."

"It makes me wonder if maybe others besides Donna and Jake wanted to come home early. Maybe it was everyone. Think about it, dear. They all had some sort of investments—Coca-Cola, Polaroid, IBM."

"Did you read this somewhere?"

"Though that isn't my point. My point is that if they'd been paying attention, reading the signs, they might still be alive."

"No."

"We have to read the signs."

"No."

"What's going on in the world— We have to pay attention, dear."

"I'm worried."

"Exactly! Their flight was still six days away when the warning sign came. They must have been chomping at the bit to get home."

"Lulu, my love, I'm worried about *you*."

Lily

On July 3, Lily was sorting through the month's unopened mail when she saw the taxicab pull to a stop at the bottom of the driveway. Raif had asked for a list of household expenses, but she'd never seen a complete accounting before. It was Robert who'd always managed their bills. "Go through your mail," he'd said. "Send me anything with a due date." The prospect was a humiliating one, but to ignore the request would have been an affront to his generosity.

When the taxicab pulled to a stop, she was sitting at Robert's desk. She was in the process of dividing the mail—more than a hundred envelopes, all told—into two piles: those that appeared personal and those that appeared business- or bill-related. She'd yet to open anything. The number of condolence cards appeared obscene. It was as the taxicab's door opened that she noticed Helen Seydel's handwriting on an envelope. She tossed the letter quickly into the personal pile.

She leaned forward in the chair—not easily given her belly—and squinted. Then she groaned: P. T. Coleman emerged from the backseat.

Lily didn't have the energy for Coleman at that moment. She didn't have access to the proper sense of humor that one required when dealing with him. Last night's shenanigans were more than enough. She was surprised and then relieved when he walked not toward the front door but toward the garage at the side of the house, in front of which was parked the Thunderbird.

With a fair amount of effort, she pushed herself up and walked to the window to watch. From his pocket he pulled a set of keys. Then he unlocked the convertible and opened the driver's-side door. He was about to get in when he stopped. He looked up and in her direction. She didn't hold up a hand to wave, but she was sure he could see her. He was staring directly at her. After several moments, he shrugged. Then he climbed inside the car and drove away.

Lily returned to Robert's desk. The truth was, she'd been hoping it was Robert who would come back for the Thunderbird, alone, during daylight hours, and talk to her. Their last conversation had been the day of the crash, before Piedmont's arrival and Raif's offer, before any of the grueling memorials and the revelation of her parents' finances.

She'd been in the tub so long that day that the water had turned from hot to lukewarm to very nearly room temperature. The skin along her arms was chilly in a pleasant way. The tips of her fingers and toes had turned soft and white, the texture pocked like the core of a ripe peach. Outside it had been close to a hundred degrees. There was no defeating heat like that. A person either stayed inside or submitted to whatever havoc the unruly humidity might inflict on skin or hair, on makeup or clothes.

Downstairs, the office extension had rung. She'd listened and waited. Through the corridors of their spacious home, she'd heard the *muh-muh-muh* of Robert's voice. He'd promised not to work that weekend. After several minutes the murmuring ceased; Lily dunked her head under the water one last time. When she came up, the extension was ringing again. This time it wasn't followed by Robert's voice. She pulled the plug from the drain and, a hand on each side of the tub, pushed herself up. She stepped carefully over the side, planting each foot deliberately on the bathmat. She wrapped her hair in a towel and pulled on her robe. Then she called to Robert. To her surprise, she heard him almost immediately on the stairs, as if he'd already been coming to her.

She opened the bathroom door, and there he was, already in their bedroom, already standing in front of her, clearly ready to knock.

"How funny," she said.

On a whim, she stood up on her tiptoes and kissed his cheek.

She moved past him to the bed. "Sit beside me," she said. "I've been thinking."

He sat beside her, exactly where she patted the mattress.

"Who called?"

"What have you been thinking?" he asked.

"Was it McGill?"

"It was," he said. "Tell me what you've been thinking."

"It's silly really."

The whites of his eyes were red, she realized. She wondered if he'd already been drinking. She glanced at the clock on the bedside table.

"Do you," she said, "do you think you know me? Do you think you have a good estimation of who I am? What my character is?"

He licked his lips, then wiped the sides of his mouth with his thumb and his forefinger. He nodded. "I do," he said. An oriole landed on the branch of the magnolia outside their bedroom window. Robert watched it; she watched Robert.

"And do you," asked Lily, "do you think I know you? I don't mean, do you have secrets I don't know about? Everyone has secrets. Lord knows. What I mean is, do you think I know you, really know who you are, as a man?"

After a moment, Robert turned away from the oriole. His eyes now were wide, wild. He had about him the air of a madman. All of a sudden, Lily didn't want to be sitting next to him. She wanted, in fact, to take back her question. She wanted him to go back downstairs. It was merely an instinct, but the instinct told her that what was coming was irreversible; what was coming was grisly to an unprecedented degree. She did not, under any circumstances, want him to speak.

That day, he'd shaken his head and appeared truly devastated when he said, "No." His shoulders had begun to shake. "No, I don't," he'd said, and then with no further warning, he told her everything.

Now, today, several weeks since learning the news not just of the existence of that other woman but of the crash and of its casualties, she covered her face with her hands. She did not cry as she had that day, but she did allow many minutes to pass in which she stared at the flesh of her palms and concentrated on the apricot smell of her apricot skin.

She returned shortly after to the business of the mail, but she found herself almost immediately confused. In a stack to the right, she'd been placing bills, in the middle were personal missives, and to the left was what remained to be sorted. When she picked up the stack on the left, she was greeted again by overseas postage. Yet she clearly remembered shoving Helen's letter in the middle pile, wanting it out of her sight. But here it was anew. At least, that was how she first encountered the letter she now saw. It was, for all time, how she'd recall its introduction to her life: as a misperception.

Picking up the envelope, she saw that the handwriting on the front did not belong to Helen. This, then, was a different letter than the one she'd already filed away. It was surprisingly thick. The script—now so obviously different than Helen's—was large and sloppy. The ink was blue. The name on the upper-left-hand side was in cursive and had been smudged at some point along its journey by liquid. Tears perhaps, more likely rain. C-something. Lily couldn't make it out. But the origin country was clear: *FRANCE*. It was addressed to Robert.

She tore it open.

She was surprised to find that inside the first envelope, there was a second, smaller envelope, which had already been opened. She pulled it out. A note that must have been hiding behind the interior envelope dropped to the floor. She picked it up.

She was now holding—it made no sense—two opened envelopes (one now empty and one still containing a letter) and a note, which was folded in two. The management of so many pieces was unwieldy. She took them to her sofa bed and sat.

First she unfolded the note. It was written in the same sprawling blue hand as had addressed the larger envelope. The fact that it was in French wasn't the problem; Lily had learned the language in school. The difficulty was in the writer's script, which was untrained. It was an apology of some sort and this, too, was addressed to Robert. The letter writer, who'd been a stewardess on the plane and somehow survived the crash, had committed an offense, and she was deeply sorry for it. The offense was in opening a letter not addressed to her and also in not immediately forwarding it to its rightful home. But this letter writer had been deeply moved by what she'd read. She'd also been made profoundly curious. There was a final apology and then nothing. The end, which was abrupt, seemed to have been dictated by the length of the page. There was a small cursive C in the corner, and that was all.

Lily put down the note and picked up the small lemony envelope. Two people had survived the disaster in Paris; why had she never before considered them or the torment they must have been feeling? From the envelope's already-opened spine, she pulled a letter that had been folded crisply into three. The handwriting here was tight and tidy. It took up all of the first side and three-quarters of the back.

Lily sucked in her breath when she saw the author's signature. The letter was from Rita.

She set it on the sofa and stood. Next she backed away from it. Whatever was inside was also unknown to Robert. This wasn't Lily's letter to read. She knew that and, at least in part, it was why she found herself initially backing away. She could tear it up, throw it away, grant that poor dead woman a modicum of privacy. But even as she considered such a gesture, she found herself advancing. She was aware of her body stooping over, her arm reaching outward, her fingers connecting with the paper.

She had the wherewithal to sit back down before she opened it. In the same way that she'd known—could feel in her bones the sureness of it—that last week's phone call from the police in the middle of the night was to deliver the news that Robert was dead, in the very same way that she'd *known* and then been absolutely wrong, Lily now felt certain that this letter would contain the world's most obvious confession. Rita was pregnant. Of course she was. What wife wouldn't have guessed immediately? And yet still, despite knowing, despite having heard the words in her head, it had taken Lily several attempts with the letter—several distinct readings—before she was convinced of the utter wrongness of her assumption: Rita was not in the least bit pregnant.

Robert, Robert, Robert . . .

I must confess I am not completely sober. This evening I was wined and dined. I was flirted with, made love to, spoiled rotten. But instead of giving the poor bloke what he wanted, I have returned to my little room to pack and to write this letter. You have been kind to me. I believe I have been kind to you. But as you've said yourself a thousand times, we have each been unfair to *her*. (I cannot write her name, even now, even so far removed from you . . .) It is time, I think, for me to distance myself. If you have not guessed—but of course you have—this is my attempt at a *Dear John*. Please do not think I am being cruel, but I have "ended" things with you in the past and you haven't taken me seriously, no doubt in part because I haven't had the gumption to make it stick. My hope is that, in writing, you will understand that this time is different. Last month, you sent me away. I was loath to be parted from you. I was loath to be treated like some disposable bobby-soxer you'd only fooled around with on a lark. Did you ever love me? I don't know. You were fond, for sure, as I was of you. But I doubt that it was love. What is indisputable now is this: my total happiness these last many weeks in Europe. How young I've felt. How unburdened. How free. I have seen the way men look at me, Robert, and it has given me such a thrill! (How good it must have felt for you to be desired by the two of us . . . I understand that now . . .) Tonight, downstairs, the dancing, the champagne . . . Somewhere in the midst of it, I came to understand this as well: My heart remains light and untethered. Your heart, on the other hand, is promised elsewhere. What I didn't know—didn't see until this journey—was that I could never have been yours. You are married, Robert. Married! This must mean something. It must! I know it does to you, deep down. To her. One day perhaps to me . . . By the time you receive this letter, I will have been stateside for several days, a week even, maybe two! You will have been wondering at the way I am so thoroughly avoiding you, but now you know . . . Do you think I am being a child? Do you think this letter is contrived? Possibly I am being silly and in the morning I will feel none of this. But tonight, just now, I feel confident. I feel open-eyed, full of life, and utterly and divinely happy.

Fondly,
I am,
Rita
6.2.62

For a long time after finishing the letter, Lily stayed seated on the edge of the sofa, staring out into the great wide nothing of the room. What she wanted was to feel a deep and satisfying hatred for this woman, this "Rita" who'd so maligned her marriage and compromised Robert's affection. Instead, with no small amount of horror and confusion, she understood that what she was feeling was sympathy, even gratitude for the letter's words. She found she was in mourning for the girl—yes: stupid, young, naïve—who had fallen just as she once had for Robert of all men. In another world, they might—and at this thought she shuddered physically, her shoulders contracting and tightening upward—dear god, they might have been friends.

Lily sat up. She took a few deep breaths. Life was funny, yes? It really was. If she'd opened this letter a month ago, she would have had a completely different reaction. The timing of a revelation changed everything, didn't it? This wasn't a profound thought, not a serious or important epiphany, but to Lily it offered a moment of unexpected lucidity and perspective. To Lily, it began to open up the world. She thought of Robert. Her pulse quickened. She thought of Piedmont. Her pulse quickened all the more. The human heart, she understood at long last, was nothing if not confused and confusing.

Oh, Rita, she thought. *Oh, Rita.*

Ivan & Lulu

"Robby's left his wife."

"I know, Lulu."

"It's an affront."

"To whom, dear?"

"To everyone."

"Why don't we stay out of it?"

"But she's pregnant. She's due any minute. She's large as can be."

"Raif says to leave her alone."

"Raif says that?"

"Yes. He asked specifically that we leave her alone. He's taken care of things."

"Is he in love? Oh, I do hope he isn't in love."

"What if he is? She'd make a wonderful mother to the boys."

"But the boys *and* a newborn?"

"It isn't our place to judge. People will have to start over at some point."

"But it's too soon for anybody to be thinking about starting over. What about Nance?"

"Don't make me say it again."

"What about poor Nance? She'd be mortified."

"Firstly, we don't even know if Raif *is* in love. Secondly—and you put me in the position of having to say this—Nance is dead. He hasn't abandoned her."

"I think we should send someone to look after her. That's all."

"Raif has expressly forbidden it."

"And what Raif says goes?"

"You know he's been instrumental in my career, Lulu."

"But this is personal. We could send Alma's sister."

"Alma's sister has her own life, Lulu. Think about what you're saying."

"But maybe she needs the work."

"Does she? Has Alma allowed as much?"

"—"

"Then why don't we hold off on being busybodies for a minute. Can you promise me that?"

"Is it true about Candy and George?"

"What did we just agree upon?"

"I didn't agree to anything."

"Are you planning on staying in your dressing gown all day?"

"Is there another memorial I don't know about? Is there a luncheon?"

"There is neither."

"Is it true?"

"It's true."

"Penniless?"

"Yes."

"But how were they living?"

"Credit. Scams. There's a suggestion afoot that they meant not to come back to Atlanta."

"They were absconding?"

"Well, that's a funny word because they had nothing to abscond with other than their credit, which was dried up."

"But then— Is it possible? Are they alive? Are they over there in Europe pretending to be dead?"

"No. Who knows why they got on that plane, in the end. Maybe they wanted to meet their grandchild."

"But how do you know they aren't in Europe?"

"I just do."

"But how?"

"Don't make me say it again, Lulu."

"But how on earth could you know for sure? Perhaps they're still alive! Imagine!"

"I've seen their bodies, Lulu."

"Impossible. You said there was nothing to see."

"I said there were *remains*."

"Remains? Remains? What kind of word is that?"

"There are certain things you've forced me to say in order to protect you. If we're done here, I have work to do."

"Are we done? It seems you're the one who makes that decision."

Piedmont

He hadn't been sleeping easily for the last several nights, not since Robert and Coleman had appeared out of nowhere in the wee hours of the morning. He wasn't convinced that they wouldn't come back for him. He was troubled that they now possessed the knowledge that he, Piedmont, the Negro boy to whom they'd given five twenty-dollar bills in order to return their car safely to Atlanta and who'd failed at his mission, was living (was that the right word? surely not . . .) on a white man's compound, spending his nights not twenty yards from where a white woman slept.

He turned onto his side. As he'd been doing since their visit, tonight he killed the lamplight immediately upon walking inside the guesthouse. He wanted to be able to see out into the night, to take in the backyard and the possible return of those men. He'd liked them well enough on the drive to Athens and the airplane. But he wasn't so foolish as to think these particular circumstances weren't extenuating. The Liberal White Man wasn't something he completely understood or trusted. But his guess was that, like all men, like the men he knew, nobody was one way all the time. Everyone slipped up. Inconsistencies were part of human nature. He'd read that in high school or maybe it was his own idea. All he knew was that Robert Tucker and P. T. Coleman had appeared in the middle of the night, highly intoxicated, it seemed to Piedmont. They'd been expecting one thing, and they'd gotten something else entirely.

It was impossible for Piedmont not to think again of Emmett Till. His mother had once called his obsession unhealthy, but there'd been as much fear in her eyes as in his own on the day they saw the newspaper and those photos of the boy's body. Emmett would have been Piedmont's age if he'd lived, if he'd never left Chicago to visit family in Mississippi when he was fourteen. But what sort of half-baked logic was that? If he hadn't gone to Mississippi when he was fourteen, then he'd have gone when he was fifteen or sixteen or seventeen. And if it hadn't been a boy named Emmett Till, then it would have been a different boy named Somebody Else. He winced. Robert and Coleman didn't seem capable of killing Piedmont; there was something lazy in their aspect. But there was also something unpredictable.

Now he lay on his side, eyes open, and thought about Emmett. He thought about his mother. And he thought about Lily. At dinner she'd been funny. She was agitated, it seemed to him, by his presence. He told her, though the thought was as new to him as it was to her, that he was planning to leave.

"Oh," she'd said. "Well, jeez." She stood up when he said this, though they'd only just sat down to dinner. She took two more beers from the icebox. She handed them both to Piedmont, along with the can opener. He pressed two triangular openings into the lids of each and handed one back to Lily. She accepted it and sat.

"Jeez, well," she said. She couldn't stop fidgeting. He thought she'd be pleased by his announcement. He'd said he was leaving in order to alleviate her nervousness. Now she only fidgeted twice as fast.

"Don't you think it's time?" he asked. They hadn't talked once about the way she sometimes threaded her fingers so slowly between his. They hadn't discussed it, but it was all he'd been able to think about until Robert showed up out of the blue.

She stood up again, but then she sat immediately back down.

"Gosh," she said. "I feel like I might cry. Is it something I did? Jeez. Is it my husband? He hasn't come back. He won't. They took the car. But of course, you do what you want. You can do anything you want. You don't need my permission. I don't mean it that way. Of course you have to leave. Gosh. What was I thinking? I must not have been thinking, Piedmont. I'm so sorry." As she talked, her fingers tapped about the table. She picked up her fork a half dozen times without taking a bite of food. Mercifully, she put the can of beer to her lips and took a sip. Piedmont had hoped this might calm her down.

"Play me something?" she asked. "Before you go? Or don't. Is it cold in here? I don't feel well, Piedmont. I think the day is catching up to me. And the beer. Ouch. It's kicking. Hold out your hand. Do you want to feel? You don't want to feel? I think I need to lie down. Don't worry about the dishes. Please. Don't leave without telling me? Do you promise? Don't leave tonight. Promise you'll stay. Thank you. I don't mean to tell you what to do. Yes, of course you understand. Of course. I have to lie down now. I'll see you in the morning. I'm sorry we won't watch the fireworks as I said. But you'll watch them for me. Don't worry. I'll be able to sleep. Tomorrow is the real show in the sky. Tonight is just a preamble. I'm suddenly so tired. I haven't been so tired in who knows how long."

During her monologue, she pushed back her chair and stood, using the table as a sort of stabilizer for her weight. She'd said much of her speech while facing the door. He couldn't see her expression; he couldn't tell if there was color in her face or not. When she walked out of the kitchen, he stood. He wouldn't follow her—that would be too much. But he moved to where he could watch her as she made her way through the rooms of the first floor. At the office she paused, turned, held up a hand, offered a wan smile, then walked inside and closed the door behind her.

He disobeyed her request regarding the dishes. It took him only fifteen minutes. Then he dried off his hands and went outside. There hadn't been a firework in the past hour. Lily was right: tomorrow was when the real show would happen. He walked straight across the yard, into his room, turned off the light, and got in bed.

He'd been like that—curled up but not sleeping, listening to the sounds of the frogs, the lone hoot owl, the crickets' incessant timpani—for several hours when he heard it.

It was a rustling not of leaves—there were no leaves—but of fallen magnolia petals, thick water-heavy petals that had fallen and then dried in the sun and now were being snapped into pieces by—by what? Something heavier than a raccoon. As much as he didn't want to, he closed his eyes. Since boyhood he'd known how to isolate and accentuate a particular sense by turning off another, like listening to his mother in the choir, quarantining and appreciating her voice alone. He dared not move. With his eyes gritted shut, he opened his ears as wide as they'd go. Yes, footsteps. But only one set.

Outside the window to the left of the front door, which was to say the window farthest from where he was still lying down, a final magnolia spine snapped. Then there was silence. Piedmont's heart raced. His thoughts now were not of Emmett Till but of his mother. Would they find his body? When they did, would it be recognizable? There were creek beds all over this city where Negro bodies could be and had been discarded. *Sweet Lord,* he thought. *Sweet Lord.* In Chattanooga, a hundred or so miles north of where Piedmont lay at that very moment, a fifteen-year-old called Larry Bolden was shot by a white policeman who wasn't then arrested. Michael and Jeremy had told him all about it. In 1958, in Dawson, Georgia, a couple hundred miles south of Piedmont, a man by the name of James Brazier was beaten to death by two police officers. His wife and children witnessed the killing. Of the incident, the county sheriff had merely said, "There's nothing like fear to keep niggers in line." In Water Valley, Mississippi—why had Jeremy and Michael given him these awful facts?—roughly 350 miles west of Piedmont, that very same year, a sheriff by the name of Buster Treloar beat to death a man called Woodrow Wilson Daniels. The killing took place in a prison. There were four witnesses, all of whom identified Treloar as the murderer. After only twenty-three minutes of deliberation, the jury, which was entirely white, freed the sheriff, who'd then said, "By God. Now I can get back to rounding up bootleggers and damn niggers." These and other wicked stories now roared in Piedmont's mind. *Dear Lord. Oh Lord, oh Lord.*

The knob on the door jiggled.

He sat up. He knew better than to be lying down when they— it, whoever it was—finally came for him. In the dark, he searched frantically for some sort of weapon—an umbrella, anything— there was nothing. And besides, to fight back would only ensure death. As it was, he might escape with disfigurement and a warning never to venture out of the dark side of town again. He'd heed the warning too. He'd crawl home if he had to. He'd beg his mother on all fours to take him back, to forgive him. He'd tell the whole truth, apologize on the spot. If he was lucky, she'd nurse whatever wounds he brought home with him. He would never, never again, abandon her. He would never fall for the generosity of another race mixer again, regardless of intention.

There was a soft rapping on the door.

It was fiendish. It was repugnant—the way he was being toyed with, being asked to open a door for an unknown enemy. This, he understood, was their true power: they could afford to enjoy it. They weren't scared of anything or anyone.

Again there was a light rapping, and then, something Piedmont had not been expecting, not in a million years, he heard the unmistakable sound of Lily's voice quietly saying his name.

His muscles—his bowels—experienced the briefest moment of relief before panic—intense, sweat-inducing panic—took over.

He opened the door only a crack. He didn't—wouldn't!—turn on a light.

There she was wearing a robe so white, it, like the magnolia blossoms, seemed to glow in the dark as if begging for undesired attention. She was gripping the doorknob. She said his name again, half whisper, half screech.

"You can't be here," he said, his voice in the same register as hers. "I'm a dead man," he said. "You're murdering me." The words spilled out of their own accord.

"Please," she said. And now he realized two things. The first was that she was crying. The second was that with the hand not grasped tightly around the knob, she was clutching at her belly.

"No," he said. He didn't mean to say it. He stepped backward into his room, just one step. His foot landed funny. He was shaking his head. But even as he was declining, even as he was aggressively fighting the urge to vomit, he knew he would consent to anything she asked.

"Something is wrong," she said. She fumbled with the light switch just inside the door. Somehow, as he'd retreated, she'd advanced. The output from the overhead was weak, but even in the muted light, he could see that beneath the place where her hand held her stomach—seemed to be holding it up, in fact—there was blood.

She stumbled a bit as she tried to move toward him. "Please," she said.

And now his body did what his brain already knew it would do. It moved toward her; it took hold of her. He put an arm around her back and another under her elbow. Her whole body seemed to push into his at that moment, as though she'd been doing all she could to maintain her upright position, but now that there was something, someone to do the work for her, she completely relinquished control and effort. As he turned toward the door, he looked down. More blood was on the back of her nightgown. Again he wanted to vomit. Instead he kept guiding her—first out the door, then across the backyard, then to the stoop that led to the kitchen. The door was open.

"Where should I take you?" he asked. He meant, of course, within the house. He meant: *Where in this home of yours would you like to be delicately placed while I ring whoever it is you tell me to ring—the doctor, the police, the ambulance . . .*

Instead she pointed to the sink. He took her there. She pointed to a narrow drawer next to it. He opened it. "The keys," she said.

He truly did not understand.

"To the car," she said. "Pick them up."

"The car?"

"I know you can drive."

"But where would I go?"

"Do you see them? Are they there?"

Her eyes were closed. Her hand was still supporting her stomach.

"They're here," he said. He picked them up.

"You have to take me to the hospital," she said. "I don't have time for an ambulance. You're all I have. Do you understand? You're all I have."

Her eyes were still closed. He didn't bother answering. He resumed his position by her side. At the stoop, he said, "Step," and she stepped down. He said it again, and again she stepped. He said it again and again until they were to the grass, and each time she allowed herself to be escorted by only his arms and his words.

After he had installed her in the backseat, he said, "Can you open your eyes? I think you need to open your eyes."

She was lying with her knees bent behind the driver's seat. Her head was behind the passenger's seat. When he turned to look at her, their eyes caught. "Good," he said. "Good girl. Keep your eyes open. Now tell me," he said. "Tell me how to go."

The sun was coming up as Piedmont emerged from the lower-level doors of the hospital. There, next to the curb of the emergency room's cul-de-sac, was Lily's car, exactly where he'd parked it five or ten or fifteen minutes earlier. Nothing would have been taken. Nothing would have been touched, though he'd left the doors unlocked and—he noticed now—the back door slightly ajar. This was the wrong side of town for such petty thievery, which struck Piedmont as an ultimately perplexing idea: that this side of town could ever be the *wrong* side of town. This was, by definition, the *right* side of town; it was the *only* side of town, unless you were like him, unless you were Negro or Colored or Black or a Brother or a Sister or whatever his mother's pastor or Michael or Jeremy wanted to call people like them. If your skin was tough as leather and your hair a constant mess of moist kink, then this—*this*—was the wrong side of town. For everyone else—for Robert Tucker and P. T. Coleman and that ghoul called Burt and even for Lily and anyone who looked like Lily, no matter how kind and generous they might seem—*this* was the only side of town. His lack of sleep was catching up with him, because now he amended his initial thought: not only was this not the wrong side of town—it was the side of town where you could own a car like this one and leave it unlocked and unattended. That's exactly what this side of town was for: casual indifference, careless nonchalance. And look how easily—because of Lily, because Lily had asked and because she was bleeding in that scandalous place that made him blush even to think about—he'd started to play the part.

Sweet Lord! How easily it had been to open that car door and lift her out, her hair sweaty, her forehead slick. (This was something he would never know: though he would think often about her, again and again about her, he would never talk to her again;

would, in fact, go out of his way to hide when, several weeks later, she and Robert and their tiny pink baby showed up at his mother's door wanting to see him, wanting to thank him — thank him for what? He would never know that either. Some things were better left indefinite, with the possibility of meaning; there was power in that: in thoughts, in ideas, in imagination, in *what ifs* . . .) How easy it had been to remove her from the car. Even swollen up with child like that, she was light to him, or seemed light to him. And he'd taken her in his arms, he realized this now — as he walked in a daze away from the hospital, the sun still rising — as though he was not a Negro or a Colored or a Boy or a Darkie or aware of color at all. No, he had taken her up and into the hospital as though color didn't exist, that's how much he was thinking only of her and what she needed. The existence of color had disappeared for Piedmont for the first time in his life and in the most unexpected of ways as he'd lifted Lily from the car (not bothering to lock it, not even bothering to close that rear door) and taken her through the glass entrance and into the arms of those nurses in their stiff uniforms and ridiculous hats, which was when — as if a great wave had come crashing over him — color came blindingly back into view. Those nurses had taken Lily from his arms, and the moment her skin no longer touched his, he'd been pushed from the hospital, shoved out, thrown out, by two large men — white men, because such terrible things as color once again existed and had never truly stopped existing in the first place — who'd called him names and, as though he were an animal with limited understanding, repeated over and over again: "Out. Out. Out."

Anastasia

L ate on the morning of July 4, having listened for the past hour to the *pop-pop-pop*s of fireworks across the city, Anastasia finally got out of bed and looked out her window. There were Tito and her brother, already in the pool. The fireworks were invisible against the bland whiteness of the sky. She yanked at her hair.

The problem was that they weren't pulling their weight. It was only Anastasia who had to keep Genie company at night, and yet they, too, enjoyed her generosity, but without any strings. This wasn't what she'd had in mind when she asked Skylar to join her. On top of that, the visitors—who'd once seemed a constant, an endless deluge of entertainment—had dried up. Gone were the days of drop-ins by unconventional men with lion cubs in their backseats; gone were the impromptu dinner parties and midnight champagne toasts. Seemingly overnight, the mansion had morphed from a fun house into a haunted one. Anastasia was bored; made positively listless by the prospect of enduring another afternoon in which she listened to Skylar and Tito romp while she counted down the minutes until Genie, who was always gone by dawn, crawled into her bed at night.

With an angry little huff, she leaned out her window.

"Hey now," she called down. "Hey now. Up here." She lit a cigarette.

Tito, who was in the shallow end of the pool, looked up, saw her, and tittered. Then he swam to her brother, who was in the deep end, and whispered something into his ear. The two of them looked up together. They were treading water. Skylar let himself sink under for a moment, then he returned to the surface blowing water from his mouth. "Come down," he called. "It's practically evening. You've been in bed all day."

Anastasia looked at her watch. "It isn't hardly noon," she said. "Are you drunk already?"

Tito whispered something else to Skylar. Anastasia wanted to stomp her feet. Every time she tried to regain her brother's attention, there was Tito cracking wise and stealing him away.

"Come up here," she said.

"You come down," Skylar said. He was still treading water. California had been good to him. He was tan and what had once been merely a lean body was now toned and sculpted. She wondered if hers was the female equivalent of his or if it was somehow inferior, the way the feathers of a female bird were always outshone by the male.

Skylar swam toward the shallow end, which was closest to Anastasia's window. When he was just beneath her, he stood and shook his head so that water whipped away from his face. His wet hair swept handsomely across his forehead. It seemed a practiced move. It made her jealous.

"Who's here?" she called quietly.

"It's too glum in there during the day," he said. "I can't stand it. Dust Mote City, and she goes on and on about that painting. The parrot never shuts up."

"Don't be ungrateful," Anastasia said.

"The coast is clear," he said. "Genie and her goon are away. The maid is doing something foul in the kitchen."

"Her name is Henrietta."

"Henrietta is doing something foul in the kitchen." Her brother walked up the pool's steps, took a towel from one of the lounge chairs, then stood directly beneath Anastasia, who was still leaned out her window from the waist up. "Toss me a cigarette," he said. She did. "If you come down, I'll tell you about a party. Tito and I are going. You have to come."

"She doesn't like me to leave without her."

"What's she going to do? Arrest you? Lock you up?"

"If I come, you'll just ignore me," she said.

"Don't pout."

"How will we get there? You said Genie has the car."

"We have a ride. Can you be ready in an hour?"

"What should I wear?"

"Something fabulous. Something that makes you look like money."

"Who will be there?"

"Everybody."

"Will we tell them who we are?"

"We'll tell them whatever we want."

"Who will we be, then?"

"Anybody," he said. "Anybody at all."

"And do you promise not to abandon me? Do you promise?"

"Be ready in an hour." It both maddened her and excited her that though he'd been back in Atlanta fewer than three weeks, he was already more popular than she, already hearing about private parties and being offered convenient rides. He blew her a kiss, unhooked his towel from his waist so that it fell to the concrete, then ran toward the deep end and cannonballed into the water, just next to where Tito still bobbed.

Anastasia stubbed out her cigarette and closed the window.

It wasn't that she didn't have anything fabulous to wear. She did. Genie Case had seen to that. And it wasn't that she was unsure about whether or not she'd go to the party; she knew she would. She must! It was that she was already feeling guilty about leaving without permission, which was a feeling that unsettled her—the guilt. It was not an emotion she'd previously entertained. Anger, yes. Embarrassment, yes. Determination, ambition, jealousy: yes, yes, yes. But guilt? No, she was certainly not one to have ever lost time to guilt. Guilt meant worrying about another person's feelings. And other people's feelings were so . . . unexceptional, so boring, so beyond one's control that there was no use fretting over them. And yet here she was sitting on the edge of her bed, rubbing her cuticles raw, fretting over Genie's feelings. Oh god! She had to get out of that house for an afternoon. She needed to escape!

It was a funny word—*escape*—because Skylar was right: there were no handcuffs. There was nothing Genie could do. She had no real power over Anastasia. She, Anastasia, could leave any time she liked. And yet if she did "escape" in a more global way, she'd be giving up this bedroom with its rose carpet and its stocked closet; she'd be giving up this comfort.

She stood in front of the vanity. She pinched her cheeks so that color rose along her cheekbones. She turned her face to the left and to the right and to the left again. She held her right hand up to her cheek. She stroked her own skin delicately with the backs of her knuckles as she'd seen done in the movies. She smiled bashfully. She blinked coquettishly. Then she pulled her hand maybe six inches away and brought it back fast against her face with a sharp *whack*. "There," she said aloud. "That'll teach you." She wasn't entirely sure what she meant, but already she felt more alive, already she felt the butterflies in her stomach flitting, lifting, moving marvelously about in anticipation of being seen.

They drove down Peachtree at a snail's pace, fireworks popping against the white sky.

"This place puts the Swan House to shame," said the man who was driving the car. "They call it the Pink Chateau. Guy who throws the Fourth of July party every year pays the city. It's cuckoo what he gets away with. To be completely honest, I was surprised it was happening this year given the politics. But who am I to say no to a free shindig?"

They had to park nearly a half mile away. The driveway was completely blocked with the cars of guests who'd gotten there even earlier. West Paces Ferry was a veritable wall of carefully abandoned Cadillacs and Jaguars and people moving down the sidewalk in the direction of the party.

"Holy moly," said Tito.

They got out of the car and took their place among the stream of people. A beer can was being kicked from a group behind them to a group in front of them.

Tito checked the passenger's door of one of the parked cars. "This is a potential dynamo," he said. "Holy moly."

Skylar swatted at him. "Don't be crass," he said. "Don't be stupid."

"I'm not going to steal anything," said Tito. "I just wanted to see if they even bothered locking doors in this town."

"Just look," said Skylar. "No touching."

"No touching?" asked Tito. He slid his hand across the fly of Skylar's pants. A group of teenaged girls wearing bikinis and with silken angel wings attached at the shoulders ran past them.

Skylar nodded toward the girls and leaned into Anastasia. "Atlanta's finest," he said. "What? Are you blushing? Don't be put out. They've got nothing on you."

Anastasia was mad about the half-mile walk. Her upper lip was sweaty. She worried that she'd overdone it with the pancake makeup. Her neckline might run if she didn't get in front of a fan fast. She slowed her pace. If she'd hoped Skylar would do the same to create some distance between them and Tito, she was wrong. He didn't. Instead it was the man who'd driven them, a man called Art Dixon, who hung back to walk with her.

"You're prettier than your brother," he said.

"What a random thing to say."

"I like him," Art said, "but I'm not funny like him. If you know what I mean."

Anastasia looked at Art without pausing her stride. She was wearing a short suede skirt in deep brown, with a fringe that showed off and then hid—showed off and then hid—each of her thighs as she walked. She liked the feel of the leather as the thin pieces swept back and forth across her skin.

"I know what you mean," said Anastasia. But to her, Art *did* seem funny, in just the same way as her brother, but somehow more devious, more dangerous.

"How did you meet them? Tito and my brother?"

"I don't meet people," said Art. "Everybody knows me already."

"I met you. I didn't know you."

"You know me," he said. "Trust me. You know all about me."

"You're a little bit of a creep, aren't you?" she said.

"I'm a whole lot of a creep."

"Drugs?"

"You want some?"

"Do you sell them? I'm assuming that's how you know my brother."

"I sell everything."

"Like what?"

"Drugs, cars." He reached into his front pocket and pulled out a joint. "Guns, women."

"You sell women?"

"I sell notions," he said. "I make concepts come true."

Anastasia picked up her pace.

"I won't bite," said Art. "You don't have to worry about me."

Thankfully, Skylar and Tito had stopped at the foot of the driveway, at the end of which was the party. The horde of people they'd been walking among surged forward. Skylar was leaned against the mailbox when they caught up to him. He'd removed one of his loafers, which he was now shaking. A tiny pebble fell to the ground.

The property itself was dizzyingly green, just as Genie Case's was. But the difference between this site and hers was that the nearest driveway was another quarter mile down the road. And this driveway dipped down through a forest of sycamores, magnolias, and wisteria. Spanish moss seemed to hang from every limb. As the drive rounded a corner and began its final rise toward the dwelling, the tree line broke open onto a manicured lawn of close to ten acres.

Anastasia sucked in her gut. The scene in front of her was like something out of one of Genie's art books, all those blurring, pulsing, moving colors. There were hundreds, maybe thousands of people. No, the view wasn't simply like *something* from one of those books, but like a definite thing. It was a particular painting, one she had looked at again and again, one that Genie had pointed out to her, in fact; had asked specifically how Anastasia felt about it. To Genie, she'd said only that it was fine. But in reality the painting had made her head buzz; had made her body swarm with energy. The name was on the tip of her tongue — not the artist's name but the title. Oh, how she loved the titles! She could feel herself tingling now in the same manner as when she'd observed the painting and then —

"Music!" she said to no one in particular. She clapped her hands together. "*Music in the Tuileries Gardens!*"

"Yes," said Art, who was once again standing beside her. He nodded his head. "I see exactly what you mean. It's like walking into a Manet canvas, one that's been brought magically to life."

"What did you say they call this place again?"

"The Pink Chateau."

"The Pink Chateau . . ." Anastasia was at a genuine loss for words.

Art held out his arm. "Here," he said. "Let me show you around."

Piedmont

The sun was fully up; it was noon; the sky was cloudy pink with the dust of last night's preliminary fireworks. Here and there were pinprick explosions of light, a taste of what the city would see at sundown. Piedmont had walked close to six miles. His feet were sore. His shirt was damp. He was aware of an odor, his odor, plus the odor of the sidewalks, of the asphalt, of the city itself—a pungent blend of overripe banana peels, cat piss, melons, stewed and stewing greens, pig fat. Name it and he could smell it. His fatigue had turned to daze, and from there it had morphed again into haze and something close to the first stages of daytime intoxication: a second beer, say, on an empty stomach. He'd moved from discomfort (except for the tendons between his instep and his heel: he hadn't realized they could ache in such a way; he'd never before associated bruises with feet, though he imagined when he finally stopped, when he finally reached a destination and there, mercifully, removed his shoes, he would find deep star-shaped bruises, the color of chewing tobacco and dirt), but he'd moved from discomfort to a state of daydreamed irreality. He had stopped thinking of Lily, stopped wondering about her body, that nightgown, its blood. He was beyond that now, somewhere floating above the city. He'd been living the past several weeks on borrowed time. He'd not been going backward—that was the wrong way to think of it. More he'd been treading in a kind of amber. He'd been play-pretending, as his mother would have put it. It was time to start thinking about what was next. It was time to start living in the real world, taking on and facing the real challenges of life, of his life, of Piedmont Dobbs's life as Member of This World. For the first time ever, he imagined leaving the South. Perhaps that had been the solution all along: to get out and start over, but to do so not simply away from his mother but away from here. Emmett Till? That boy's problem was that he had come south. If he'd stayed home, he'd still be alive. He'd be Piedmont's age, off doing his own thing in his own big city somewhere in the middle of the country, far away from here.

This was what Piedmont was thinking about—his head so high up in the clouds, his shirt now not just damp but actually wet with sweat—when a gold sedan pulled to the side of the road in front of him. It took him longer than was reasonable—blame the heat, blame the lack of sleep—for him to realize it was Michael and Jeremy. Somehow, in this city of half a million, they had found him. It had taken them over two weeks, but they had found him at last.

Piedmont shivered in the warm breeze of a different passing automobile, one that honked as it whizzed by. A sheet of newspaper wrapped itself around his shin and then continued on.

"Motherfucker," said Jeremy, who'd rolled down the passenger's-side window and then leaned out most of his torso. "Piedmont Dobbs. Why the hell you on the side of the highway? Where in all get-out you been?"

Piedmont stopped, nearly at the car's bumper, and looked around. It was true. He was no longer walking on Peachtree Avenue. Somehow, without even realizing it, he'd wandered onto the expressway.

"Get in the car, son." Jeremy disappeared back into the car. A moment later the backseat door was pushed open. Piedmont heard Jeremy shout against the traffic, which seemed to have increased with his body's return to reality. "Get in," he yelled again, and Piedmont, the tendons in his feet now bellowing their approval, now reasserting their epic pain, did once again as he was told.

"We heard things about you," Michael said, as he pulled the sedan back into traffic. More sheets of newspaper hit the windshield and slid away as the car gained speed.

"What did you hear?"

"We heard you were shacking up with some chick."

"No," said Piedmont. "That's wrong."

"Miss Carvie's been worried sick. You sure you're not a yard Negro?"

"No, no. Never."

"We heard you were living in a house with a really big yard."

"I was getting paid."

"That's what a yard Negro would say."

"I do what I want."

"He does what he wants. You hear that, Jeremy?"

"I hear that, Michael. Sounds like an addict's excuse to me."

Piedmont wasn't exactly sure what they were talking about. They were somehow the same and not the same as the last time he'd seen them.

"You aren't secretly playing the part of a race-mixing yard Negro in a white lady's bed?"

"No," Piedmont said. "Absolutely not."

"You can't be messing with white girls."

"I'm not," Piedmont said. "I wouldn't." Their anger was newly palpable.

"You know what?" It was Michael talking. "I bet that white lady wants him to conk his hair. I bet he's going to do it, that's how much he hates himself. How low he's going to sink. Might as well drive him to the market right now and buy him up some eggs and lye. Get him a fine-toothed comb and a tub of Vaseline.

He can spend all day in front of the mirror conking his hair so it's fine and straight as a white man's."

Piedmont had seen photographs of zoot-suiters and their slicked-back, well-oiled hair, but he'd never once thought of mimicking their style.

"You going to degrade yourself? You going to try to become one of them? Because guess what? You'll never be one of them. You can straighten your hair all you want, you'll always be just like us."

Piedmont was shaking his head. He felt unmoored, unsafe, and left out.

"Listen up, hustler. We've been looking for you."

"I'm no hustler," Piedmont said, and this made them laugh.

Michael turned in his seat. "Is that blood?" He gestured toward Piedmont's shirt with his chin. "You been fighting? He's been fighting." He slapped Jeremy on the shoulder and turned back to the steering wheel.

"Nah," Piedmont said. "I'm not fighting."

"Good," said Michael. "Good. We found you in the nick of time. We got business to settle."

"Business?"

"You a boy or a man?"

"What?"

"A boy or a man?"

"Man," said Piedmont.

"Exactly. You're a man. But all those white folks you been hanging out with?"

"I don't know what you're talking about."

"Of course you don't because we haven't told you yet."

"Tell me what?"

"Listen up. Pay attention."

Piedmont bit at his lower lip.

"I'm trying," he said, but their rhetoric was scattered. It seemed they were mixing and matching lines they'd overheard. Or maybe it was Piedmont who was scattered. Maybe Jeremy and Michael were making perfect sense. Maybe they'd been making perfect sense all along.

"Which is it?" asked Michael. "You with us or what?"

"I'm with you," said Piedmont. His answer was both true and not true. He wondered what it would feel like to be thrown from a moving car. He wondered if Michael and Jeremy were capable of such violence. Two weeks ago, he would have said no. Now he wasn't so sure. He was suddenly worried about Lily, about her property. If they truly had been spying on him, then they knew exactly where he'd been hiding out while his face and ribs recovered.

"Yeah," said Michael. "Yeah. I thought so. Go ahead, show him."

Jeremy jackknifed his body, looping an elbow over his seat. "Check it out," he said. He nodded at the floorboard behind the driver's seat and removed a towel that was there. Piedmont followed his gaze.

In a pile that suggested no rhyme or reason were dozens and dozens of guns—pistols, revolvers, at least one sawed-off shotgun. The pile clinked and clanked.

Piedmont looked at Michael, who flipped down the rearview mirror and studied his reaction.

"What do you think?" asked Michael. He was grinning.

"I don't understand," said Piedmont. He shook his head and looked at the pile again. His chest tightened.

"We're sick of this shit," said Michael. "News people, the mayor and his wife, television shows, the goddamn president of the United States—they're all going on and on about this airplane that went down in Paris, France, on Planet Earth. They jabber away about the movers and the shakers, about all the important folks we lost that day. The Reverend himself comes on the radio and tells us that we better behave, that we should hang our heads in sadness at our loss. You know what, though? It isn't *our* loss. You understand? It isn't our loss at all. It's their loss. We have losses. Every day. Every single day we suffer losses. But no one talks about those. We get no letters of sympathy. We get nothing. Just ignored."

Piedmont closed then opened his eyes.

"We're going to a party."

"A party?"

"A rich white party with a bunch of rich white folks. You get it yet?"

"No," said Piedmont. "I don't get it."

"These are bad people," said Michael. "These are people who do not care about us."

Piedmont listened as best he could, but his focus remained on the bouncing pile of metal on the floorboard beside him.

Michael elbowed Jeremy. "Show him the burp gun."

"Burp gun?" asked Piedmont.

"Burp gun," said Michael, moving the sedan into fifth and pushing into the gas. "You know. *Machine* gun."

Jeremy bent over. From the floorboard in front of him he produced a gun the likes of which Piedmont had never seen before, had never even known to imagine.

Any sort of clarity he'd momentarily experienced during the intense heat of his long solo perambulation along the expressway was gone. He felt every bit the child again. *Here is a boy,* he found himself thinking, *who knows absolutely nothing at all.*

More than anything, he was scared.

Anastasia

nastasia slipped outside and onto the back veranda of the Pink Chateau. She'd gotten separated from Art and Skylar and Tito twenty minutes earlier, and ever since she'd been drifting from room to room in sheer delight of the splendor. This home, not Genie's, was where the real money was. Here the marble walls glowed white-pink; the statues glistened; the windows were leaden and clear. Here was none of Genie's morbidity.

Outside, overhead, afternoon fireworks flared white and ghostly against a cloudy sky. A group of men on a slate veranda were talking about Jackie Kennedy or, rather, talking about Norman Mailer who'd written about Jackie Kennedy in *Esquire*.

"He's a smug prick," one of the men said. "The article was all about him."

"Did you even read it?"

"I didn't need to. Where were the nudie pics? I wanted nudie pics."

"Don't mind him," another one of the men said. "He's just jealous they never take anything of his."

"I wouldn't write for that rag if . . ."

"Sure, sure. Sure, sure."

"You know the chap who beat out Arnie Palmer last month?"

"Jack Something."

"Name doesn't matter. He's twenty-two years old. Twenty-two! Can you imagine? How does he sleep at night?"

"Probably well."

"And this wall in Berlin is officially in Stage Two. I'm telling you, between Germany, herbicides, and the twenty-two-year-old, the world is ending."

To Anastasia, this group of men also reeked of money. She moved closer.

Genie's aging eccentrics—the ones whose visitations had suddenly dried up as if they'd been ordered to stay away—told stories of sailing with pirates off the coast of Africa and eating monkey hearts with tribal kings. They talked about safaris and drag races and picnics enjoyed on the edges of volcanoes. But for all their skill with narrative, these people had always seemed covered in cobwebs. There was a layer of dust, of antiquity to what they said and how they said it. It seemed that whatever fortunes had once made possible their adventures were now distant, dwindled, and severely diminished.

These men on the veranda wore shiny new suits with initials embroidered onto the shirt pockets. Their teasing, so it seemed to Anastasia, was good-natured, informed; their posture carefree, unburdened. She doubted that any of them cried themselves to sleep at night, but if they did, she guessed they hid it from their lovers instead of flaunting it, instead of requiring constant handholding and nonstop doting. These were the men to whom, when she'd gotten into Genie's car last month, she assumed— through of series of dreamed-about balls, dances, and coming-out parties—she would be given access. Instead she'd been made the paramour of a homosexual geriatric. She pulled back the elastic of one of her bracelets and let go. It slapped against her wrist, leaving a red mark in its wake. The men hadn't yet noticed her.

"Bully," she said under her breath.

She put down her drink and, with the studied nonchalance of Audrey Hepburn or Elizabeth Taylor, walked to the other end of the veranda, where she paused, her hands on the railing, to look out at the vast back lawn of people and a dreamlike swimming pool, its pale marble steps leading right into the water. What numinous occurrences had happened here? She consciously arched her back and leaned onto her forearms as if at great ease, as if without a care in the world, as if she were completely unaware of the men.

"Now that," one of them said at last, speaking loudly enough so that Anastasia would have to hear him, "is an American woman."

She waited. Then, slowly, slyly, with such great patience she astonished even herself, she turned her face—her arms still on the railings in front of her—and looked at them. They were, all four of them, watching her. She smiled.

One of them held up a tumbler. "Join us?"

She turned back toward the lawn of people. In the distance, she thought she saw Skylar wave. It might have been someone else, a stranger.

She pushed herself from the banister, again so slowly she could have giggled at the perfection of the performance, and then sauntered in the direction of the men.

"What are we drinking?" she said.

"Gin," said a man who was dressed all in white. The others seemed to understand that he had rights of first refusal. He was the one who'd called her an American woman. "These are my friends from New York. You can call them New York. They're indistinguishable."

"I wouldn't say that," said one of them.

"They're here to steal my art," said the man in white. "Should I let them steal my art?"

"I think the gallery's made a generous offer," said one of the New York crowd.

Anastasia didn't bother looking at the other men. Dominance had been established. Worth had been made clear. This man was the one she wanted. "What's your name?" he said.

She held out her hand. "I'm Anastasia," she said.

"P. T. Coleman," said the man in white. He brought her hand to his lips and kissed the knuckle of her middle finger. She thought she felt his tongue on her skin.

"This is the girl I was talking about!" said one of the others. Anastasia quickly regarded him. He was wearing a brown suit. It wasn't as nicely cut to his figure as she'd thought from a distance. His hair, she now saw, was receding at the temple.

"Do I know you?"

"The girl who looks like the water fountain statue," said the man in brown. "On the front lawn, just on the other side of this house. You remember. The one who's staying with your aunt." He said all this to P. T. Coleman, not to Anastasia.

Coleman turned to her.

"Is that you?"

Anastasia blushed. She wished she had remembered the man in brown sooner. His name was Ed Klein, the fellow who was both business and personal, the one with whom Genie had dined, the one who wanted the god-awful Gauguin, the one whose company had so confounded Genie that she'd crawled drunkenly into Anastasia's room on all fours and then seduced her with such authority that it seemed her plan all along.

"I think I see someone," Anastasia said. She began to move away, but P. T. Coleman, this man in white—such a gesture of confidence!—took hold of her elbow.

"Do you know Genie Case?" he said.

"I do," she said. "Yes. I know her." Anastasia worried that her voice had wavered; that her confusion was visible. She hated feeling the fool.

"Genie Case," said P. T. Coleman, "is my aunt."

Anastasia hiccupped.

The nephew! At last! She was overcome with delight. Here finally was the true owner of Genie's art collection, the actual heir of all the riches that Anastasia had been enjoying these last few weeks. Even before she knew who he was, *what* he was, she'd been attracted to him. Was this what fate felt like? Did it have a sensation all its own? She hiccupped again.

"Here," said Coleman. He held out his glass. "Have a drink."

As she tilted the glass up and back, she allowed her gaze to wander. Behind this small group of men, in the distance, crazy-eighting around an ivy-covered cottage and the wide blue pool, was a conga line being led by a juggler. The juggler may or may not have been Tito. He was a wearing a mask, but Anastasia thought she recognized the yellow trousers.

"You want to see the sights," said Coleman.

"My brother is here somewhere. We got split up. I should probably find him," said Anastasia, though even as she said it, she was unsure.

"Good," Coleman said. He held out his arm. She took it. Why on earth would she not have taken it? "I got split up from someone too. I'm supposed to be keeping an eye on him, keeping him off the booze." Coleman winked. "We can look for them both together."

He led her down the stairs and onto the lawn and into the sea of people. She licked her lips. The taste of juniper was still there. She felt almost tipsy with self-worth. *My god!* She must have looked dazzling by this man's side.

Genie & Claude

W hen they were still children, there were certain weeks in the summer when Genie and her brother, Claude, would be dropped off at their uncle's cabin, what had once been the family's homestead. It suggested a far more modest lifestyle than the one in which Genie and Claude were being raised. Their father never got out of the Model T on the occasion of these visits, and their uncle never greeted him. The few times the children had dared speculate aloud on the long-standing but quiet feud, they'd been shushed by the backhand of their mother.

The summer before their uncle died, an event that allowed their father finally to sell the family land to the city, construction of the first high-voltage transmission line was visible from the cabin's back porch. It would open up the town. The state—the South itself—would never be the same. They'd heard their father say as much.

The cabin was five miles north of the heart of Atlanta, which in Genie and Claude's youth still looked like the country. But that line between the Georgia Railway's hydro plant and the substation at Boulevard in Atlanta would change everything.

Mere mention of the transmission line caused their uncle to spit, but Genie and Claude loved the sound of its construction. Its hugeness confounded them. They spent their afternoons at the cabin's creek bed, lifting stones, searching for crawdads, trying to conceive of such a structure. The year was 1912.

"I hear it's fifty miles long," one of them might say.

"I hear one hundred."

Genie and Claude, separated by fifteen months, were thick as thieves. They were thick as thick could be. Their uncle had once referred to them as the Gold Dust Siblings. He took the origin of the phrase, along with any explanation, to his grave.

In the dappled sunlight that sneaked in through the thick foliage overhead, the brother and sister ran from rock to rock; they carried large sticks as though they were swords; together they learned the lay of the land to a nearly instinctive degree. They ran and jumped and skipped across those thousand rural acres — though they would never know it, would of course never be told — in much the same way as their father and uncle had once had done, toward the end of the turn of the century.

Genie and Claude took turns with a blindfold, one wearing it, the other giving orders. "Lift your right leg. Higher. No, higher still. Good. Now step. Yes. Good. Turn left. Not that far left. Good."

Perhaps it was Genie's idea to go out the open window one night after their uncle had fallen asleep. More likely it was Claude's. He was older. But it was Genie who took the steep hill toward the creek at a full-tilt run in spite of the dark. In the morning, her legs would be scratched from ankle to thigh from the orchard grass that they rushed through, but that night, running ahead of her brother toward the sweet babble of the water below, she couldn't feel a thing. It was the first time they'd left the homestead after dark and without permission.

At the edge of the shallow water, Genie paused. She stood up straight. In her excitement, she'd not considered Claude's position. She'd assumed he was close by, his footfalls merely a beat or two behind. But now, at the water, standing still, she found she was alone. She had time to be scared for only a second or two before she heard him, circling through the woods, his steps coming fast in her direction. She knew her brother's cadence by heart. Like a cat, he could choose to wispy-run or heavy-run, depending on his mood. That night, to give Genie warning, he heavy-ran.

She braced herself for a friendly attack, some late-night extension of the day's earlier make-believe. Her heart beat wildly, both wanting and not wanting to be found, both wanting and not wanting to be tackled.

He rushed her from the side, pushing her down into the soft earth and twigs. He dug his knees into her lower back. They gasped for air, Genie trying desperately to hold back laughter.

Suddenly, Claude bent over and bit into Genie's shoulder. She yowled, then pushed up onto her forearms, knocking Claude over and onto his chest. She crawled quickly on top of him, pinning him so that his stomach was on the ground and his face in the grass. He was laughing and all Genie could think to say was, "You won't be laughing long," before bending over herself and biting him on his neck. She rolled off of him and the two of them howled at the moon.

On their elbows now, both with bites that would be bruised but not bloody by morning, they crawled side by side along the bank of the creek bed. They crawled until their shirts were torn and their limbs muddy. They crawled until they were so tired, they considered sleeping in the open air. They crawled until they were at the foot of the hill, at the top of which was the cabin, inside of which was their uncle snoring soundly on a thin twin mattress in front of the unlit hearth. Before Genie could stand, brush off her knees and arms, Claude put a hand on hers.

In a whisper, he said, "I love you." If she hadn't known better, she'd have thought he was crying. But she'd never seen her brother cry, and so she knew this to be an impossibility.

Genie, filled up with gratitude, filled up with her own feeling of perfect sibling love for her perfect brother and her dearest friend, but also filled with the turmoil of youth and the fear of being fooled, pulled her hand away from his and jumped up quickly. She clucked down at him in the dark. "Love?" she asked. "Love?" She hoped to impress him; she hoped to sound as old and wise as he. "What do you know about love?" It was a question she'd heard her own mother ask of her father late one night when she'd sneaked downstairs past bedtime. She said it now not understanding its effect, not knowing that she would spend the rest of her life wishing to undo this single moment, wishing to go back—decades in the future, decades even after his unexpected death on a different continent—and say, simply, "I love you, too."

Robert

By sundown, Coleman had found Robert but he'd lost the girl. The two men were standing now in the ballroom of the Pink Chateau, at the center of which was a life-size ice sculpture featuring four rearing stallions. The carving had melted down so that the animals appeared swaybacked. Their pointy hooves dripped gloomily into marble buckets on the floor.

"Shit a monkey," said Robert. "Am I high?"

"Is that a question?" said Coleman. "Are you really asking me that? Are you being funny? Because you made me swear not to give you anything and I haven't. You have an ant on your shoulder. Get rid of it, please. What happened to the girl who was just standing here?"

"What girl?" asked Robert. "What are you talking about? Look." He grabbed Coleman by the elbow. "Isn't that Piedmont? Is the kid following me? Is that Lily's boy? Does that mean Lily is here? What the hell?"

Coleman was still looking at Robert's shoulder.

"Snap out of it. Look."

He did.

"Cocksucker!" Coleman said. "You're right. That's him, and

why not? It's July Fourth. Everybody's out and about. Should we talk to him?"

"Does he look about ten years older to you? Does he look bigger? He looks bigger to me."

Piedmont spotted them before Coleman could answer.

"Is he going to run for it?" asked Robert. "Or attack?"

Piedmont looked left, then right.

"Attack," said Coleman. "I say *we* make a run for it. I need to find that girl."

Robert gripped Coleman's elbow more tightly. "You're not going anywhere."

The kid, looking directly at them, shook his head. Then, still quite slowly, he nodded once.

"What's that mean?" asked Coleman. "Is he giving us a signal? Is that a signal? Is he dressed like one of the waiters? Is that a costume? Where's the girl? What did you do with her? The one in the suede skirt."

The kid gestured with his head toward an adjacent room, which appeared to be empty except for a few people passed out on a set of matching couches.

"He wants us to follow him," said Robert. As he spoke, he pushed Coleman through a small crowd of people toward Piedmont, who'd situated himself in a corner. He seemed to be playing at seriousness, at some sort of faux espionage. "What are you doing here?" asked Robert. "How did you even find us? Is that blood on your arm?"

"Find you?" said Piedmont. "I didn't find you. I'm not looking for you, but listen—"

"Is Lily here?"

"You don't know where she is? They haven't phoned you?"

"Who's *they?*"

"Do you even care about her?"

"Watch it, kid."

"I feel sorry for you is the truth."

"Is this about the other night?" asked Robert.

"I'm talking about your wife. I'm telling you there's a problem, and you're asking me about the other night?"

"There's a problem?"

"Listen," said Piedmont. He snapped his fingers. "How doped up are you two? Can you hear me? Can you drive?"

He was talking to Robert, not to Coleman, whose head was going back and forth, following the voices, but whose eyes were now closed.

"I'm sober as a new day," said Robert. "Where is Lily? Tell me. What's the problem?"

Piedmont shook his head. He looked newly smug. "She's having your baby," he said. "She's at the hospital. I drove her there last night. If they hadn't kicked me out, I'd be there now. She's all alone." He paused. "What's your excuse?"

Robert didn't have an excuse. But he did have a purpose. "I get it," he said. "You win. You're a better man than me by tenfold. I get it. I'm a fuck-up. But I'll do better. I'll make it right."

"Master Robert has had an epiphany. Amen. Good job for you. But in the meantime, listen up. You need to get out of here now," said Piedmont. His voice turned to a whisper. "Shit's going down. Shit's going down real soon."

"What sort of shit is going down?" Coleman asked the question, his eyes still closed, his head tilted toward the ceiling, a vague smile on his lips.

Robert was less than interested in Coleman's antics—whether they were antics or whether he was truly as buzzed as he now seemed—and more interested in Piedmont's demeanor, which he realized wasn't forced or performative at all. In fact, the kid looked solemn; he looked downright unhappy.

"You following what I'm saying?" said Piedmont, talking again only to Robert. He had no time to waste on Coleman. "There are people here who have plans."

"Plans?"

"Bad plans."

"Bad plans?"

"Folks in the world are angry. You get that? You understand what's going down? This is bigger than you and me. There's a movement afoot."

"A movement?" This didn't sound like the Piedmont he'd spent a couple hours with in the middle of the night. This sounded like half-baked zealotry.

"They've been listening to the radio. I'm serious. My friends have guns."

"Guns? What for? Friends? What have you gotten yourself mixed up in?"

Piedmont snapped his fingers. "Enough with the questions," he said. "Listen. Do you follow me? You need to get out of here now. This party? Firecrackers, booze? Same time every year like nothing ever changes? You know how that makes them feel? Makes *us* feel? They're going to teach y'all a lesson."

"What kind of lesson?"

"They want to put things in perspective. They want attention. They want to be seen. You understand? We're tired of this. We're sick of living like this. You know there was a lynching here? An entire family? On this property? And y'all come here to drink and whoop it up like nothing ever happened?"

Piedmont's confidence had a stirring effect on Robert. He looked directly into the kid's eyes, and in them he saw panic and confusion, but above all he saw resolution. Here was a man—a Negro man, a Colored man, but also simply a Man—who had had enough. There were thousands of young men just like him —hundreds of thousands in Atlanta alone—who likewise had finally had enough. It was a wonder it had taken so long. Robert had spent the last week feeling sorry for himself, wishing he'd never cheated in the first place, and longing for the company of his wife. He'd spent the three weeks before that pining for a dead girl and ignoring his wife. Piedmont had spent his entire life waiting to be seen, to be heard, to be treated like a human being. Context was everything.

"Yes," Robert said. "Yes. I follow. We need to leave."

"You need to leave *now*. Go be with your *wife*."

"This isn't a joke."

"This is not a joke."

Robert nodded and once again took Coleman by the elbow. "Come on," he said. "We need to get out of here."

"But the girl," said Coleman. "I want the girl."

"Forget the girl," said Robert.

"Those thighs," he said.

"Forget the girl." Robert grabbed Coleman's arm and walked him swiftly out of the house and across the lawn. "It's time to find Lily."

Ivan & Lulu

"You know what the real travesty is?"

"Are you dressed, Lulu? Do you have your face on? Please come out of the bathroom. Unlock the door, please."

"The real travesty is that you're determined to trot me about as though nothing has happened."

"No one is pretending nothing has happened. The entire city is in mourning."

"It's been only four weeks. Four weeks! And can you hear that? Can you hear the fireworks? It's as though they've all forgotten."

"Please unlock the door. Thank you. Look at you, Lulu. You're beautiful. You're a vision."

"I'm not going."

"It's difficult for me to take you seriously when you say things like that because you're already dressed. If you weren't going, then you wouldn't be dressed. But look: you've got the right gown on, just as we talked about. Your hair is done perfectly. Alma did a very fine job. It's that simple, then. You're coming."

"Don't talk about Alma. You aren't kind to her."

"How am I not kind to Alma?"

"You don't care about her nephew. He's still missing."

"There's nothing I can do."

"You're the mayor."

"My hands are tied. We've never even met Alma's sister."

"I'm tired."

"You don't look tired."

"I'm devastated."

"You look just fine to me. It's time to leave. It's the Governor's Mansion, Lulu."

"The Governor's Mansion. Ha! You make me sick. I do not like that man."

"He's coming around."

"He ran on segregation."

"Isn't a person allowed to change his mind?"

"But has he changed? Has he really changed, dear?"

"You know he helped get the Reverend released from jail."

"If I have to hear that story one more time . . . He refers to him as Daddy King. It's insulting."

"We're leaving now," said Ivan. "The car is here."

"You can't make me."

"Don't push me, Lulu."

"I dare you," she said. "I dare you to make me go."

"I'm warning you."

"Warning me? Warning me?"

"One more word . . ."

"Are you going to hit me?"

Ivan sat suddenly on the bed.

"Oh," he said. He clutched at his chest. "Oh, oh."

"What is it, Ivan? Are you ill?"

"Oh god," he said. He hiccupped.

"Tell me, dear. Tell me. What do you need?"

"Forgive me," he said. He slouched forward, his head now in his hands.

"Forgive you?"

His shoulders heaved. It was difficult to understand him when at last he spoke again. "I should never talk to you like that."

She sat down beside him.

"You take such good care of me, Ivan."

She put a hand on his thigh.

"Do I take as good care of you as you do of me?" she asked.

She squeezed his knee.

"I'm afraid I haven't been a very good wife these last few weeks," she said. "I haven't comforted you the way you've comforted me, Ivan. Not since we lost them."

His body convulsed when she said this. At what felt like long last, he let out a single immense sob, an undertaking of such force that it seemed his whole person had been waiting an entire lifetime to finally produce and release the effort.

"Oh, my love," she said. She put a hand to his heart and gently pushed him down so that he was lying on the bed, she beside him.

He covered his eyes and turned away.

"Oh my dearest, sweetest Ivan."

"Hold me," he said. His chest and shoulders were shaking.

She curled her body tightly around his.

"Lulu," he whispered. "Lulu."

"I'm here. I'm right here, love."

"Oh, Lulu," he said. He gulped for air. "I miss them. I miss them all so much."

She cupped his head in her hands. She kissed his eyes, his nose, his chin.

"Yes, dear heart. Yes, I know. I've known it all along."

Robert

The Thunderbird was half in the ditch and half on the road. The left headlight must have been busted because only the dry creek bed on the passenger's side was illuminated. Street-side, except for what the moon allowed, all was dark. The fireworks had stopped hours earlier.

Robert opened the door. Because of the angle, because of the way his side was dipped into the ditch, he nearly tumbled out. In fact, he did tumble out slightly: he landed on one knee but was able to catch hold of the door handle before slipping any further into the ditch.

He hauled himself up and dusted off his slacks. A twig snapped in the woods beyond the creek bed. Reflexively he straightened his back and cocked his head, an almost canine pose. He thought he could hear whispers, then footsteps and the crunching of leaves, the brushing aside of branches. He called out. No one answered. He groped his way around to the driver's side and opened the door.

In the backseat, the girl in the suede skirt was clearing her ears and shaking her head. She'd caught up to them just as they were leaving the party and asked for a ride.

She'd actually been wearing her seat belt. Robert couldn't believe it. Quite possibly it was the first time a seat belt had ever been buckled in that car.

Up front Coleman was draped over the steering wheel, murmuring. "*Hehwuzat,*" he said. "*Hehwuzat.*"

Robert grabbed him by the shoulder and pulled him up and away from the wheel. The back of his skull made contact with the seat harder than Robert intended. Coleman lifted his hand and rubbed the spot but didn't complain. A small trickle of blood ran from his ear horizontally toward his nose. Robert tried not to stare. He thought he might puke.

"Hell was that?" Coleman said more clearly, now rubbing the back of his neck. "A deer?"

"There was no deer," said Robert. His mouth tasted of iron.

They'd taken the turn from Tuxedo onto Valley at a wide angle. He'd had his eyes closed—he was so exhausted—but had opened them as they took the perilous turn. The velocity had pushed his torso into the seat, reminding him momentarily of the midnight flight in Coleman's new plane. He'd gulped in the night air and felt first a sort of faintness at the speed of the turn, but then, the faintness abating, another brilliant rush of life. *Life!* he'd thought. *Life! Life!*

They'd taken the turn in fourth gear, and Robert had registered the magnificent white-brown magnolias lit up by an audacious moon. In the neon of the headlights, he'd registered the green, green grass to the side of the road where there was no sidewalk and no shoulder but merely a foot's width of flat earth before the shallow dry ditch; he'd registered the image of a traffic symbol floating in the air—not floating, obviously, but attached to a thin post made invisible by the nighttime—and he'd registered the row of arborvitae, too, but by that time it was too late. By that time they were already plowing into the trees, and his forehead was already headed haphazardly toward the dash. He'd known better than to let Coleman drive, but as they'd left the

Pink Chateau, he'd felt no moral high ground from which to deliver any kind of ultimatum. Maybe it was a true desire for self-destruction, this willingness to be reckless again and again and again.

Coleman was talking, perhaps had been talking the entire time that Robert was—what was he doing?—just standing there dazed, pondering, trying not to look at the line of blood that was moving southward on Coleman's face.

"Give me your hand," Coleman was saying. "Get me out of here. I need help. Lift me up." The girl was still cleaning out her ears. Perhaps she had a concussion.

It was then, at that very moment, that they heard the sound. It was similar to a barking dog—no, not a barking dog, more like a smothered dog, like a dog being held down against his will—this horrendous sound rose up from somewhere nearby so that the hairs on the back of Robert's neck quite literally stood up, as did the pores on his arms individuate themselves, as if suddenly chilled by an unanticipated cold front.

The cry ended long enough for Robert's and Coleman's eyes to meet. "No," said Coleman. "Don't help me out. Get in. Get back in the goddamn car."

Robert shook his head. He looked up at the night sky. Was he aware that he was shaking his head? That was unclear. "But you heard it," Robert said. It might have been a question. It might even have been an accusation.

"I'll leave you," Coleman said. "So help me god, I'll drive away and leave you where you stand. Get in the car."

"You're bleeding," said Robert.

"*You're* bleeding," said Coleman.

Robert put his fingers to his forehead. They came away wet. He wiped the blood onto his pants and then stumbled toward the front of the car.

"Don't go up there. Don't you dare go up there. The minute

you see it, you lose all plausible deniability. Get back in the car or get out of the way," Coleman called. "I'll run you over. I'll do it."

Robert passed in front of the headlights and looked into the ditch. Then he looked back at Coleman, who—though he'd likely never admit it, not in a million years, not tonight, tomorrow, not ten years from now—appeared terrified by what Robert would say.

Robert looked again into the ditch. His shoulders slumped. He wanted to cry. "It's an armadillo," he said at last. "You've hit an armadillo."

The windshield of the Thunderbird was cracked. But even through the distortion, Robert could see the terror leave Coleman's face.

"An armadillo?" Coleman asked. "In Atlanta? I heard they were coming up from south Georgia, but I never quite believed it." He slapped the steering wheel in awe. "An armadillo. In Atlanta, Georgia."

With no nod toward modesty, the girl in the back climbed into the front seat.

Almost clinically, Coleman brought the butt of his palm to his cheek and wiped at the line of blood. He looked at what the gesture had produced, as if assessing the relevance or weight of the evidence that his open hand had brought away. He smiled. "I am a goddamn lucky man." He said this to the girl. "You know that? I've been kissed by angels. An armadillo? An armadillo?" He howled into the night.

The girl stuck a finger in her ear and wagged it back and forth as though trying to remove water.

"You shouldn't go with him," Robert said. "You should go to the hospital. You should come with me."

"You're going to help her? You?"

"Get out of here, then," said Robert. "Go already."

Coleman put a hand on the girl's knee. He slid it up her thigh.

"Yeah," he said, looking at Robert. "She's fine. She's going to be just fine."

"What about the human condition?" Robert asked. "What about comporting ourselves differently moving forward? What about being better than your old man?"

"To hell with mankind," Coleman said. "To hell with you and my old man and everything and everyone. There's just me, Bucko. There's always only me."

What scared Robert more than anything was the calmness with which Coleman spoke. An outlandish idea, but his verdict just then was that it was the calmness of money; it was the flatness of privilege. It was part and parcel of that ubiquitous gesture by any man with a certain thickness of bankroll in his back pocket. Robert wanted to punch Coleman then, which wasn't a new sensation. He also wanted to punch himself, which was also not a new sensation. It sickened Robert to no end that even at a moment such as this, he could be jealous of another man's bank account.

He put his hands in the air and stepped back, the attitude of someone about to be shot. Behind him, the injured animal grunted.

Coleman pulled away. After a minute or two, the pink taillights disappeared into the night, and Robert was left alone with the dying armadillo. He sat down by the side of the road, his feet only a few inches from the thing. It was on its back, its feet in the air. There was nothing dignified in its position, and there was nothing for Robert to do but wait, which he did. The armadillo breathed slower and slower. Robert just breathed.

The version of Robert that existed even an hour earlier might have pointed a finger at Coleman, might even have decried the injustices of life, the unfairness of it all. He might have focused on the irony of the situation—alone, in need of a hospital, just as Lily had been not twenty-four hours earlier, if the kid called Piedmont was to be believed. The old version would have snorted at the absurdity, scoffed in indignation at his sorry lot in life without once considering or acknowledging his own obvious role.

But this current version of Robert was quiet, contemplative. He felt newly aware, at long last, of the choices he'd made. He could practically see his life on a grid in front of him. He could plot the moments, the turns, the twists, the nosedives. From the upper-left-hand corner of the grid to the lowest-right-hand extreme, he could see the penciled-in dots, see exactly where and how he'd gotten himself—*he!* of his own volition!—exactly to this spot now.

His path was clear. It led only toward Lily, toward his wife, who'd been waiting—he knew it, he could feel it in his bones—for this precise and particular discovery.

But first there was the armadillo.

Anastasia

t most, it was an hour until dawn. The moon was at a funny angle, somehow still visible between the buildings. The streets were empty. And the drive, despite the wind in Anastasia's hair, was uncomfortably quiet. There was a sulfurous odor in the air. Her head felt foggy and thick. She tried not to think about the ringing in her ears or about the man who'd gotten out of the car or about the face he'd made as he looked into the ditch or about the howl that had come from P. T.'s mouth after his friend had said, "It's an armadillo." She focused instead on the cathedrals, which they were now passing. Lights from inside both churches were on, and the stained-glass windows above their dueling entrances appeared garish, almost neon, against the sky. In just over an hour, the sun would begin its rise, converting the temperature from tolerable to ungodly.

The car slowed, then turned.

"I thought you were taking me to your place," she said. "Why are we at Genie's?"

"You're a good kid," P. T. said, "a real French fry. You're fun. I had a nice time walking around the party with you. You're a looker. There's no doubt about it. But I try to keep my distance from my aunt's little numbers. It's better for the family dynamic if I drop you off and call it a day."

Anastasia turned away and bit back tears. She hated when she got ahead of herself. She hated giving any man the upper hand. If it hadn't been for the sudden sight of Tito, crouched behind a large sycamore, midway down the drive, Anastasia might have actually let herself start crying. Instead there was Tito, who huddled down lower as the headlights from P. T.'s car lit up the flora that lined Genie Case's property.

Anastasia glanced at P. T. It was clear he had already forgotten her; he was already five miles away; and it was obvious he hadn't seen Tito.

They came to a stop at the top of the roundabout. P. T. didn't even turn off the ignition.

As she opened the passenger's door, he touched her leg. "Don't be blue," he said. "Genie'll take care of you."

It was the last thing in the world she wanted to hear. She moved his hand away and got out of the car. The headlights shone milky pink onto a hydrangea bush just ahead. The hood of the car was badly dented.

"There's blood on the fender," she said. She was glad she hadn't looked into the ditch. She was glad she couldn't picture the dead thing.

In the dark beyond, Tito stood—his white shirt and yellow pants aglow—and gave a little wave. "You should leave," said Anastasia, directing her gaze for a final time at the car's driver.

She shut the door and looked again toward the sycamore, and again Tito stood and again he waved in her direction. "Go," she said.

Coleman swatted at something invisible on the steering wheel. "I do as I'm told," he said, and just like that he drove into the night, as though for him she'd never even existed.

Tito ran to Anastasia, practically into her arms. He was sweaty, frantic. "Oh," he said. "Oh." His eyes were puffy and the knuckles on his right hand were swollen and at least one was split and bloody. She noticed this, the state of his knuckles, because of the glint of the sapphire he was wearing on his pinkie. It was Genie Case's ring. Anastasia would never forget it. She'd been wearing it that very first day, at the Radisson.

It was only after Anastasia noticed the bright blue stone, its quick bright wink in the light of the porch, that she noticed the torn skin on Tito's hand, the raised bruising that seemed to spread from one finger to the next.

She took in the ring and its strange position on Tito's pinkie. She took in the state of his hand. Then she looked him in the eyes. "What happened?"

From inside, the parrot squawked.

"Oh," said Tito. He bounced in place and clutched at her forearms. Little tears leapt from the corners of his eyes. He was crying, yes, but his actions were somehow counterfeit. She distrusted him — this sudden show of crazed and sweaty affection — now more than ever.

"Oh! You got out! You're safe!" said Tito. "Skylar was so worried."

"Worried about what? Where's Billy?" she asked.

"Oh. Oh. Did you see the guns? We were so scared."

"What guns? What are you talking about?"

"It was madness," said Tito. He bounced up and down; his voice was a high-pitched whisper. "There were three of them, but then one of them went berserk. They made us lie down on our stomachs. They turned off the lights. At least two of them had machine guns. The woman next to me wet her pants. She was crying. It was awful. Oh!"

"Are you making this up?" asked Anastasia. "When was this? What are you talking about? At the party? Someone tried to hold up the party?"

"At the Pink Chateau. They didn't *try* anything," said Tito. "They did. They did it. We thought you were still inside. There was some sort of disagreement between them. The two who had guns started shouting at the one who'd been going around with a garbage bag. He looked like a kid. He looked too young to be wrapped up in that sort of thing. They were yelling at him to take wallets and watches, all the jewelry from the women. He was doing it too, doing just what they told him to, but he was moving too slowly. They started shouting at him, telling him to move faster. All of sudden he just stopped. He threw down the bag. He started talking about a movement. It sounded crazy. He made no sense. He just kept asking, 'Where's the movement? How's this a movement?' Then he called them thieves. The pair of them, the ones with guns for chrissakes, he called them thieves! Of course they were thieves! That's when we slipped out. We weren't the only ones. I saw at least a dozen people running across the yard. Somebody must have called the cops. Don't you think? Oh god, we thought you were still in there, at the Chateau. Skylar felt terrible. Oh. Oh. Oh."

"Stop saying that. Is Billy here? Is he inside? Where's Genie? Is she here, too?"

Tito tightened his grip on Anastasia. In fact, where his fingers dug into her, her arms stung.

"You're hurting me," she said.

He gripped tighter.

"Billy had an idea," said Tito. "Because of what he saw, because of what those kids did, Billy came up with this crazy plan. But you've got to believe me. It was his idea. Not mine. Okay? You believe me, right?"

"Let go," said Anastasia. "Let go of me." She allowed her voice to rise. She didn't want to give in to his hysterics, but his panic —feigned though it might have been—was so palpable as to be contagious.

She shook her arms loose. He looked down, surprised almost, as if he'd forgotten he was holding her—either that, or he hadn't believed her capable of extricating herself.

"Take me to Billy," she said. She rubbed herself where he'd held on too tightly. The position—each hand clasped onto an opposing forearm—gave her the look of someone old, decrepit, borderline deranged.

He nodded. "Yes," he said, now playing a more somber and controlled role. "Of course." He reached for her hand, but she pulled back. "Fine," he said. "Come. Just remember. This was all his idea."

He moved then toward the front door, which Anastasia saw was already ajar. Slowly, she followed. With each footstep toward the house, she became more and more aware of the fact that she was utterly unprepared for whatever was happening inside. If she found Genie Case and Billy sitting on a couch together reading, she would have been unprepared. If she found them in the pool, skinny-dipping in the last of the moonlight, she would have been unprepared. If she found them each in their own beds asleep— given Tito's current condition—she definitely would have been unprepared. Yet even this self-knowledge—this expectation for the unexpected—left her somehow breathless, somehow even more terribly taken aback when, having walked in and closed the door behind her, she saw, at the foot of the stairs, Genie Case bound and gagged and her brother, Billy, who sometimes went by Skylar, standing over her.

Robert

It was nearly dawn by the time the armadillo stopped breathing. By then, the front of Robert's shirt was caked with blood. The wound on his forehead was worse than he'd first suspected. The skin between his lip and nose was busted too. He'd collected a few handfuls of magnolia leaves and some of the downed arborvitae and covered the animal as best he could. It wasn't much, but it was something.

In the hour or so since Coleman and the girl had sped off, only one other car had driven by. Robert had raised his hand—a plea for help, a gesture of request—but the happy couple slowed only long enough for Robert to see the expressions on their faces, lit up by a single silver sparkler that the girl held out her window, change from gay curiosity to downright horror. The boy behind the wheel floored it; the girl dropped the sparkler and pulled in her arm abruptly.

He must have been a truly gruesome sight. Robert wanted to weep.

Twenty feet away, the sparkler flickered and crackled against the asphalt, as the oxygen burned and the glint moved steadily down the shaft until it popped a final time then fizzled into a pile of aluminum dust. The air smelled freshly of rotting eggs.

Who knows who called the medics—maybe Coleman had

found a pay phone, made a final grand gesture by way of a phone call; or maybe the young couple had been too frightened to stop but not too insensitive to go for help. It didn't matter. Robert was grateful. He was grateful for everybody and everything.

Life, he thought again for not the first time that night. But his heart now felt deflated; it was no longer filled up, puffed out with the audacity of self-importance and delusion. *Life* . . .

When they helped him into the ambulance, he didn't resist. When they guided his head toward the pillow, he was as gentle as a baby lamb. He closed his eyes and concentrated on the sirens overhead. They could take him wherever they wanted. He would do whatever they said. Never again would Robert Tucker put up a fight.

Anastasia

It was amazing how quickly she understood what and why and how it was all happening. Billy and Tito had already emptied the safes, the one in Genie's third-floor bedroom behind the self-portrait and the one in the second-floor study. From the dining room, they'd opened the many corner cabinets and found the silver. They decided against the china; it would be too cumbersome. And so now, in all, at the foot of the stairs, next to the chair in which Genie sat, bound and with a silk handkerchief shoved into her mouth, there were two duffel bags filled with loot, several wooden boxes, and the Gauguin, shrouded by a blanket.

Anastasia, once she understood, which again was nearly immediately, had gone straight to Genie's dressing room, where she located an ivory in-laid box in which Genie kept her more everyday jewelry. Even her everyday jewelry had value. Tito had already thought to remove what she'd been wearing that evening.

Anastasia was upstairs still, in Genie's closet, just to see, just in case there was something she couldn't live without, when Billy called to her.

"It's time," he said. "Our ride is here."

"Yes," she said. "I'm coming." She slipped a mink shoulder wrap from a hanger. It was far too hot out to wear this summer, but she could use it as a pillow on the long trip to wherever they were headed. One day it would be winter somewhere.

Downstairs, Genie's eyes were wide. Her right socket had swollen considerably since Anastasia first walked in. Tito must have only just hit her before she arrived. Billy was at the front door; Orvil's birdcage was at his side. The parrot looked sluggish. Someone had already moved the painting and duffels to the car.

Genie moaned loudly and wagged her head.

"Let's go," said Billy. "Quick."

Anastasia paused at Genie's side. She looked at Billy. "Not the bird," she said.

"He's worth something."

"No," said Anastasia.

A few of Orvil's feathers fluttered to the floor.

Billy sighed audibly and chewed at his lower lip. He was annoyed. But she knew he would do as she asked. "Fine," he said. "But hurry up in there. We need to skip town." He pushed the birdcage away from him.

Outside, it was early morning. The sun was rising. Soon it would be fully light out.

She waited until Billy was out of the house before she set down the ivory box and the mink throw. She knelt next to Genie, who stopped moaning as soon as Billy was gone.

Slowly, maintaining eye contact all the while, Anastasia removed the handkerchief from Genie's mouth and wiped her chin with her thumb. The old woman jerked her head away from Anastasia's hands. She stared at the floor.

"I love you," Genie whispered.

Anastasia tried to caress her cheek. This only made the old woman weep. "Please," said Genie. "Please. Why are you doing this?"

"You don't love me." Anastasia also whispered when she spoke. She rose up a little and kissed the woman's forehead.

"I do love you." She was whimpering now, almost whimpering, something close to a mewl. "I won't tell. I won't."

Anastasia's lips were still against the old woman's skin, and she spoke now into it, her own breath echoing back into her mouth in a not unpleasant way. "I know you won't tell," she whispered. "I know you won't."

Genie pressed her forehead into Anastasia's lips, but only for a moment. She raised her head finally. For what felt like several moments, the women looked at one another.

"Untie me," Genie said. "I love you. Untie me."

Anastasia stood up. "You don't even know me." She dusted off the hem of her skirt, though nothing was there, nothing could have been there. "You don't know me at all, which means you can't love me." She picked up the stole and the jewelry box. Outside, a car horn honked. "My godparents," said Anastasia, "weren't even on the plane."

Genie, as the girl spoke, allowed her head to roll back, and as Anastasia delivered her confession, the old woman gazed at the chandelier overhead. Then, though it started as something close to a hiccup and from there increased, expanded, grew to outlandish proportions, she laughed. Genie, the old woman whose hands and feet were still bound to a chair pulled out of her own dining room, was laughing uncontrollably.

"Stop it," said Anastasia. The girl looked anxiously toward the front door. It was even lighter now. She could hear the car—whatever ride her brother had arranged—idling in the roundabout. She thought, in the distance, to the east, she could hear the revving motors of a neighbor's lawn crew.

Genie laughed so long, so hard, that there was fresh saliva on her chin. Anastasia did not attempt to wipe it off.

"You think," Genie said, snorting as she caught her breath finally, "you think I didn't know?" And here the old woman's smiling and wheezing morphed into something like earnest physical pain. "I knew before I brought you home. I knew when I watched you dive." The old woman's demeanor turned suddenly and deathly serious. "Oh, sweetie," she said, "I knew every person on that plane."

Anastasia should have walked out right then. She should have untied the woman, walked out the door, and told her brother to floor it. She didn't.

"But why?" the girl asked. "It makes no sense."

Genie shook her head. The earnest pain had morphed again, now into genuine sadness or what seemed to Anastasia to be genuine sadness. "I was lonely," Genie said. "And you looked so dumb out there. You looked so gullible. I knew I could have you. Before I even met you, I knew having you would be easy."

Anastasia ran outside before Genie could say any more. She didn't bother shutting the door. It was everything she'd ever feared: in her life, she had learned nothing.

Robert

S nap out of it."
   Overhead, there was a loud pop, two hands being
brought forcefully together in an intentionally unpleasant way.

"Snap out of it, I say." The voice was familiar. All Robert had
to do was open his eyes, and he'd see the face and then place the
voice.

"Up," said the voice. Something kicked at Robert's shins,
which was when he realized he wasn't lying down, as he'd initially
thought, but sitting somewhere, his cheek pressed flat against
something hard and cold. More than anything, he hoped he was
in the back room of a police station somewhere. Anywhere, he
prayed, other than a bar.

The chair he was sitting on—he could feel it now, the ache
in his lower back and the numbness in his quads that suggested
he'd been in this position for at least a few hours—was abruptly
pulled out from beneath him. His knees landed hard on the floor.

Unless he was prepared to stay that way forever, prairie-dogged
on a linoleum floor in exquisite physical discomfort, he had no
choice but to open his eyes.

The first thing he saw was a hand stretched out: an offering.
Without looking up, Robert grabbed it. He was pulled to his feet,

where, once erect, he discovered that the hand belonged to the worst possible person; it belonged to Raif Bentley.

"No," said Robert. He tried to sit back down, he tried to back away in fact, but Bentley held on to his hand.

"You're awake," Bentley said. "Good."

Robert was shaking his head, which was freshly bandaged. "I didn't ask them to call you." The words spilled out quickly and without thought. "I need you to know. I didn't ask for this. I don't deserve your help."

Bentley let go of his hand. Instead he held him now by both shoulders. "Don't test me," he said. But he smiled as he spoke, which Robert didn't like at all. It was exactly what he'd feared from Bentley: he was as decent as ever, possibly more. The world around them had gone to hell, and Bentley still had it in him to smile. At him. At Robert Tucker.

"I have something to show you," Bentley said. He turned as if to walk out freely of the room they were in, which Robert only then realized wasn't part of a police station or courthouse. Beyond the swinging door with its large glass window, a man walked by dressed entirely in blue; a surgical mask dangled beneath his chin.

"Where am I?" asked Robert, who now grabbed at his friend's elbow.

"You passed out in the ambulance."

The events of the night came back to Robert in a single nasty flash. "Is Coleman here? The girl? Are they all right?"

Bentley stopped at the door. He seemed to be studying Robert, assessing his spiritual constitution. "You're done with Coleman. That's non-negotiable. He isn't a good man. You are. You've fucked up. But you're ready. I can see that now. You're done with the past. It's time to move forward."

Robert nodded. "Yes," he said. "I am. I never—" But he could find no more words than those.

....

There were two things Bentley wanted to show Robert. The second one was Lily, who was sleeping when they walked in, her body angled away from the curtain, her knees drawn up fetal-like. Bentley had arranged for a private room. He was that kind of friend.

They hovered by the door, not wanting to wake her.

"She looks like an angel," said Robert.

"You should know she's asked something of me and I've done it. I didn't wait for your approval, and I didn't bloody well need it anyway."

Robert was only barely paying attention. He found it difficult to take his eyes away from Lily.

"There's a Negro she's asked me to see about."

"His name is Piedmont," said Robert, not yet looking away from Lily. "He's gotten himself mixed up with a bad crowd."

"Yes," Bentley said, "at the Chateau. It'll be in the paper. That's unavoidable, I'm afraid. But I've already talked to Ivan. He's going to keep the kid safe."

"How?"

"I make it a point not to ask certain questions."

Robert nodded.

"I know what you're thinking," said Bentley. "And you're wrong. Money has nothing to do with it. It's called friendship. It's called being a good person and making the right decision. It's called being there for someone when he needs you so that he's there for you when you need him."

Robert rested a hand on Bentley's forearm. "Yes," Robert said. "I believe you."

This—standing in the doorway, watching Lily sleep—was where they were now, the long night behind them and much of the morning too. But before taking Robert to see Lily, Bentley had taken him first to the fourth floor of the east wing of St. Joseph's Hospital on Courtland Street.

They had walked corridor after corridor, each hallway seeming to alternate between blinding brightness from the burgeoning afternoon sun to yellow dimness where shades had been pulled to muted mustard darkness where no windows existed at all. They walked and walked, Bentley in front, Robert behind. If there were thoughts in his brain, he wasn't aware of them. Instead, he was aware of his breathing, slow and somewhat labored. His lower back was wet where his shirt was somehow still tucked in. He looked down; the front tail of the oxford was brown with dried blood. Had it been only four weeks since the crash? One month nearly to the day? Was that all? For one month, then, Robert had tried to rid himself of the reminders of time and body. For one month, he'd been gliding, he'd been rolling, he'd been sliding straight downhill, waiting, waiting, waiting to make contact with anything, anyone solid enough to stop him.

Ahead of him, his friend walked with none of the apparent effort of movement that Robert's body required. But that was no longer a fair assumption. A person could look one way and be another. Bentley could wake up in the morning, put his pants on one leg at a time, tighten his tie, feed his boys, start the car — he could do all these things with the same apparent breezy instinct he'd been doing them all this life, and inside he could be dying. Inside, he could be beating his chest with his open palm. It was staggering: the myopia Robert had been indulging in for so long.

At the end of a narrow and dark hallway, Bentley finally stopped. There was no door that Robert could see. There was only a large window, but the window didn't let in any sunlight. He wondered what they were doing here; what lesson he'd been brought here to learn. He wasn't annoyed. Not in the least. He was ready for an education. A stroke victim who'd been brought back in the nick of time, he was hungry and ready for knowledge, for the synapses to connect correctly with the muscle. He wasn't beyond saving, Bentley was right: there was still hope — for everyone, for anyone. There had to be.

"This," Bentley was saying, his finger pressed against the glass wall, "is what I wanted to show you."

Robert turned to see.

Before him, on the other side of the partition, were a dozen or so sleeping babies, swaddled in pinks and blues.

Robert nodded. "Sure," he said. "I get it." And he did get it: the lesson Bentley was teaching him was that life, its forward movement, its upward trajectory, was all that mattered for everyone—for Bentley, for Piedmont, for that girl in the suede skirt who may or may not have had a concussion and who might or might not be getting the help she needed. Time was necessary, its passage essential, in order to make all of this breathing going on all around them—so many lungs! breathing so much air!—in order to make it valuable, worth something. Take away time and what did you have? You had life without consequence and where was the beauty in that? Yes, Robert understood the lesson.

"No," said Bentley. "You don't get it. You don't get it at all." He pressed his finger once more to the glass in front of them. "That one," he said, "right there. Middle of the second row, blue blanket." He waited. "Do you see which one I'm pointing to?"

Robert looked at Bentley. Then he looked again at the babies. He found the second row, identified the middle infant, swaddled in a blanket of the lightest, faintest blue. He nodded.

"That one," said Bentley, "is yours."

Piedmont

"M a?"

"—"

"Ma? Are you there?"

"—"

"I know you're there because you accepted the charges. Please talk to me."

"Are you . . ."

"Yes, it's me."

"Are you going to break my heart again?"

"—"

"I didn't raise a boy who couldn't take a lick."

"I know you didn't."

"Not that I ever raised a hand to you."

"I know you didn't."

"Neither did your father."

"I know that too."

"What I mean to say, what I mean is that I thought I raised someone with a backbone."

"You did."

"Someone who faced rejection by standing up and trying again."

"You did."

"Why'd you run off?"

"I was angry."

"Then I raised a coward."

"I was confused."

"Then I taught you nothing."

"You taught me everything."

"I'm confused every night, Piedmont. I go to bed confused. I wake up confused. That's life."

"Yes," he said. "I understand that now."

"I imagine you want to come home all of a sudden."

"I do."

"How do I know it's for good?"

"What can I say?"

"Tell me you went out into the world and learned a lesson."

"I did."

"Tell me what you learned."

"I went out into the world. I went out into it, and I broke my own heart. I saw a real-live airplane take off. I drove a Thunderbird convertible. I was pulled over and beaten up. I held five twenty-dollar bills in my hand. All five of them were stolen from me. I saw a car full of guns, which is more guns than I ever care to see for the rest of my days. I was shown kindness. I slept near a swimming pool. I stood where an entire family once hung by their necks from a single tree. I pressed a magnolia flower between the pages of an encyclopedia. I gave the flower away. I played a baby grand piano. I played it like I was Oscar Peterson or Jelly Roll Morton or Nat King Cole. I danced very slowly with a white lady. I fell in love. I saved a life. It's possible I saved two lives."

"Is that all?"

"Yes. That's all."

Robert

In the future, once a year on June 3, Robert Tucker would sometimes allow himself the fantasy of what might have happened if the plane hadn't crashed, if it had instead taken off. Eight or so hours later, it would have landed in New York; another five hours after that, it would have landed in Atlanta. Robert and Lily would have been at the airport, as promised, waiting at the gate for her parents.

Robert, in his fantasy, is standing with McGill, smoking a cigarette; McGill is there to cover the mayor's press conference and the subsequent welcoming home party.

Robert and McGill watch as the plane lands.

"Lily's folks are back," says McGill.

"That's right," says Robert.

"Baby is due?"

"Next month."

McGill nods. "Fortuitous." He says the word flatly.

Robert stubs out his cigarette. He is thinking about Rita. He is thinking about her last letter, which—if the plane hadn't disintegrated—he would have received mid-June, at the earliest. But because this is merely a dream, one both manufactured and impossible, he pretends to have read the letter. He pretends to know their affair is over.

Robert's wife, in his conception of this day, is sitting with a group of other women, with Jane and Polly and Agatha and Martha. Standing near them are the Bentley boys—all three having been dressed up and trotted out in matching blue suits by the nanny.

"Raif's on the next flight," says McGill. "Wonder who's going to stick around to ferry him home."

Robert is barely listening. The plane has come to a stop a few hundred yards from the floor-to-ceiling windows of the terminal. Detached stairs are being wheeled toward the door by three young Negroes in jumpsuits. They unroll a red carpet that extends nearly to the airport's exterior entrance one level beneath where he stands with McGill, but Robert is focused on the aircraft's door. He watches as it separates from the seal first a few inches, then returns, then is swiveled open by a uniformed stewardess in blue. She's undoubtedly French. She has one of those wonderful pursed mouths with cheeks constantly being bitten from the inside. She looks up at the terminal window and waves to no one in particular.

The crowd inside cheers.

What Robert wants, somewhat obviously, is to see Rita as she disembarks. He wants her to sense his presence, to find him in the crowd above. He wants her to locate him in some mystical way, to feel from several hundred yards away his yearning for her, but also his appreciation for finally letting him go and for having made the decision on her own to continue her life without him.

In Robert's invention of this day, the crowd around him slowly thins, McGill himself disappears, and, from a platform high above, it is Robert all alone who is watching, waiting, searching the endless stream of passengers for Rita, girl about town.

But this, of course, is not what happened on June 3.

Instead, the plane exploded. Instead, the people aboard died; and when they were finally home from the hospital in the house that had been purchased for them by their dear friend Raif Bentley, it was Lily who delivered to Robert his lover's final letter.

She found him one night in the study. There were still so many boxes in the house, many of them remaining to be unpacked. The baby was upstairs sleeping. Robert was sitting in his office chair, the one that Candy and George Randolph had given him last Christmas.

"This was my favorite place while you were gone."

He'd patted his thigh. "Sit with me," he said.

She'd shaken her head. "Not tonight," she said. "I want to go stare at him while he sleeps."

"Kiss me, then," he said.

She leaned down and kissed him.

When she stood up, he saw the letter in her hands. He recognized the envelope instantly, its light yellow color. She held it out to him and he took it. Then he looked up.

"Before you read it," she said, "I want to say I'm sorry."

"Okay."

"Don't talk yet."

He nodded.

"I'm sorry I opened it. I'm sorry for how it ended with her. I can only imagine how it must feel. I'm mad at you, Robert. I'm mad still. But I want to tell you I understand. I want to tell you that I understand how big the heart is, how capacious an organ. There's so much room inside. I see that now." She was quiet for a minute. She was thinking of Piedmont no doubt. She'd told him so much already. "That's all I've got."

"I can talk now?"

"You can say anything you want."

"Is it very important I read this letter?"

She thought about that. He had the impression that he'd surprised her with this question; that she'd been prepared for many possibilities but not for this.

"Yes," she said at last. "I think it is."

"Thank you," he said. "Then I will."

She bent low a final time and kissed him again, but now only on the forehead.

"When you're ready," she said, "come watch him sleep with me." At the doorway, she turned. "But only when you're ready."

Lily

Many days later, they returned the baby to the basket in the backseat and pulled around the buckle to keep it from shifting as they drove north out of the city. Lily kept her head turned toward the window. She was contemplative, not sullen. Robert let her be.

An hour before, Piedmont Dobbs had declined to greet them, to meet with them at all. Lily had been surprised by this, though Robert had warned her repeatedly in the days leading to their visit that she shouldn't get her hopes up.

"He was inside," she said as, rebuffed, they'd taken the steps back down to the first floor, the same steps they'd only minutes earlier climbed. "I know he was inside. I could feel it."

"I think you're probably right," Robert had said. He was holding the baby and walking behind so that Lily could use the banister and set the pace. She was still a little wobbly on her feet. "But his mother said he was gone, and that means he didn't want to see us."

Lily considered this. The stairwell was dark, it was August, the heat was relentless, and the railing seemed to give, spongelike, where her fingers came into contact with it. She tried to conjure an image of Piedmont taking these stairs, first as a child, then as a teenager, and finally as a man. He had them memorized, no doubt, their intricacies and minute peculiarities. He could take them at a full-tilt run with his eyes closed. That's what she suspected anyway.

In the car, many, many hours later—the baby asleep in the basket in the back, Atlanta a few hundred miles behind them, Raif Bentley's farm in Virginia still ahead—she would allow herself to cry as she gazed out the window, her head turned away. She wouldn't mind if Robert saw. There was nothing he didn't know about, nothing she hadn't told him about her own heart. She'd fallen for Piedmont. She believed he'd fallen for her too. But she wasn't naïve. And she believed Piedmont wasn't either. There was no place for them in this world. In another, perhaps. In twenty years, fifty, maybe a hundred, there would be another Piedmont and another Lily, and they would look and act and talk just the same as the originals. But they'd be together, they'd be allowed to be together, they would know how to navigate the world hand in hand. Or so Lily liked to imagine and would continue to imagine from time to time as she and the baby aged alongside Robert, who would also age.

That Robert hadn't made fun, hadn't gotten angry, hadn't laughed or sworn or called either of them names, that he'd simply sat at the side of the hospital bed and listened as she told her story, that he'd done so was one of the reasons she was with him now, why she'd asked before they even left the maternity ward if he wanted to see—just see, no pressure, no expectations—if they could start over.

What he'd said, and this was maybe the real reason she was with him now—exiting the apartment building where Piedmont Dobbs lived once again with his mother, about to drive north for the remainder of the summer and possibly even the fall—what he'd said was, "No. Not start over. Let's never start over. Let's start now. As we are. As you are. As I am. Let's start like this."

She'd nodded, stupid little tears springing to her eyes. "It's the hormones," she'd said. "I'm not sad."

"I know," he said.

"Do you think"—she bit at her lip—"do you think it will be different?"

Robert looked down at the baby, who had been placed in Lily's arms by the nurse assigned to them. "I don't know," he said. The baby's eyes were closed, but his head jerked gently side to side. "Look," said Robert. "He's already fighting."

Lily had looked down that day in the ward. At her side was her baby, her son. She would love him and she would love Robert too again one day, sooner in fact than she thought. She would love them in ways she'd formerly not known were possible—she would love them to the brink of language, the place where words butted up against emotion. But just then she wasn't thinking of them, she was thinking of Piedmont, the boy who was really a man, who'd driven her to the hospital and saved her life and possibly also this baby's.

And now, several weeks removed from that hospital bed, having walked up the three flights of stairs with Robert, then turned around and walked back down, having secured the baby safely in his basket in the back of the car, Lily turned once more before getting into the car herself. She looked up at the brick apartment building. She counted the floors. In a center window, she thought she saw a dark shape step quickly out of view. It could have been Piedmont. It could have. She raised her hand to her chest and closed her eyes.

"Are you ready?" asked Robert. He was on the driver's side, his hand on the latch.

She nodded, her eyes still closed, her face still turned up toward the window where Piedmont might once have been standing or might not have been standing at all.

"I'm ready," she said.

They were on the dark side of town, and a hot summer breeze swept up from the asphalt, putting the whole city in motion, a kind of fast-forward of movement and life. In the breeze, hints of tar and sulfur, pipe tobacco and pork beans, Pine-Sol and peaches and always Coca-Cola. Cars whizzed by; sidewalks filled in as if on cue. Men strutted, women sauntered, kids hopscotched down one alley then back up another.

This was life, a version of it.

This was Atlanta.

This was 1962.

Acknowledgments

Special thanks to

Jeff Clymer
Rion Amilcar Scott
Bobbie Ann Mason
Michael Trask
Leon Sachs
Eleanor Ringel
Patrick Smith
Carvie Williams

If it weren't for my father, Jack Pittard, and his endless supply of anecdotes, memories, and stories about Atlanta, this book would not exist as it is.

It if weren't for Helen Atsma's unabashed enthusiasm and unwavering editorial support, this book would not exist at all.

Works Consulted

Abrams, Ann Uhry. *Explosion at Orly: The Disaster That Transformed Atlanta.* Atlanta: Avion Press, 2002.

"Article Regarding Harry Belafonte and Associates Denied Service." June 1, 1962. The King Center. http://www.thekingcenter.org/archive/document/article-regarding-harry-belafonte-and-associates-denied-service.

Balcomb, Theo. "A Promise Unfulfilled: 1962 MLK Speech Recording Is Discovered." *All Things Considered.* NPR. January 20, 2014. http://www.npr.org/2014/01/20/264226759/a-promise-unfulfilled-1962-mlk-speech-recording-is-discovered.

Branch, Taylor. *Pillar of Fire: America in the King Years, 1963–65.* New York: Simon & Schuster, 1998.

British Movietone. "Orly Plane Crash I—No Sound." Filmed May 1962. YouTube video, 2:13. Posted July 21, 2015. https://www.youtube.com/watch?v=aYaqdWYmQxo.

British Pathé. "Orly Airport Boeing Crashes in France (1961)." YouTube video, 2:20. Posted April 13, 2014. https://www.youtube.com/watch?v=XwvzB_IA94A.

"Civil Aviation Disasters." Pilot Friend. http://www.pilotfriend.com/disasters/crash/af.htm.

"Civil Rights Movement." John F. Kennedy Presidential Library and Museum. https://www.jfklibrary.org/JFK/JFK-in-History/Civil-Rights-Movement.aspx?p=2.

Dartt, Rebecca H. *Women Activists in the Fight for Georgia School Desegregation, 1958–1961.* Jefferson, NC: McFarland, 2008.

Esquire. April, June, July, August, 1962.

"FBI FILE NY 105-8999." The Malcolm X Project at Columbia University. http://www.columbia.edu/cu/ccbh/mxp/.

"Flyer Advertising SCLC Benefit." The King Center. http://www.thekingcenter.org/archive/document/flyer-advertising-sclc-benefit.

"Georgia Cold Cases." The Georgia Civil Rights Cold Cases Project. April 30, 2015. https://scholarblogs.emory.edu/emorycoldcases/georgia-cold-cases-2/.

Godbold, E. Stanly, Jr. *Jimmy and Rosalynn Carter: The Georgia Years, 1924–1974.* Oxford: Oxford University Press, 2010.

Golden, Randy. "Airplane Crash at Orly Field." About North Georgia. http://www.aboutnorthgeorgia.com/ang/Airplane_crash_at_Orly_Field.

Grady, James H. *Architecture of Neel Reid in Georgia.* Athens: University of Georgia Press, 1973.

"Great Monkey Hoax, The." Museum of Hoaxes. http://hoaxes.org/archive/permalink/the_great_monkey_hoax.

Haine, Edgar A. *Disaster in the Air.* New York: Cornwall Books, 2000.

"History of Georgia Power." Georgia Power. https://www.georgiapower.com/docs/about-us/History.pdf.

JET Magazine, March 8, 1962.

Karazin, Christelyn D. "Swirling in History Part Ten: Vintage Swirl." Beyond Black & White. March 1, 2013. http://www.beyondblackwhite.com/swirling-history-part-ten-vintage-swirl/.

Kennedy, Randall. "Lifting as We Climb: A Progressive Defense of Respectability Politics." *Harper's Magazine,* October 2015, 24–34.

Kruse, Kevin M. *White Flight: Atlanta and the Making of Modern Conservatism.* Princeton, NJ: Princeton University Press, 2007.

Link, William A. *Atlanta, Cradle of the New South: Race and Remembering in the Civil War's Aftermath.* Chapel Hill: University of North Carolina Press, 2013.

LIFE, June 1, June 8, June 22, June 29, 1962.

LIFE: The First Fifty Years 1936–1986. Boston: Little, Brown, 1986.

Maddox, Lester. *Speaking Out: The Autobiography of Lester Garfield Maddox.* Garden City, NY: Doubleday, 1975.

Mann, Barry Stewart. "The Story of the Orly Disaster." Unpublished notes for oral history performance.

McGill, Ralph. "Violent End of a Quest for Beauty: In Stricken Atlanta, a Legacy of Art Lives On. Those Who Cared for the Important Things." *LIFE,* June 15, 1962, 30–41.

Mitchell, William R., Jr. *J. Neel Reid, Architect: Of Hentz, Reid & Adler and the Georgia School of Classicists.* Photography by James R. Lockhart. Savannah, GA: Golden Coast Publishing, 1997.

Mixon, Gregory, and Clifford Kuhn. "Atlanta Race Riot of 1906." *New Georgia Encyclopedia*. September 23, 2005. http://www.georgiaencyclopedia.org/articles/history-archaeology/atlanta-race-riot-1906.

Playboy, April, May, June, July, August 1962.

"Report to the American People on Civil Rights, 11 June 1963." John F. Kennedy Presidential Library and Museum. https://www.jfklibrary.org/Asset-Viewer/LH8F_0Mzvoe6Ro1yEm74Ng.aspx.

Rooney, Donald R. "Orly Air Crash of 1962." *New Georgia Encyclopedia*. December 9, 2003. http://www.georgiaencyclopedia.org/articles/history-archaeology/orly-air-crash-1962.

Russell, James M. *Atlanta: 1847–1890: City Building in the Old South and the New.* Baton Rouge: Louisiana State University Press, 1988.

Short, Bob. *Everything's Pickrick: The Life of Lester Maddox.* Macon, GA: Mercer University Press, 1999.

"SNCC Constitution." The Martin Luther King, Jr., Research and Education Institute, Stanford University. http://kingencyclopedia.stanford.edu/encyclopedia/documentsentry/sncc_constitution/.

Wainstock, Dennis D. *Malcolm X, African American Revolutionary.* Jefferson, NC: McFarland, 2008.

Whisenhunt, Dan. "50 Years Later, Orly a Painful Memory." *Reporter Newspapers,* May 4, 2012. http://www.reporternewspapers.net/2012/05/04/50-years-later-orly-a-painful-memory/.

Whitaker, Mark. "Interracial Couple in 1950s: Bravery, Faith and Turning the Other Cheek." CNN, October 17, 2011. http://www.cnn.com/2011/10/17/us/interracial-parents-courtship/.

X, Malcolm. *The Autobiography of Malcolm X.* With the assistance of Alex Haley. Introduction by M. S. Handler. New York: Grove Press, 1965.

Zainaldin, Jamil. "Charles Lindbergh's Atlanta Legacy." *SaportaReport,* September 16, 2013. http://saportareport.com/lindberghs-atlanta-legacy/.

About the Author

Hannah Pittard was born in Atlanta. She is the author of four novels, including *Listen to Me* and *The Fates Will Find Their Way.* Her work has appeared in the *Sewanee Review,* the *New York Times,* and other publications. She is a professor of English at the University of Kentucky, where she directs the MFA program in creative writing.